THE SECOND RIDER

Alex Beer

THE SECOND RIDER

*Translated from the German
by Tim Mohr*

Europa
editions

Europa Editions
214 West 29th Street
New York, N.Y. 10001
www.europaeditions.com
info@europaeditions.com

Copyright © 2017 by Limes Verlag, a division of Verlagsgruppe Random House
GmbH, München, Germany
First Publication 2018 by Europa Editions

Translation by Tim Mohr
Original title: *Der zweite Reiter. Ein Fall für August Emmerich*
Translation copyright © 2018 by Europa Editions

Library of Congress Cataloging in Publication Data is available
ISBN 978-1-60945-472-2

Beer, Alex
The Second Rider

Book design by Emanuele Ragnisco
www.mekkanografici.com

Cover illustration taken from a photograph by Austrian National
Library/Interfoto/Alamy Stock Photo

Prepress by Grafica Punto Print – Rome

Printed in the USA

War has a long arm.
Long after it is over,
It continues to claim victims.
—MARTIN KESSEL

THE SECOND RIDER

1.

VIENNA, NOVEMBER 1919

J ost! Private Jost!" rang out from the underbrush, but he
ignored the call. He knew that no living person was
addressing him. The voice was only in his head. Along
with all the others.

Though the war had been over for a year already, the memories refused to recede. When he closed his eyes everything
was so piercingly clear that he might as well have seen them
yesterday: the dead, the dying, the maimed. Even smells: the
cold sweat mixed with the smoke of the grenades. But most of
all he heard the sounds of combat in his ears, the shouted commands, the barrages, the explosions, the screams of anguish.
They'd found a new home in his head and taken over his body.

No, he'd never returned from the battlefields of Galicia.

Dietrich Jost stared at his hands, which trembled uncontrollably, and glanced at his feet, which were having difficulty
walking on the rough terrain. Before the war he'd been a well-
to-do zookeeper, now he was nothing. A war trembler. A
pitiable cripple who had to live in the poorhouse and beg for
food. Someone who'd been betrayed by the country he'd given
everything for. The bureaucrats labeled him neurotic, a hysterical faker, just so they didn't have to pay him a war victim's
pension. Was an amputated leg really worth more than a broken psyche?

"Jost! Private Jost!"

With quivering knees but a resolute stride he walked
deeper into the woods, left the trail he'd been following, and

pressed into the brush. The hunter's blind, where the money and papers were waiting for him, had to be right around here somewhere. With those things he'd be able to book his passage from Trieste to Santos and start a new life overseas. Brazil would be his salvation. The whoosh of the ocean would wash the voices from his head and the sun would fade the horrific images.

At the office of the emigration agency he'd seen photos of beautiful, well-fed women with chubby-cheeked infants on their hips and smiles on their faces. He'd find a wife and leave his old life behind. His old life in this shit hole, Vienna.

The Kaiser had gone into exile, the crownlands had been split up, and Austria was but a pitiable remnant barely in a position to survive. Just like its citizens. Everything was in short supply. Food, coal, soap and clothing. People were starving, freezing, stinking. They fought each other over rotting horse meat or moldy potatoes and shared their beds with fleas. There was no work and no medicine, which meant even more crime and sickness.

The once glamorous seat of the empire had become a filthy, bloodthirsty beast that he would soon escape. He'd died in Galicia and would be born anew in South America.

"Jost! Are you deaf or what?"

The voice was very close now. Next to him. And it was real. As real as the cold steel of the pistol barrel now pressed to his temple.

Jost squeezed the words out: "P . . . P . . . Please . . . don't."

"I heard you wanted to reach a beautiful place. And I'm here to help."

A loud bang broke the stillness of the woods, and the voices in Jost's head went silent forever.

2.

I nspector August Emmerich sat in the tram running from
central Vienna toward Hütteldorf, pulled his wool cap
down over his face, crossed his arms on his chest, and
leaned back. He was tired—no wonder, it was late after all, and
he'd barely closed his eyes the night before. The children of his
partner, Luise, who'd lost her husband in the war, were con-
stantly sick because it was impossible to heat the apartment
well enough. They hacked their lungs out and cried a lot.
Three little beings who'd picked a bad time to be born. On the
other hand, was there ever a good time?

He let his heavy lids close for a moment, and savored the
pleasant temperature. It had recently become possible to heat
the trolley cars using the overhead electrical lines, and the conductor was making good use of that on this particularly cold
day. He probably knew that a cold bed in a cold apartment
would be waiting for most of the passengers. Coal was scarce
and maintaining a fire in an apartment was a luxury that only
very few could afford. It made this short, warm break all the
more welcome.

Emmerich yawned and leaned his head against the window
as they passed Casino Baumgarten, which with its ostentatious
façade was reminiscent of better times. What surprises would
the night bring? He glanced at Veit Kolja, the man he'd been
tracking for more than three months and who was now sitting
two rows in front of him—it was all up to him and him alone,
Inspector Emmerich, as to whether this crook could be

stopped, and it was looking good. Kolja had a large jute sack in his lap, and Emmerich hoped he was leading them to his stash.

Food, clothing, and medicine were scarce, and Kolja was one of those profiting from people's hardships. He was the leader of a smuggling ring that had stockpiles of contraband in secret locations and traded their supplies for money, jewelry, and other valuable items.

When this time of misery and need was finally over, Kolja would be unspeakably wealthy or, if it was up to Emmerich, in jail. In the deepest, darkest, dampest hole. Forever. Because, after all, what was sleazier than getting rich off people's pain and misery?

In the past few weeks he had put everything into making sure he'd be able to arrest Kolja and his men. He'd followed and observed them, he'd stood by in rain and cold, he'd even greased the palms of a few informers. It was tedious and exhausting, but it had paid off. He was nearly there. He could feel it. He was on the verge of breaking up the smuggling ring and arresting those responsible for it, which he hoped would earn him a promotion . . . as long as nothing messed it all up at the last minute. Or more accurately, nobody.

His boss, District Inspector Leopold Sander, once a highly decorated officer in the Imperial and Royal Army, who knew a lot about military command but not the slightest thing about police work, had hit upon the brilliant idea of giving him an inexperienced sidekick—Ferdinand Winter, a rookie who'd just finished his training and was more a hindrance than a help.

Winter, who was sitting next to him and dressed, like him, in plainclothes, put everything in jeopardy with his prim appearance. He gave off an air of nervousness. His legs fidgeted and his fingers tapped on the wooden seat as if he were trying to send Morse code messages out into the night. It drew the attention of the other passengers. Most of them were factory workers on their way home from a long, draining shift. An excess of energy like Winter's stood out. And standing out was pretty much the last thing that should happen when tailing a suspect.

"Settle down," hissed Emmerich rudely. He refused to show respect for the rookie until he earned it. He gave the young man a withering look.

Winter had big, bright blue eyes, gleaming blond hair, perfect skin, and soft hands. He chose his words with care. Guys like him weren't used to working. Guys like him weren't made for times like these. Emmerich knew delicate lads like Winter from the orphanage where he'd spent his childhood. The nicer and more innocent they were, the higher the odds were that they wouldn't survive.

Ferdinand Winter was definitely one of them. One of the nice, innocent ones. As far as he'd been able to figure out, Winter was the pampered son of a rich Vienna family whose money was no longer any good. Inflation took whatever the war had left, so the kid had been forced to deal with reality. Which wasn't bad in and of itself, thought Emmerich—except that it had affected Emmerich's sphere of responsibility.

"Satzberggasse," announced the conductor as they approached the second to last station. But Kolja remained seated, motionless. Where was this son of a bitch heading?

"Settle down, for god's sake," Emmerich whispered, since Winter had started to get antsy again. "We're heading for the edge of town, not the front."

"Hütteldorf, Bujattigasse," called the conductor a few minutes later. "Last station. All passengers please exit."

The remaining passengers stood up slowly and reluctantly. The warm break was over, and life waited outside.

The two police officers got into the line of people sluggishly pushing their way out the tram door onto the platform and then down the two steps onto the street. From there the passengers scattered in every direction.

Emmerich put a hand on Winter's shoulder from behind so he wouldn't follow too closely on Kolja's heels. "Easy," he said once the suspect was out of earshot. "He's a pro. The best thing is for you to stay a few steps behind me."

They followed Kolja at a safe distance as he headed directly toward Gasthaus Prilisauer, which suited Emmerich just fine, a shot of schnapps sounded good to him right then. Or better yet two shots.

But the smuggler had other plans. Just before the pub he turned left, went through Ferdinand Wolf Park, followed the Halterbach drainage canal to the point where it emptied into the Wien river, crossed the Bräuhaus bridge, and then, turning to the right, left all civilization behind.

"Everything alright? You're limping," said Winter, behind him, a little too loudly. Emmerich turned a deaf ear. "Nothing but woods here," said Winter, stating the obvious, and Emmerich had to resist stuffing his mouth right there and then.

"Wait here," he ordered, after Kolja, with his sack, climbed over the damaged wall that ringed the so-called Lainzer Tiergarten, an extensive area in the eastern section of the Vienna Woods. "And don't leave this spot." He came across more like a kindergarten teacher than an aspiring police inspector.

"Alright, alri—" Winter started to say before holding his tongue and pressing his lips together.

Emmerich nodded. At least the kid was a fast learner.

He gave his pistol, a Steyr repeater, the once-over and double-checked that he had his brass knuckles, then hopped over the wall. When he landed on the other side he had to stop himself from crying out in pain. There'd been shrapnel from a grenade lodged in his right leg since the battle of Vittorio Veneto, and it caused him constant trouble. In the last few days it had been worse than ever. The doctors had diagnosed it as arthrofibrosis, which was a fancy word for a miserable condition.

Emmerich massaged his knee, which was ever stiffer as a result of scarred connective tissue, then stood up straight and braced himself against the wall. Good thing he'd left Winter behind. He didn't want anyone to know about his wounded leg, and the kid was already suspicious. He couldn't afford to be shifted to desk work if he was deemed physically unfit. Now that he had Luise and her children to look after, he needed the extra pay that came with his current duties. Then there was the fact that he was just thirty-six and couldn't possibly imagine spending the rest of his career as a pencil pusher. He wasn't cut out for that. He was a detective. He hunted down criminals, on the streets, that is, not on paper. He also wasn't prepared to give up his dream of one day being promoted to the *Leib und Leben* division. The men who worked in that division, under the direction of the famous Carl Horvat, were the most elite members of the police force. They handled cases of murder and grievous bodily harm. He'd wanted to join their ranks for as long as he could remember, and he wasn't going to be stopped now that he was so close. Not even by his bad leg.

Emmerich grasped his talisman, a silver charm dangling from his neck on a leather lace, gritted his teeth, and limped off into the woods. Luckily Kolja had lit a lamp, which Emmerich used to track him, and thankfully the pursuit didn't last long. The lamp stopped moving after just a few meters, and Emmerich hid himself behind a thick tree trunk. What was the smuggler up to? There was no bunker or anything else that could be used to stash things around here.

Kolja began to whistle a song, put down his sack, and pulled something out of it. An axe.

Emmerich's stomach began to ache. Not from fear or hunger, but because it was dawning on him why Kolja had come here. Not for the purposes of his business, but to collect firewood.

While Kolja hacked at a thin beech tree, Emmerich, disappointed, used the opportunity to slip away.

"False alarm," he whispered as he slung his leg painfully over the wall. "Winter?" The kid wasn't standing where he was supposed to be standing. "Winter?"

Emmerich sat atop the wall and looked around. He'd had a feeling that his new assistant spelled trouble. What was he supposed to do now? What a useless dilettante. Where had he gotten to?

A yelp behind him answered his question.

"Winter!"

Emmerich hopped off the wall again, ignored the searing pain that shot through his body, and hobbled into the darkness, which was only dimly illuminated by the moon.

Had Kolja not come here alone after all? Had the smuggler discovered the inexperienced Winter and dragged him off? Had an animal attacked him? Or had he gotten into it with some other firewood collectors?

Something underfoot made Emmerich stumble and broke his stream of thoughts. He grasped at the air with his hands but found nothing to grab onto and fell face-first into the cold slush.

The smell of the dirt and the metallic taste of blood in his mouth sent a quick series of memories shooting through his head. Trembling ground, thundering cannons, splitting helmets, and the most horrible conflict of all: the survival instinct versus military commands. He had to pull himself together. He had to get going. Must get up. Must go on. Forward. Never give up. Never surrender.

He was startled when someone grabbed him by the arm and pulled him up.

"Damn it, Winter," he wanted to say when he realized who it was, but he stopped himself when he saw that the young man's hands were smeared with blood. "What happened?"

Winter turned and pointed toward the edge of the woods. "You have to come with me."

After he'd made sure his new assistant was unhurt, Emmerich brushed the dirt from his pants, straightened his cap, and listened. Silence. Kolja had taken a break from his task.

"Where?" he whispered.

Winter motioned for him to follow and set off. Straight into the brush but not in Kolja's direction.

The kid moved fast, with long, hurried strides. He wasn't bothered by the uneven ground or by low-hanging branches. He just walked on, farther and farther into the thicket, until the brush was so dense that you couldn't see your hand in front of your face.

Emmerich struggled to keep up, but didn't want to reveal his problem by asking Winter to slow down. He was overjoyed when Winter finally stopped. "So?"

Winter didn't answer, but instead looked around searchingly. "You mind?" He held up a little pocket lamp.

Emmerich thought for a moment and then nodded. If they were to come upon Kolja or some other soul he would just say they were poor people looking for firewood.

Winter turned on the lamp and shined the light on the forest floor. "It had to have been right here somewhere," he said. "I heard noises and wanted to check on you . . . "

"Check on me?" Emmerich interrupted.

Winter nodded with childlike seriousness. "And I stumbled over a root and fell on him."

"On who?"

"On him."

The light of the lamp finally came to a halt and, like a theater spotlight, illuminated a ghastly scene. The star of the macabre stage was a dead man whose pale visage was framed by coagulated blood, the consistency of which was more reminiscent of tar than of the sap of life. Viscous, sticky, and horrible smelling.

"Haven't you ever seen a corpse before?" asked Emmerich when he saw Winter's face, which was suddenly whiter than the dead man's. It was meant as a rhetorical question, which is why he nearly choked when the young man silently shook his head. Ferdinand Winter must have been the only person in this entire country who'd never seen a dead body before. "Where the hell did you spend the last five years?" This time the question was a serious one.

"In the Imperial and Royal Army's telegraph and communications division."

Emmerich made no comment, silently took the lamp from Winter, knelt down, and shone light on the full length of the corpse. From the worn-out shoes with paper-thin soles past the ratty trousers, the twine used as a belt, and the jacket made almost entirely of patches, to the glassy eyes that seemed to peer into the distance. A stare into eternity that Emmerich knew all too well—he had seen that stare far too often in his life.

The dead man had an entry wound on his right temple and an exit wound on the left. Emmerich took a step back and felt around on the ground, finding what he had expected: a gun. More precisely a Steyr M1912, the standard-issue pistol of the Imperial and Royal Army.

With expert hands he searched the clothes of the man, put the gun in his pocket, and turned to Winter. "So far, so good," he said. "Let's go back into the city."

"But—" Winter began, but Emmerich left him standing there and marched off toward the tram station.

"We can't just leave him lying there. We have to do something."

Emmerich suppressed a sigh. "You want to take him on the tram? Feel free to go back and carry him here. Then the three of us can hop on."

Winter stared at the ground. "Sorry," he said. "I have a lot to learn."

"We can get started with that right away." Emmerich pulled a small brown card out of his pants pocket. On it was the number 165. "This was on the dead man. We're going to figure out his identity now and inform any family members he may have. While we're doing that, the patrolmen from the commissariat can take care of the body."

Winter didn't have to say anything, his look spoke volumes. He'd never seen a card like this, which is why Emmerich turned it over to show his assistant the stamp on the reverse side.

Asylum Society
18 Nov. 1919
for
homeless in Vienna

"165 is the bed number. And see these holes?" Emmerich pointed to the edge of the card. "It's been punched five times, which means the dead man stayed there five nights. That's the maximum. They won't let anyone stay there longer than that."

"You think that's why he—"

"—Blew his brains out?" Emmerich nodded. "That and a thousand other reasons. Poor bastard. Who could blame him." He rubbed his leg as inconspicuously as possible and looked in the direction of town, where the headlight of the 49 tram was finally coming into view. Hopefully the conductor had the heat up because the cold had crept deep into his bones.

The inspector's wishes were fulfilled, and for the second time that day he was able to enjoy a warm break. "Wake me up when it's time to get off," he said, leaning back and pulling his cap down over his face.

"Where exactly are we going?"

"First to the commissariat, then to the homeless shelter."

"And then?"

"Then the situation will be taken care of and we can set our sights on the smuggler again."

3.

The men of the detective corps were spread around the twenty-two station houses of the federal constabulary because they worked directly with the uniformed guardians of public order. Since they spent most of their time on the streets, the lower ranks of police detectives did not have their own offices and instead worked at large tables in the main room of whatever station house they were assigned.

"It's about time that the overhaul of the police system was instituted and we got our own desks," complained Emmerich when he saw that constable Rüdiger Hörl, a dumpy, half-bald fifty-year-old who was on overnight standby duty, had taken over their work space again. "You can put this stuff right on." He grabbed Hörl's khaki uniform jacket and chocolate-brown cap from the table and threw them to him. "There's a body in the Vienna Woods that needs to be taken to the coroner's office."

"The woods are huge. What, am I just supposed to hope to get lucky searching over a thousand square kilometers? Easter's not until April." Hörl didn't seem too happy that Emmerich had brought him work to do.

"Over Bräuhaus Bridge, then go to the right over the wall into Lainzer Tiergarten, then about two hundred meters into the brush."

"Get out of here," said Hörl. "I'm not running a courier service for stiffs. Especially not for ones who've made pendulums out of themselves."

"He didn't hang himself, he shot himself," Winter spat back.

"Even worse. More of a mess. And besides I've got things to do." Hörl pointed to a wooden bench where two women were sitting and staring at the floor. "I need to take care of these gracious ladies."

"What were they engaged in?" Winter looked at the two of them, who were dressed nicely and also seemed well fed. They didn't look like pickpockets or prostitutes.

"What else? They wanted to earn a little on the side. These days it's not just the poor, uneducated women who turn tricks. The finer women have also had to learn that life isn't always a bowl of cherries. Isn't that right?" he yelled in the women's direction, causing them to turn red and hang their heads even lower.

"Let them go," Emmerich suggested. "A couple of part-time prostitutes are the least of our problems."

"Says you!" Hörl turned to Winter. "If you value your balls at all, don't get lured in by ones like this. Go to the official ones. The ones who do it on the side like this don't have a health department license. Indulging yourself with one of these is like playing Russian roulette."

He gave the young man the kind of smug look a teacher might offer upon dispensing some important life lesson to a departing pupil.

The two women's discomfort was palpable.

"You can go, ladies." Emmerich opened the door and turned to Hörl. "You, too. To the Vienna Woods in your case. And the next time you address women, I expect more decorum."

"Thanks," the two women breathed before they disappeared into the cold night.

Hörl shook his head. "He is the most ferocious dog I know. But when it comes to whores, he turns into a gentleman," he hissed to Winter. "Better get used to it."

"Why is he like that?"

Hörl laughed. "Nobody can read Emmerich. That's another thing you'd better get used to straightaway."

Hopefully the homeless shelter isn't something I have to get used to, thought Winter when they reached the building on Blattgasse.

A throng of men, of all ages, from whiskerless youths to hunched old men, had assembled before the large gate. There must have been several hundred, and most of them had no hat or gloves or even a proper winter jacket. They shivered as they waited for the place to open. They pressed closely together, as a wind carrying the smell of snow had kicked up.

The freezing, emaciated bodies shifted a few steps back as a portal in the lock gate was opened and a bearded man stuck his head out. "Cards first!" he yelled. "No exceptions."

Immediately a host of brown cards were held aloft, and one man after another shuffled forward past the envious glances of those without cards, and presented their valuable slips of paper to the housemaster, who punched a hole in each and let the lucky holder enter.

Finally Emmerich and Winter made it to the front.

"Wait, wait, wait, not so fast." The housemaster blocked the entrance with his stocky frame. "This card's no good. Five nights and then you're out."

"My card's good every night." Emmerich pulled out his badge. "We're not here to cause any trouble. We just have a few questions."

Ha," snapped the bearded housemaster. "No trouble, my ass. That's what you coppers are all about."

Emmerich planted his hands on his hips and stared silently into the man's eyes. The housemaster turned away, looked at the wretched figures waiting to get in, and sighed.

"Do I have any choice?"

Emmerich spared the housemaster the answer, shoved him aside, and pulled Winter in through the gate.

"Cards? Anyone else with a card? Nobody? Then I'll distribute the new ones now," they heard called out behind them, at which point skirmishes broke out.

Winter turned around, shocked, but was pulled forward into the home by Emmerich. "They're fighting for the rest of the spots," he said dryly. "It's nothing to do with us."

Before Winter could give any thought to the poor souls outside, a wiry man who was apparently one of the wardens stopped them.

"Hey, you two, not so fast. You already been checked for vermin?" He shot them a disparaging look. "I don't want you bringing in lice or something worse, you miserable rabble."

Emmerich held his badge with its embossed eagle up to the guy's face. "This is the only creature on our bodies."

A look at the eagle turned the warden obsequious. "Most honorable inspector," he said bowing slightly. "I am at your service."

"The most admirable type of person. Kissing up to power and kicking the downtrodden." Emmerich looked the man up and down, full of disgust. The people seeking shelter here might have seemed repellent on the outside. But they were a thousand times more palatable to Emmerich than this bootlicker. "What do you know about the man who spent the last five nights in bed number 165?"

"165? No idea. We don't ask for their names or backgrounds. We don't ask them anything. And even if we could . . . We have two hundred beds, and their occupants change every five days, how could I possibly remember anything?"

A thought suddenly occurred to Emmerich. "Where is bed 165?"

The warden told them how to find it. When they entered the dorm room, they were hit with stifling, fetid air.

While Emmerich strode stolidly into the room, Winter visibly cringed. "Perhaps we should question the housemaster," he suggested.

Winter looked anxious to flee as quickly as possible. The world outside had been tough since the war, but compared to this place it didn't seem so bad to him.

"You heard what the warden said: they don't take any personal information. The homeless get a bed and a warm meal. Nobody cares about anything else. If anyone will know anything, it'll be the man's comrades in misery."

They went through the dorm room, a long, narrow room with fifteen beds lined up against two opposing walls with no more than an arm's length between them. It was dim, so it was hard to read the numbers which were written on the wall at the head of each bed.

"Here." Emmerich pointed to an empty bed, stopped in front of it, then sat down on it. Comfortable it was not. There was no mattress, just two tattered blankets on wire mesh strung from a metal frame. There was a pillow, too, with a blue patterned case that was so greasy that its shine was plain to see even in the dull light of the room.

Emmerich stood up again. "Could I please have your attention," he called, garnering nothing more than a yawn from the men lying in the other beds. "We need some information in the man from bed 165."

"He's downstairs getting our soup," said a voice.

"We looking for information about the man who probably spent the previous five nights in bed 165," Emmerich corrected. "Anybody know his name?"

Again only yawns, coughs, and a quiet murmur.

The bells in the tower of the nearby Weißgerber church struck eight times, and the present company showed more interest in the whereabouts of their soup than in the concerns of the two inspectors.

Emmerich searched his pockets, fished out a half-empty packet of tobacco, and held it up.

"Oh yeah, now I remember," said the man in the next bed.

"Me, too," said one on the opposite wall. "I was here the last two nights, I spoke to him."

"His name was something with D," said another man.

Then it was quiet again.

Emmerich understood, felt in his pockets again, and conjured up a packet of rolling papers and a banknote.

Expectant silence. The men watched suspiciously and then ravenously as Emmerich began to roll a cigarette.

"Pfff," one whispered. "He should offer more than that."

"The longer you wait, the less will be left." He lit the cigarette, took a few deep breaths, and then blew out a cloud of smoke.

"Dietrich Jost," said the man from the next bed, causing insults and curses to fly.

"That's better. It's not so difficult." Emmerich motioned for Winter to take notes.

"He served in Galicia," said another man. "Three years."

"He was a zookeeper before the war."

"But he couldn't work afterwards because his nerves were shot."

"His old lady left him, too. She couldn't take it anymore. The constant trembling." The man in the bed next to Jost's put out his arms and flailed about wildly. "It really was shit sleeping next to him."

"So he was shell-shocked?"

"Oh yeah," came the answer in unison.

Emmerich knew a lot of men who'd lost not their lives but control over their bodies on the front. Their limbs twitched uncontrollably, and they often had difficulty speaking.

"Would he have been capable of loading and firing a pistol in his condition?"

"Definitely not," said the man on the opposite wall, and all the rest agreed.

Emmerich rolled another cigarette, which was met with loud protest by those present, protest that Emmerich studiously ignored. He needed to think. Was it really possible that Dietrich Jost hadn't killed himself?

"Did he seem distraught by his circumstances?"

"Distraught?" The man in the next bed fixed on the banknote and the tobacco that Emmerich had put down next to him. "Not really. He was a little . . . well, you know." He twirled his finger next to his temple. "Said some crazy things and had convinced himself that he was going to emigrate to Brazil soon." He started to laugh. "He liked the idea. And he had this one friend, who always looked out for him with a bit of money here and there. What was his name again? Something with Z."

"Zeiner," another man interjected helpfully. "Harald Zeiner. Good guy. Had a big heart."

"Just had it good. Nobody looked after any of us poor bastards."

"What's with the cig anyway? Who gets to smoke it? And why all the questions? Did Jost get into some kind of trouble?"

"Where can I find Zeiner?" Emmerich ignored the questions.

"He doesn't have a fixed address. He sleeps here and there. The best place to find him is at the Kitty Bar. He started working there recently."

"Kitty Bar? Where is that?" Emmerich, who knew Vienna nightlife well, had never heard of the place.

"How should I know where it is? Do I look like someone who could afford to hang around in some fancy bar? I'm happy if I can afford a swig of the cheapest stuff, forget a glass or a bartender." The man was starting to get agitated. "What is with the cig?"

"Does anyone else know anything?" Emmerich called out through the room, but there was no answer, just unhappy grumbles.

"I think I know what bar he means," whispered Winter.

Emmerich looked surprised, stood up, and thanked the homeless men. "It's been an honor, gentlemen." He tipped his cap and headed for the exit. He left the goodies on the bed.

Wild shouts and curses rang out even before they'd left the room.

"I'd wait a minute," said Emmerich to the man they encountered in the hall carrying a large pot. "Don't want to upset the soup."

4

I want to be absolutely sure it wasn't a suicide," said Emmerich when they were finally back out on the street, able to breathe in the cold, clear air. "Dietrich Jost fought for God, for Kaiser, and for *Vaterland* and paid a dear price. Nobody kills a war veteran without getting punished. Not in my city. So where's this Kitty Bar?"

Winter ran his hands over his face as if he could wipe away the invisible sheen of misery and suffering that clung to him from the shelter. "I think he meant the Chatham Bar."

"The Chatham Bar?" Emmerich was visibly surprised. "Have you ever been in there?" It was a crazy bar better known around Vienna by the name *Je t'aime* Bar. And it wasn't a reference to the romantic type of love.

"I only know their ads. With the black cat sitting in front of a champagne glass. Never been inside."

"Then it's time you were."

"A day of firsts," mumbled Winter, following his superior as he headed in the direction of Dorotheergasse in 1st district.

"Evening," said Emmerich to the overgrown bouncer as he reached for the doorknob when they arrived.

"Get the hell out of here," said the man, blocking their way. "We don't let in the likes of you."

"Aha, and why not?" said Emmerich, sticking out his chin.

"Because you stink. And anyone who can't afford soap can't pay for drinks either."

Winter sniffed his underarms. The long day and the visit to the homeless shelter had indeed caused an olfactory effect.

"Now fuck off, and fast." The bouncer made a hand gesture as if shooing away stray dogs.

Emmerich looked the man over. His scarred face left no doubt that he'd spent a lot of time in the ring, and Emmerich decided he'd be better off not starting a fight. The guy was large, and nearly six feet tall . . . He wouldn't be able to take the boxer on his own. And he couldn't imagine Winter was of any use at all when it came to street fighting. It was a shame he couldn't just identify himself as a policeman—but then the joint would empty out immediately.

"You always run into people a second time," he promised, and trudged off with Winter in tow. They went around the corner to the service entrance, and Emmerich banged on the door.

"Garbage collection," he said when a young woman in a checkered apron opened the door.

"What? Now? At this hour? Hang on, they don't do the rounds until the day after tomorrow. And since when do you collect the stuff door-to-door?"

"Didn't you read the notice? It's a new city service." Emmerich tipped his cap and bowed slightly. "So where are the bins? We don't have all night. We have to keep a tight schedule or we'll catch hell from city hall."

The woman hesitated for a moment, squinted her eyes, and then stepped aside to let them in. "Around the corner to the left."

Emmerich followed her directions, grabbed a stinking bin full of cigarette ash and broken glass, and carried it out. Winter did the same.

"Christ, Hilde, what's with the wine?" yelled a man. "The guests are complaining."

"Go ahead. We can handle this."

Emmerich waited until the woman had disappeared,

dumped the contents of the bin against the exterior wall of the building, then put it back in its place inside. Then he and Winter slipped into the bar.

They were immediately enveloped in a warm cloud of perfume and the haze of countless cigarettes. The buzz and hum of voices filled the room; a woman dressed completely in lace belted out a popular song accompanied by a man on piano.

Die Männer sind alle Verbrecher,
ihr Herz ist ein finsteres Loch,
hat tausend verschied'ne Gemächer,
aber lieb, aber lieb sind sie doch.

Men are all criminals,
their hearts a dark hole,
with a thousand different loyalties,
but they're lovable, lovable all the same.

The place was decorated in Secession style. It had a timber ceiling, and marble tables, Thonet chairs and plush red sofas sat all around the room, over which hung little dim lamps.

The guests, predominantly men with fat wallets, were dressed in the latest fashions and smoking cigarillos. They talked animatedly.

"We could have just shown our badges," said Winter.

"We could have. But sometimes it's better to stay anonymous—you'll learn that, too." He marched to the bar, took off his cap, and waved over a barman. "I'm looking for Harri."

"Who?" The barman, whose nametag identified him as Franz, gestured to a few guests calling for schnapps that he'd be right with them.

"Harald Zeiner. He's supposed to be working here."

Franz's brow furrowed. "There's no Zeiner or Harald on

the staff." He paused for a second and then winked. "At least not on the official staff."

"Perhaps we're in the wrong place . . . " Winter looked questioningly at his boss.

"I don't believe so." Emmerich thanked the barman and turned to his underling, who was now looking at the scene around them with big eyes. "You have any money with you? I bequeathed all of mine to the brothers in misery back on Blattgasse."

Winter reached into his pocket and pulled out a few crowns. Emmerich took them out of his hand and ordered two beers.

"Thanks, keep the change," he said when the desired items appeared.

"We're not allowed to drink on the job." Winter stared at the tankard Emmerich was holding out to him.

"Cheers," Emmerich said, taking a big sip. Boy, did that taste good. It was the little things that made life worth living.

Winter didn't seem to be enjoying the moment quite as much. With his head hanging and his arms pressed to his sides he seemed more like a wet poodle than a young police inspector who'd just put an exciting day behind him.

"What's wrong?"

"We smell." Winter motioned to two women in expensive evening gowns and fur stoles who had just slipped past them, looked at them for a moment, and then quickly turned away. "And it's so elegant and classy here."

Emmerich laughed and gulped down the rest of his beer. "I'll show you how elegant and classy this dump is." He went over to a narrow door with etched glass and opened it.

Winter stared at his boss and at the still full beer in his own hand. Had somebody put something in the boss's drink?

"It's a broom closet," he said. It was maybe four square meters and full of cleaning equipment.

Emmerich pulled Winter into the little room, closed the door behind him and knocked three times against the back wall.

"What are we doing in here?"

Before Emmerich could answer, a small slat opened through which a pair of watery blue eyes appeared. A moment later the wall opened as if by some ghostly hand to reveal another dimly lit room that was divided into small booths. Giggling, groans, and the squeaking of bedsprings left no doubt as to what was happening here. *Lebenslust*, in order to forget the gray squalor for a few sweet moments.

"What delight can I offer the esteemed gentlemen?" A blond dandy with slicked-back hair, a handlebar mustache, and exaggerated gestures raised his right eyebrow and looked the two of them over.

"We've heard such good things about Harald Zeiner that we thought we'd drop by."

"Harri!" The well-groomed man smiled and rubbed his hands. "Unfortunately the Styrian stallion is busy at the moment. Might I recommend someone else?"

Emmerich waved his hand. "We'll wait."

"Certainly." The dandy sauntered over to a booth and stole a glance inside. "It won't be more than a few seconds," he said when he returned. He pulled out a large wallet. "A lively three-way in booth number three. Unfortunately I need to take payment in advance." He named an exorbitant sum.

"That's not necessary." Emmerich walked right past him. "We don't have any explicit services in mind and it won't take long."

Surprisingly, the man did not try to stop them, and instead went back to his spot by the secret door.

Emmerich pulled aside the heavy red curtain that shielded the occupants of booth three from curious glances. A fat man with a sweaty, flushed face was standing in the middle of the small space buttoning his pants while another sat behind him on a narrow bed counting a stack of banknotes.

Emmerich cleared his throat. "Harald Zeiner? I need to talk to you."

The man on the bed stared at him, dumbfounded.

"Who's this guy?" The fat guy fiddled frantically with his belt. "Is he from the vice squad?" He stumbled out in a panic, which nobody could blame him for, since "crimes against nature" were punishable by a jail sentence of one to five years.

Emmerich didn't even look at him. "It's about Dietrich Jost," he said to Zeiner.

"What about him?" asked the man, completely shocked.

"He's dead."

"Dead? That can't be . . . "

Winter tapped Emmerich on the back. "Boss," he whispered.

"Just a second . . . " Emmerich brushed him off and turned his attention back to Zeiner. "He shot himself. At least that's what it looks like at first glance."

"Shot himself?" Zeiner shook his head in disbelief. "But . . . but he was in no condition to handle a weapon . . . "

Emmerich felt a more forceful smack on his shoulder. "In a second," he repeated angrily, but this time it wasn't Winter; it was the brawny bouncer. He put Emmerich in a headlock and dragged him into another booth.

"You always run into people a second time," he hissed in Emmerich's ear. "Who knew it would be so soon?"

The dandy was waiting for them. "You didn't really think you could walk in here and act like you run the place, did you? Because I run the place." He pulled out his wallet again. "Now you're going to pay."

"I've got nothing." Emmerich grinned. He wondered where Winter was. "I don't have so much as a *heller*."

"Then you'll pay in another currency." The man hauled off and punched Emmerich right in the face.

He spat blood and tried to extricate himself from the hold, but it was as if he were in a stockade. The greasy man gave Emmerich a left hook. He was just winding up to kick him between the legs when a dull thud rung out. In the next instant the bouncer loosened his grip and then fell groaning to the floor.

Emmerich wanted to make use of his regained freedom to repay the dandy for his punches, but then there was a clink, and when he looked up Winter was standing there with just the handle of his beer tankard in his hand. The two other men were now both lying unconscious on the floor.

"I hid behind the curtain. I didn't know what I should—" Winter explained.

"Well done." Emmerich patted him on the shoulder and stepped over the puddle that had formed on the floor. "Shame about the beer though." He pulled the curtain closed and went back to booth number three.

It was empty.

Zeiner had disappeared into thin air, and there was nothing else for Emmerich to do except to issue a description of the escapee and then call it a night.

Arriving home, he closed the door quietly behind him, took off his jacket and cap, and crept into the kitchen. He poured himself a schnapps. Hopping down from the wall had been a silly and stupid thing to do. His leg still hurt, and he hoped the alcohol could numb the pain enough for him to fall asleep.

He leaned against the stove, which, surprisingly, was still warm, and closed his eyes. It was nice to have a proper home.

With his salary and the money Luise was able to make working at home they were able to afford this two-room apartment with a little kitchen. They'd been living here together for a year. Their home was modestly furnished, but they enjoyed the luxury of having it all to themselves. They weren't forced to take in subletters or boarders, and they shared the bathroom on the hall with just one other person, old Frau Ganglberger, rather than an entire floor of people.

The idea of having his own family had always been an abstract fantasy for Emmerich, but then he'd met Luise and discovered a whole new side of himself. He'd found himself to be a devoted husband and caring father despite the fact that he'd never liked children and had shunned the mysteries of love up to that point.

Thinking of the children, it occurred to him how quiet it was. No coughing and no crying disturbing the nighttime silence. He peeked into the bedroom where Emil, Ida, and little Paul were sleeping peacefully next to each other in the big bed.

"There you are." Luise came out of the living room and nuzzled his back.

"Were you able to find cough syrup?"

"Cough syrup and pork belly. I rendered it and made schmalz. Ate it with acorn bread. There's some left over if you're hungry."

He wanted to kiss her but stopped himself when he saw that her face was paler and more worried looking than usual. "What's going on?"

She took the glass of schnapps from him, took a big slug, and crossed herself. "I have a bad feeling," she said. "That something's going to happen."

"Come on." He took her hands in his and held them tightly. "You're just tired and overworked. Go to sleep, I'll be right in."

She went over to the stove and put glowing coals into a heavy clothes iron. "Something's going to happen," she repeated, spread the ironing cloth out on the dining table and took a threadbare shirt from a basket of freshly washed clothes. "Back when Xaver died, when the war made me a widow and the kids orphans, I had the same feeling back then."

Then Luise said nothing more, she just silently ironed.

5.

Harald Zeiner wandered aimlessly in the night trying to get his thoughts together.

When the police inspector had told him that his friend had shot himself, he'd been shocked at first, then confused about the circumstances, and finally pieced together a ghastly puzzle. Murder. Everything suddenly made sense: Jost's unexpected optimism, his constant yammering about Brazil . . .

But since his evening meal just now, Zeiner was no longer so sure about his hypothesis. Was his suspicion that Jost had been murdered just a figment of his imagination? Or had he been taken in like a stupid chick by the assurances and pretty words of a cold-blooded murderer?

What was true and what was a lie? He of all people should have been able to see through it since he made his money fooling other people.

He lit a cigarette, crossed Nußdorfer Lände, and climbed down the sloped, brush-covered bank of the Danube canal, known colloquially as the Vienna Arm. There he stared at the dark water slowly flowing toward Port Albern, where it would join the Danube and then flow on toward the Black Sea.

Maybe Jost really had committed suicide, he thought. The thought had crossed his own mind many times, and he'd gone through the various methods in his head. Jumping into water had never been an option. At least not the Danube. That river would carry him east, where he had served—and he never wanted to go back there again. Neither alive nor dead.

He looked up at the stars. How indifferent they were. Some thought they guided mankind's fate, but in reality they couldn't care less.

"Enough whining," he admonished himself. Moaning wasn't going to make things better, and it wasn't going to bring Jost back to life either.

Zeiner inhaled so deeply on the last of his cigarette that the ember nearly burnt his finger, then flicked the butt into the water.

All of a sudden he heard a rustling behind him. Before he could turn around there was a cracking sound and a dull pain went through his skull. He wanted to scream and to defend himself, but his body refused to listen. He slowly tipped forward and a moment later was swallowed by wet cold.

He floated eastward for a few meters with his face up. The last thing he saw before the dark flood engulfed him was the stars in the firmament looking down on him utterly impassively.

6.

Emmerich was tired. It hadn't been the children keeping him up the previous night but the aching in his leg and Luise, who had puttered around anxiously until the morning hours. He would give a kingdom for a proper cup of coffee right now.

Instead he took a gulp of cold tea and choked down a dry piece of bread. Then he headed for the commissariat.

"Morning." He yawned, pushed back a strand of his brown hair, and rubbed his stubble. Hörl was finishing the night shift. "Anything new?"

"We just got word. A guy fitting Zeiner's description was just fished out of the Danube."

"Dead or alive?"

"Dead, of course. In these temperatures you freeze as fast as you drown."

"Damn it," said Emmerich. "Any details?"

"Whether he froze or drowned?"

"No, you clown. Where did he fall in? Where was he pulled out? Accidental or suspicious? Is the body clearly identifiable?"

"Here's the report. Same size, same facial description, same clothing as in the description. I don't know anything more than that." Hörl handed the report to Emmerich along with Zeiner's file from the criminal registry in which he was listed for gross indecency and theft. "I'll send somebody over to have a look at the body. I hope it wasn't murder, otherwise we'll have to pass the case to *Leib und Leben*."

"I'll take care of it." Emmerich rolled up the papers and shoved them into the inside pocket of his jacket. He saw any chance to distinguish himself to the elite division as an opportunity. "You find anything on Dietrich Jost?"

Hörl shook his head. "Seems to have been clean. Either that or he never got caught."

"A very good morning, gentlemen."

Winter, fresh as spring, entered the station house and earned a grunt from Hörl and a roll of the eyes from Emmerich for his abundance of energy.

"We found Zeiner."

"That was fast. Shall we question him right away?"

"Good luck." Hörl clapped Winter on the shoulder as he put on his jacket.

"What does that mean?" said Winter, turning to Emmerich.

He just shook his head, handed him the report that Hörl had given him, and pointed to the door.

"Where are we going?"

"To the turnips."

Winter had figured out that it was better not to ask his boss too many questions, and followed him silently to the Vienna Arm.

There, despite the early hour, brisk activity prevailed. Barges filled to the brim with white turnips sat anchored at the port. Turnips were a sought-after commodity, since they kept well and could be eaten all winter long. Little surprise then that there was already a huge swarm of stalwart housewives aggressively haggling over the prices while a horde of children circled the boats and carts like vultures waiting for a chance to pilfer the coveted goods.

"Piss off, you scallywag," sneered one merchant as he smacked a filthy little chap on the head. "The bastards," he said, turning to Emmerich, who had come up beside him.

"They make off with anything that's not nailed down. If you don't pay attention they'll steal the bread right out of your mouth."

Emmerich nodded. Hunger was harder to bear for children than for adults. "A body was supposed to have been dragged out of the water here. You know anything about it?"

The merchant sighed. "I only saw it from a distance. Terrible thing. You should ask the dockworkers over there. They fished him out." In that brief moment of inattention, a throng of children had snuck up again. "Gang of thieves," grumbled the man, kicking the nearest one in the butt. "No five-finger discount here!"

Emmerich winked at the children and approached a few men who were penny-bowling. They'd propped a narrow board up on a rock to create a bowling alley. They were taking turns rolling *heller* coins down the incline, hoping to get them as close as possible to a stick stuck upright in the ground. Whoever was closest won all the coins.

"Morning, gentlemen," Emmerich interrupted the game. "I was told you made a rather macabre catch this morning."

"You can say that again," said one of the workers, a stocky man with a nose covered with red veins.

"Wasn't the type of catch you'd want to eat," said another, who had a pockmarked face.

Emmerich looked around. "Where'd you take the body?"

"Over there in the bushes. We covered him with branches and told the children scary stories so they'd stop poking him with sticks."

Emmerich nodded. You really had to worry about the next generation. And about the current one, too. These men seemed unaffected by their discovery. A life full of deprivation numbed people. "You notice anything unusual?"

"He was wet," said one of the men. He laughed and rolled his next coin down the board.

"And cold," said another.

His coin landed so perfectly next to the stick that his buddies let fly a barrage of curses. Winter blushed.

"Did you see him jump?" Emmerich gestured to Brigitta Bridge, which connected the 20th district to the 9th.

The men said no and started another round of *heller* rolling. "We would have heard it. He must have jumped in further up."

Emmerich left the dockworkers to their game and went over to the bushes. Winter trudged reluctantly along behind him. "You have to get used to corpses!" said Emmerich. "They're part of the job. And of life."

The first thing he noticed was that the body was naked except for underpants. "Didn't he have anything on?" he called to the dockworkers, at which point they became oddly quiet.

"Jesus! Stripping a corpse? Is nothing sacred anymore?" Winter held a handkerchief over his mouth and nose in disgust.

"Decent clothes are hard to come by," stated Emmerich, kneeling beside the cold, sallow corpse.

The eyes were closed, the mouth slightly open. Death had contorted his face, but it was still unmistakably the corpse of Harald Zeiner.

"Do you think he did it because of us? Because he was afraid he'd be arrested?" murmured Winter.

"Be a man and put the handkerchief away," grumbled Emmerich. "And as far as your question . . . If everyone in the city who was engaged in some illegal activity were to throw himself into the Danube, there'd be more bodies than fish in there." He looked out over the water, flowing murky and gray.

Winter hesitantly put his handkerchief back in his pocket. "Maybe it was an accident? Maybe he was drunk and fell in?"

"You don't just fall into the Danube canal. And besides . . .

Doesn't it seem odd to you? First the dubious suicide of Jost, and then his best friend just happens to fall into the Danube? The whole thing stinks." Emmerich found two cuts on the back of the dead man's head and pointed to them.

"Couldn't he have hit his head on rocks in the river?"

The inspector ignored his junior partner and continued to examine the corpse. The body showed no signs of a struggle, though there were scars from the war and from a hard life of deprivation.

"What's with his mouth?" Winter took a tentative step closer. "Could that be from chewing tobacco?"

"What?" Emmerich pushed the head to the side, and when he still couldn't see anything he grabbed a small stick and pushed the jaws open. The dead man's mouth was indeed stained yellow. "No, that would be more brown." He went so close that the tip of his nose nearly touched Zeiner's blue lips. "Everything's yellow, strange. The medical examiner is going to have to look at it."

A group of curious children had gathered unnoticed and was watching the scene.

"Eew, they're going to kiss," yelled a girl with a runny nose.

"If you touch him, his ghost will come for you tonight and drown you," said another.

"Then you'd better take care." Emmerich jumped up, raised his arms suddenly and gave a bloodcurdling scream.

The children shot off like a school of startled fish—all except one little boy, about the same age as Emil. He just stood there and smiled. His clothes were shabby but clean, and there was a bulge on the side of his patched pants—part of a turnip peeked out.

Emmerich had an idea. "Do you have any change with you?" he said, turning to Winter. "I forgot to throw some in my pocket."

Winter unenthusiastically pulled a few crowns out of his

pants pocket and handed them to his boss, who in turn held them out in front of the boy.

"Did you see them fish the body out?" The boy nodded solicitously. "Did you also see them undress him?" More nodding. "Did you see where they took the clothes?" The boy pointed to a barge at anchor behind the dockworkers. "If you bring me everything in the pockets of the clothing, you get a reward." He turned back to Winter, who was staring at him with his mouth open. "It's easier this way," he said.

The boy crept past the men like an old pro, climbed silently onto the barge, and disappeared. A moment later he was standing in front of Emmerich and handed him a lump of wet paper.

"That's everything," he said.

Emmerich handed him a crown along with a second coin. "Do you know where the nearest police station is?" The boy nodded as earnestly as a professional courier. "Go bring a patrolman here. Tell him—" The boy sprinted off even before he could finish the sentence.

Emmerich examined the mushy lump in his hand and, disappointed, had to concede that he wouldn't be able to reconstruct the letter or whatever it had been. Then he carefully picked apart the white lump. His face lit up.

"Are you thirsty?" he called to Winter, who was standing idly by the corpse.

"Thanks, but water is the last thing I feel like now."

"I'm not talking about water."

When the boy returned—he had two patrol officers in tow—Emmerich pressed another crown into his palm. The tot dashed off, beaming.

The inspector ordered the officers to take the dead man to the medical examiner. "Let's go," he said to Winter and then he strutted as confidently as possible to Liechtensteinstraße. His wretched leg. If the pain didn't let up soon, he would have to come up with some way to deal with it.

"What's the story with the smugglers at this point?" asked Winter, who, naturally, once again had no idea where his boss wanted to go.

"They won't get away from us. They'll be plying their miserable trade as long as there is hardship in the city—and I fear that will be quite some time."

"So what are we going to do now?"

Emmerich stopped at a tram shelter on the 36 line. "We're going to ride out to Nußdorf and enjoy a glass of wine at Poldi Tant."

7.

"Incidentally, I don't have any more money with me," said Winter when they exited the tram at Nußdorfer Platz and headed toward a rustic tavern.

Emmerich took in this information without reacting, opened the door, and stepped into the establishment. It was *Frühschoppen* hour, and the rustic wooden benches and chairs were full. A large green-tiled stove gave off cozy heat, and a Schrammel-music quartet was playing typical Viennese songs.

Und wenn ich einmal sterben sollt',
so soll es dorten sein,
wo auf den Bergen ringsherum
wächst Österreicher Wein.
Als Abschied singt mir ein Lied,
vom deutschen Vaterland,
dann senkt mich in ein kühles Grab
am blauen Donaustrand.

If someday I must die,
let it be that place
where on surrounding hills
grow Austrian grapes.
As goodbye sing me a song
of the German *Vaterland*,
then lower me into a cold grave
on the blue Danube strand.

The morbid, melancholy music did nothing to diminish the merry mood of the wine drinkers. Boisterous laughter and banter filled the room, toasts were offered, and guests happily raised their glasses.

"*Mahlzeit*, gentlemen." The two inspectors were greeted by a rosy-cheeked, buxom middle-aged waitress in a green dirndl. "Should be a couple spots opening up in the back in a moment. You can have a look at the menu in the meantime."

Sure enough, two old men with Kaiser Franz Josef-style sideburns soon stood up and staggered toward the exit.

"We don't have any money," whispered Winter to Emmerich as he headed for the vacant seats.

"What will it be, gentlemen?" The woman in the dirndl had followed them to their places and now waited expectantly with a pencil in her hand.

Winter stared at his hands as Emmerich discreetly flashed his badge to her. "Food safety inspectors," he said. "We got a complaint about the schnitzel and the Grüner Veltliner wine."

The woman's face flushed. "Who lodged a complaint?"

"Anonymous report. But we have to take it seriously, of course. Can't risk any threats to the general health. If the hygiene standard isn't up to scrub, you'll have to shut down. Or at least pay a hefty fine."

She put her hands on her hips. "You are free to taste the schnitzel and wine. There are no grounds for any complaint."

Emmerich sighed. "Then bring us two orders."

The inspector could tell his young colleague was embarrassed. He was shifting uneasily in his chair. He certainly hadn't imagined his new job this way. But he would learn.

"Did we really come here to scam food?" whispered Winter.

Emmerich placed a tattered pack of matches on the table. On it was an image of a man in a red doublet hoisting a large tankard to his lips. Above that were emblazoned the words "POLDI TANT. Nußdorfer Platz 4."

"Zeiner had it in his pocket, and the Danube canal starts two hundred meters from here. I think he must have been murdered around here somewhere and thrown into the water."

"*Bitte schön!* Two schnitzels and two glasses of Grüner Veltliner." The waitress put down the food and drinks and stood in front of the two guests with her arms crossed.

Emmerich sniffed his wine and held the glass up to the light. "Seems heavily sulfured," he said, shoving a portrait of Zeiner toward the indignant woman. "Ever seen this guy?"

While the woman studied the photo, he took a large swig and then began to dig into his schnitzel. Only now did he realize how hungry he was. Breakfast had been pitiful.

"He was here yesterday with two other men. Just before closing time. They sat over there, the three of them." She gestured to a table next to the tiled stove and then stared at Winter, who was sipping at his wine.

"Seems . . . overly sulfured . . . it's true," he said quietly and looked up fearfully as if he were meeting the eyes of a dangerous predator.

"Can you describe the other two?" Emmerich had already put away half his schnitzel and was working on the side dish— potatoes with parsley.

The waitress shrugged her shoulders. "Nondescript faces. They had a heated argument. Didn't hear what about."

"Anything else?"

Who do I look like, Mata Hari? I'm just a simple waitress, not a spy. I make sure people get their food and don't eat and run. That's it."

"Could you possibly come to the Margareten commissariat and look at a few mug shots later?"

The woman narrowed her eyes. "I thought you were food safety inspectors."

Winter slunk so far down in his chair that he nearly disappeared beneath the table.

"We are," said Emmerich, casually finishing his wine. "The two men violated the Health Code, paragraph 126, clause 10."

She seemed satisfied with that answer, since her facial expression loosened, she nodded, and she shifted her attention to other guests.

"Are you not going to eat that?" Emmerich took Winter's plate and started to inhale his portion.

Winter didn't object. "Have a look," he said, gesturing to a woman at another table who was eating *Kaiserschmarrn*. "Her lips."

They were stained yellow.

Emmerich called the waitress over again. "So that's the way it is," he said, pointing discreetly to the woman at the other table. "Charging exorbitant prices for dishes and then preparing them with some cheap substitute instead of real egg yolks. Boy, if I were to mention that to my bosses—"

The woman went pale. "It's nothing unhealthy, there was no other choice for years, and the taste is acceptable. They don't notice the difference. Perhaps you'd like to try it?"

Emmerich nodded. "If possible, with stewed plums or applesauce," he called after her, then turned back to Winter. "We have to find out who those men were that Zeiner met last night. They could be important witnesses. Maybe one of them is even the murderer."

"So you're sure it was a murder?"

"There were two murders." Emmerich finished Winter's schnitzel, and the *Kaiserschmarrn* was served shortly thereafter. This, too, he consumed as ravenously as if he hadn't eaten for weeks. When he was finished, he stuck out his tongue. "Yellow?"

"Just like Zeiner's."

"Most egg substitutes have coloring in them so that the dish at least looks the way it used to. The stuff can really stain your mouth."

"How long does it last?"

"Depends on how often you brush your teeth."

Emmerich stood up and a stabbing pain shot through his leg again. He turned away so Winter wouldn't see him grimace, reached for Winter's wine, which was still sitting nearly untouched on the table, and gulped it down.

"The schnitzel wasn't veal, it was horse," he said to the woman as he made his way out. "But at least it was fresh. And I'm willing to make an exception and turn a blind eye to the sulfur and egg substitute. *Auf Wiedersehen.*"

"What's that paragraph about that you mentioned from the Health Code?" asked Winter as they walked toward the Danube canal.

Emmerich shrugged. "No idea. I don't even know if there is a Health Code."

8.

They'd searched the Danube Promenade, Josef von Schemmerl Bridge, and the Nußdorf weir system without finding any signs of a crime.

Winter suggested they extend the search radius to include the Kuchelauer harbor, but Emmerich aborted the search. First, he was sure that the murder hadn't been committed so far away. And second, every step meant an unspeakable ordeal for his leg. He needed pain medication. Desperately.

"Let's ride to the medical examiner's," he said in the hopes of not only learning more information about Jost and Zeiner, but also of getting hold of some medication. Even if they were primarily concerned with the dead there on Spitalgasse, doctors were doctors, after all, and they could issue prescriptions.

The closer they got to the building—a three-winged structure behind which rose the hulking Fool's Tower, a round, prison-like building where mental patients had once been shut away—the more nervous Winter became.

"Corpses, corpses, always more corpses," he mumbled, though Emmerich was able to hear him.

"Don't get so worked up," he growled. "At least here they've been washed and nicely laid out. You should have seen the dead on the battlefield. Mangled and covered with blood." The pain had left him short-tempered. When he noticed Winter's shocked expression he regretted his outburst immediately. The youngster couldn't help his inexperience. On the contrary, he was doing his best to be useful. "You'll see," he said, patting him on the shoulder. "The medical examiner's office is nothing to worry about."

Winter forced a smile, which quickly faded again when a fetid smell reached his nose.

"That's not the bodies," Emmerich attempted to calm him. "It's from the Alserbach." He pointed to a drainage canal where filthy, brown water flowed behind a low wall. "So here we are."

The Forensic Institute housed a morgue, where the deceased from the general hospital were laid out behind thick black curtains, and a room for safekeeping corpses undergoing court-ordered examinations. In addition, there was a chemistry lab, a little kitchen, and a conference room for the medical examiner's commission. But the heart of the complex was the room where autopsies were performed—a sort of amphitheater, the roof of which had skylight windows to provide as much light as possible on the subject of examination below.

The dead man lying on the metal table in the middle of the room, pale blue, waxy, and completely naked, was none other than Harald Zeiner. Bending over him and prodding around in the opened corpse was a young man in his mid-twenties at the most.

"There's no lecture today," he said without looking up. "Professor Hirschkron is at a conference, and Professor Meixner is out sick."

"And who are you?"

Emmerich, who was ill at ease with the fact that an inexperienced little bastard was poking around in his corpse, regarded the coroner with eyes narrowed in suspicion.

The young man looked up, surprised. "I am Aberlin Wiesegger, the new assistant. And you are?" Even close up he didn't look a day over twenty-five.

Emmerich looked him up and down. His white apron was

splattered with reddish brown droplets, and in his hand he held something that looked like a large pair of tweezers.

Apparently the view of the exposed organs, all glistening in various shades of red, was too much for Winter. Out of the corner of his eye, Emmerich saw Winter's gaze bounce as casually as possible around the room before finally alighting on an enameled tub next to the dissection table. Emmerich himself, meanwhile, was focused on Wiesegger, who was eyeing him like a combative dog.

"I am Inspector First Class August Emmerich," he said a little too loudly while presenting his badge.

"I see. So it's you I have to blame for the two suicide victims."

Emmerich narrowed his eyes further still until they were just slits. What did this bloody—literally bloody—newbie know anyway? "You believe the cases to be suicide?"

The youngster put his tool down on a side table. "The entrance and exit wounds on Herr Jost are typical of suicide. And this gentleman . . . " he motioned to Zeiner, " . . . shows no signs of a defensive struggle."

"And what about the wounds on the back of his head?"

"They are most likely from rocks in the canal, which the current dragged him over."

"Jost trembled from shell shock. How would he have loaded and discharged a weapon?" Emmerich interjected as Winter continued to stare at the tub.

"Where there's a will, there's a way." Wiesegger bent over the corpse again, extracted the liver, and placed it on a metal scale. "How else would you explain the gunshot residue on his hands?"

Emmerich thought for a moment. "The murderer could have put the gun in his hand and pulled off an extra shot," he speculated. "In which case we'd find another bullet in the woods."

"That wouldn't prove anything. If he trembled so much it's

quite possible he missed with his first shot and had to fire a second time." The young doctor noted the weight of the liver and then looked at Emmerich again. "Modern techniques are able to confirm whether two bullets were fired from the same weapon—the order in which they were shot, however, nobody can determine."

Emmerich could see his theory was on shaky ground. "But you can't rule out the possibility of another party?"

Wiesegger shook his head. "My esteemed Herr Emmerich, I cannot rule it out any more than you can prove it. Naturally murder is possible. There are no indications either way. But in my view, suicide is the more likely scenario. Times are hard. Many people lost everything as a result of the war—including their perspective on the future. The suicide rate is higher than ever, and the two men that you sent me fit the profile perfectly."

"Is that your final word?"

Wiesegger nodded. "That's what it will say in my report."

He turned his attention to a young man, probably a student, who had just entered the room. "I'm nearly finished," he said. "Bring him on in."

"What's the story with the coloration around his mouth?" Emmerich was clutching at straws. Perhaps the yellow film wasn't from an egg substitute after all, but from some sort of poison.

"Harmless. I'd guess it's Dottofix. The coloration would have disappeared the next time he brushed his teeth. If it would make you feel better, I'll take a swab."

Emmerich nodded. "Uh . . . there was one other . . . one other concern," he stammered.

"Just a moment please." The budding coroner went over and turned a faucet on, letting water run into the tub. A few seconds later the door opened and the student pushed a heavy stretcher into the room. On it was an obese body covered with frost.

"Could you please give him a hand?" Wiesegger asked as the student shoved the stretcher alongside the tub.

"Excuse me? Could you possibly—" Winter didn't realize at first that he was being spoken to. Only when someone tapped him did he awake from his trance. "We need to transfer the man into the tub, to thaw him out," the student explained. "The cooling unit in the morgue has gone haywire and froze all the bodies."

Winter caught his breath. "So that's why the tub is there," he sputtered.

"We get a lot of frozen bodies in the winter," said the young man as if it was the most normal thing in the world.

"I'll do it," Emmerich hurriedly volunteered. "Wait for me outside, I'll be right there."

In actuality his goal wasn't so much to spare Winter as it was to get him out of the way so he could ask for pain medication unobserved.

The relief on Winter's face was obvious. He scurried out of the examination room as if he were fleeing a burning building. Emmerich helped hoist the overweight body into the tub and waited until the student had left the room again.

"What else can I do for you?" asked Wiesegger as he threaded thick black twine through the eye of a long needle.

Emmerich cleared his throat. "An old war wound has been giving me trouble since yesterday. You don't happen to have any pain medicine handy, do you?"

The coroner pushed the needle through the skin between Zeiner's collarbones. "As you can see, my patients are immune to pain, one and all. As a result I am never faced with the trouble of having to administer analgesics."

"Could you possibly write me a prescription?" Emmerich was reluctant to have to ask the youngster for something. But what else could he do?

"Unfortunately I don't have a prescription pad. Who am I

to order around a pharmacist anyway?" He didn't pay any further attention to Emmerich; instead he methodically stitched Zeiner's chest closed.

Emmerich could tell that Wiesegger was lying, but he didn't want to debase himself further by begging or telling him anything more about himself or his suffering. "Thanks a lot." He wanted to throw the youngster into the tub with the fat corpse but let it go and hobbled outside, where Winter was waiting for him.

"Does this mean we can focus on the smugglers again?" he asked.

"Nope. Just because that guy can't prove it doesn't mean it wasn't murder, not by a long shot. We're sticking with this case." The pain was seeping into his hips at this point, and it took a lot of self-control to conceal his bad mood. "Listen, I have to take care of something," he said to Winter. "See what you can find out about Jost and Zeiner in the meantime. The best thing to do is to go through the rogues' gallery and the penal records again. Hörl's often sloppy. Maybe he missed something."

"Will do. By the way, are you feeling alright? You look sort of . . . sick."

"Don't you worry. It's just from the over-sulfured wine at Poldi Tant."

Emmerich, his head held high, turned into the next side street, where he leaned against the wall of a building and caught his breath. The pain was barely tolerable.

The first pharmacy he found had no more analgesics in stock, and the second one wouldn't let him buy on credit, even though he showed them his badge. With his teeth gritted, he limped out and nearly fell over a disheveled man who was sitting on the cold ground reaching two arm stumps out toward him.

"Alms," croaked the beggar. "Alms for a poor war invalid."

Emmerich examined the haggard face of the bearded man and rummaged through his pockets in the hope of finding a coin or a cigarette or something else that might appease the man's suffering a little, but all his fingers found was emptiness.

"Sorry," he said as he watched with repulsion the way people hurried past averting their eyes. They didn't want to be confronted with the cripple, a symbol of loss. He reminded them too much of their own losses and fears.

"This is how Vienna treats its heroes!" yelled Emmerich as an older woman wearing a large hat and a fur stole switched to the other side of the street to avoid the beggar. "This man lost everything because he fought for you!"

The passersby stared at the ground and rushed away, leaving the street suddenly empty.

"Please go away," said the mutilated veteran, staring with glassy eyes at the empty hat sitting in front of him. "You're driving away my customers."

Emmerich, his pulse racing, closed his eyes for a moment and without saying another word limped to the nearest bar.

The owner, sufficiently impressed by Emmerich's badge, handed over a liter of rotgut swill.

"I'll bring the money by tomorrow," mumbled Emmerich, opening the bottle right there. The first slug practically stripped the lining of his throat and brought on a fit of coughing, but soon warmth and numbness spread through his body, and the pain in his leg dulled to a bearable level—the only thing that couldn't be dulled was the wrath of the world.

He hobbled back to the beggar, put down the half-full bottle in front of him, and headed back to the commissariat.

"Find anything on Jost?" he called to Winter, who was sitting at his desk studying a file.

"No, I—"

"No?" Emmerich took the papers out of his hand and

looked them over. "These are documents about the smuggling ring. What are you doing? I told you to gather information on Jost and Zeiner."

"Yeah, I know, but," Winter tried to explain himself but Emmerich wasn't going to take any excuses.

"When I tell you to do something, then you have to do it. Got it?"

"But—" Winter started again but was once again interrupted.

"No buts." Emmerich had gotten loud. "When your superior officer orders you to do something, you're to listen. If you had served, you would understand that."

Winter, who looked as if he might break into tears at any moment, motioned behind him. "It wasn't my—"

"EMMERICH!" This time it wasn't Emmerich who interrupted Winter but a large man in his early fifties. He had a full head of brown hair, a rich, bushy beard, and the taut demeanor of an officer of the Imperial and Royal Army. District Inspector Leopold Sander, war hero, recipient of various distinguished service awards, and his new boss. "What's with the show?"

"Forgive me, Herr District Inspector, but he failed to follow my orders. I can't tolerate such impudence."

"Officer Winter bears no such blame. I personally gave him new orders. And as far as the subject of impertinence and failing to follow orders . . . You can certainly imagine my surprise when I learned that you had, without authorization, set aside the investigation of the case of the smugglers to go chase after some chimeras."

"Not chimeras. Homicides."

"Are you working for the *Leib und Leben* division all of a sudden? Because if in fact the case actually has to do with homicide, it belongs to them."

"Before I turned it over I wanted to make sure that we're

indeed dealing with murder. I've just begun the inquiry and will soon be able to say with certainty."

Sander straightened himself so that he was a good head taller than Emmerich. "Have you consulted the medical examiner?" he demanded.

"Yes, Herr Wiesegger believes anything is possible."

"And what does he believe probable?"

Emmerich looked at his hands. He couldn't lie to Sander, because he'd surely get a copy of the report sent to him. "Suicide," he mumbled.

"Suicide," Sander repeated loudly and clearly. "So according to the expert opinion of the medical examiner, it's suicide. Goodness, Emmerich, what in god's name could possibly make you keep pursuing the case?"

"I have a feeling. And anyway, Wiesegger is young and inexperienced. There's a good chance he missed something. I would like Professor Meixner, or better yet Professor Hirschkron, to do another autopsy."

"Wiesegger is supposed to be brilliant. Not for nothing did Hirschkron make him his assistant. You need to put a little trust in the competence of the Vienna Medical Examiner's office. It is world renowned, after all."

"If you would give me one week, then—"

"Thousands upon thousands of upstanding people are being bled by unscrupulous price gougers every single day, and Mayor Reumann has sworn that it will no longer be permitted." Sander grabbed him by the shoulder. "The city council wants results. You are the best man for the case, and for that reason I cannot permit you to let your attention be diverted by some fantastical ideas. Do you understand, Emmerich? The city is counting on you." He thought for a moment and then looked him in the eye. "I am counting on you."

"But—" Emmerich began, but Sander held up his hand and silenced him.

"What is it with you? Have you been drinking?" He sniffed the air.

Emmerich clenched his lips together, took a deep breath, and shook his head.

Sander squinted his eyes and twitched the tip of his nose. "Right," he said after a few seconds, "so everything's settled." He put on his gray felt hat and made as if to leave. "I want you to report to my office tomorrow morning at eight, Emmerich. Good day." The district inspector disappeared through the door at a measured pace.

"I have an idea how we might nab Kolja . . . " Winter tried to defuse the uncomfortable situation, but fell silent when he saw Emmerich's face. "Wasn't trying to cause offense," he mumbled and stuck his nose back into the file lying on the table in front of him.

Emmerich ignored him, bummed a cigarette from Hörl, and went out into the fresh air. There he leaned against the wall of the building and sucked in the blue smoke.

The pain was wearing him down, and he thought seriously for a moment about whether he had imagined the whole thing. Perhaps the shell-shocked vet Jost had gotten lucky with a shot. Perhaps Zeiner was so upset by the death of his friend that he had jumped into the water. Perhaps the deaths really had been just the desperate acts of hopeless, broken men. Perhaps, perhaps, perhaps . . . Too many question marks. Too many uncertainties.

Emmerich had had enough, and he did something that he had never done before. He let work be work and simply went home.

9.

Perhaps I should rethink my relationship to my job and approach it more like Hörl from now on, thought Emmerich as he hobbled up the stairs. He never took his career too seriously and seemed well served by this attitude. It would certainly also be nice to be able to spend more time with Luise and the children . . .

"*Grüß Gott*, Frau Ganglberger. It's an honor, Frau Pospischil," he called as he passed the *bassena*, the public water faucet on the building façade, where the women were sharing the latest gossip.

Suddenly they both fell silent. Frau Ganglberger made a face as if she had just seen a ghost. "Oh god," escaped her lips. "You . . . home . . . already . . . no, no, no."

Emmerich froze. "What is it?"

"Herr Emmerich . . . Herr Emmerich." She threw her hands onto her head. "I don't know what I should say."

"Did something happen to the children? Or to Luise?"

"No . . . well, yes . . . it's . . . "

Emmerich didn't wait for her to finish; instead he stormed inside and up the stairs.

Luise'd had a bad feeling, it suddenly occurred to him, and I didn't take her seriously. If something has happened I'll never forgive myself . . .

His hand trembled as he pulled the key out of his pants pocket, and it took three tries to put it into the lock. "Luise!" he yelled as he was unlocking the door. "Emil! Ida! Paul!"

"Auguuuuust." It was Paul, the youngest, who came running toward him with open arms and latched onto his leg before he could even enter the apartment.

Emmerich lifted him up and hugged the scrawny boy, who was as light as a little bird. He loved this child, loved his little family, and he would do anything he needed to do to protect them.

"Where are Emil and Ida? And where's your mother?"

"With the man." Paul motioned into the apartment with his eyes wide.

Emmerich put the boy back down, put on his brass knuckles, and entered the kitchen. "Who are you?" he asked the stranger who was sitting at the kitchen table. The man was gaunt, his skin had an unhealthy yellowish tint, and he had a dirty bandage wrapped around his head. His cheeks were sunken, his eyes sat deep in his dark-ringed eyeholes. Luise, Emil, and Ida sat silently opposite the man and now looked at Emmerich, terrified. It was cold in the apartment. The stove must have gone out, but nobody seemed to have noticed. "Who are you?" Emmerich repeated. "And what do you want with my family?"

Instead of introducing himself, the man said: "I could ask you the same question."

As it slowly dawned on Emmerich who this man was, it became so quiet in the room that even the tiniest sounds could be heard: the rustling of a mouse in the wall, the rattling of a horse-drawn wagon passing somewhere outside, and the excited chatter of the neighbors at the *bassena*.

"This is Xaver," Luise interrupted the silence. "My husband." The pain in Emmerich's leg suddenly vanished, along with the rage at Sander's appearance and his doubts about work. August Emmerich didn't feel anything at all anymore. "I . . . I didn't know. I had no idea." Luise's voice faltered, and since she was staring at a piece of paper it wasn't clear whom she was speaking to. "I'm . . . I'm so sorry." She put the piece of paper down on the table and started to sob.

Emmerich saw the paper was the certification that her husband, Xaver Koch, had been killed in action. He wanted to hug Luise but stopped himself at the last second. Luise—beloved, best friend, and loyal confidante. *His* Luise . . . Was she still? She'd fallen head over heels for his beautiful brown eyes, that's how she'd described it back when they first got together. They'd gone to the park, together with the children. He'd stolen a kiss in a moment when they weren't paying attention. He'd been alone for so long. And now? Now this life, which she and the children had so enriched, was suddenly in danger. And he couldn't even summon up any rage for the man who seemed more like a lump of misery than a human being.

"Luise," he said softly, "you're not to blame—"

"He's right," said Xaver. "Mistakes happen in the chaos of war."

"You were in a prison camp?" asked Emmerich, tormented. He suddenly felt sympathy for this cadaverous man.

"Siberia," he said taciturnly, holding up his hands, which were missing several fingers.

Emmerich nodded. He'd heard many reports about the miserable conditions in the Russian ice desert and the mass deaths of the innocent soldiers interned there. How they dropped like flies. Frozen, starved, or worked to death. Compared to their fate, everyday life in Vienna was a piece of cake.

Looking at the utterly unexpectedly reunited Koch family, who were convulsively trying to somehow come to grips with the situation, he felt an all too familiar emotion: he felt shut out. He was just a bystander. They were a family. Bound by a holy oath and by blood. He was the outsider.

Emmerich slipped off the brass knuckles, opened the glazed swing door of the cupboard where Luise kept the good china she'd received as a dowry, and pulled from behind a tablecloth the tin where he kept his rainy-day money. Then he packed his few belongings in a small case.

He ran his hand over each child's head and left the apartment without another word.

10

Anatol Czernin stood on an upside-down fruit crate at the edge of Holzplatzl, where the local forest owners came to sell bundles of firewood, and blew on his fists. It was one of those mornings when it was so cold he couldn't feel his toes or the tip of his nose. The cobblestones were covered with frost, and the breath of the people who walked around the market square formed little clouds in the air.

Nobody was paying attention to him. They passed by as if he were invisible. There were too many of his type. Broke war returnees who couldn't find jobs and muddled through as day laborers, scavengers, or beggars. Not much of a life, but what else could they do? There were worse occupations—like Harri Zeiner's trade. No wonder he'd become a little peculiar.

Harri, the paranoid bastard, had shown up at his place the night before, hysterical. He'd dreamed up some crazy story about Jost being killed, whereupon they confronted the supposed killer. As if he had nothing else to worry about. At least there'd been a warm meal in the offing.

The thought of food brought Czernin back to the here and now. He was hungry and needed money. "Ladies and gentlemen," he called out, clapping his hands together. "If you would give me your attention for a moment . . . "

Two snotty-nosed children stopped and stared at him with open mouths.

"Stop a minute," he called after a group of women. "I'm about to perform the street ballad of the six killers. Guaranteed to entertain. It'll give you shivers down your spine. And if you like it, you can thank me with a coin or two . . . "

It took a while, but finally a small group of curious onlookers gathered around him. Czernin took off his hat and placed it in front of him and began to sing an old folk song:

Es klopft so grauslich an der Tür:
Ach, Weib, geschwind, öffne hierfür.
Vielleicht ist es ein armer Mann,
der sonst kein Obdach finden kann.

A ferocious knock was at the door:
Woman, he said, go open henceforth,
could be it's a man so poor,
he's unable to find another shelter.

He cleared his throat. The cold had gotten to his vocal cords, and snippets of memories flashing through his head made his throat tighten.

Das Weib das ging und eilt sogleich,
bekommt in der Tür schon den ersten Streich.
Sie morden Herrn und Knecht
und Magd und rauben bis in den hellen Tag.

The woman she did and off she dashed,
and for it she was the first to be slashed.
They murdered man and minion and maidservant too,
and looted until the day sky was blue.

"Boo," one of the two children protested, holding his hands over his ears. "He's singing it wrong." The little brat threw a rock at him and then ran off, laughing.

"*Es war heut Nacht ein Angstgeschrei . . .* " he continued

singing, "There was a cry of fear last night," but the crowd had lost interest and wandered off in all directions.

"A few *hellers*," he called, holding up his hat. "You heard the first two verses, after all." He was ignored; it was as if he didn't exist at all. "Fine," he mumbled. "Guess it'll have to be the other method." If they wouldn't give him money voluntarily, he'd just have to take it.

He kicked the fruit crate angrily, as if it were responsible for his lack of success, and then he tromped across the street to the Kosmos cinema. The matinee was about to start. He bought a ticket with the last of his money and sat down in one of the rear rows. Soon the lights would go out and the guests would shift their attention to the screen—then it was easy pickings.

Much to his enjoyment they were showing a historical film, and he watched the start of it spellbound before he finally began to dedicate himself to the other viewers' belongings.

First he carefully pulled the purse of the woman sitting in front of him under the row of chairs, removed everything he deemed valuable, and then shoved it back into place. He repeated the procedure with an old woman sitting a few seats to the right, who grunted rapturously whenever Emil Jannings appeared on the screen in the role of King Ludwig.

Grinning with satisfaction, Czernin leaned back to count his loot when he suddenly felt a cord around his neck. Sorry, he wanted to say. I'll give it all back. But all that escaped his mouth was a gasp. He grabbed at his neck and tried to get his finger under the cord but wasn't able to. Help! he wanted to scream, somebody help me! but he couldn't produce so much as a peep.

So he'd nicked a few things—that was no reason to choke him half to death. What was wrong with people?

Czernin felt the pressure in his eyeballs, desperately mobilized his last reserves of energy, and kicked the chair in front of him.

"Shhh," was the only reaction he got.

The assailant could let up anytime now. He'd learned his lesson. He wouldn't be so quick to steal in the future. He tried to reach back and attack the choker, but his body was no longer following his commands.

What was going on? What did the guy want? One last thought went through his head before everything went black: What if Zeiner had been right?

11.

The pain in Emmerich's leg had been overshadowed by the one in his head. The piercing pain in his temples was barely tolerable, just like the throbbing at the base of his nose and the dragging pain in his neck.

Groaning quietly, he opened his eyes and was suddenly wide awake. This was not his bed, and it also wasn't his home.

He sat up and looked around: sunlight pressed through thick full-length curtains and bathed the room in a dim light. He could make out a high ceiling, tiled walls, and two rows of beds lined up close together, from which he could hear moans and snoring. At first glance it reminded him of the homeless shelter which he'd visited two days before—except that it smelled different here. Clean and sterile. Clinically clean. He was lying in an infirmary.

What had happened?

His memories consisted of scattered images which made no sense. There were turnips, wine, amputated arms, and murdered men all whirling around in his mind.

He touched his head and felt a thick bandage, which brought back another image . . . a bandaged man at his kitchen table. Xaver Koch.

This image let loose an avalanche—Sander's appearance at the station house, Luise's desperate facial expression, the children's dismay, his wordless exit, the visit to Beppo's Bar . . .

"Good morning!" A nurse in a high-necked, floor-length outfit pulled back the curtains, and Emmerich covered his face with his hands to protect his eyes from the bright light. "Aha," she said, pressing her lips tightly together. "Our liquor casualty has come back to life."

"Coming back from the dead is all the rage at the moment."

Emmerich pushed back the covers and looked down. He had on a white knee-length garment that reminded him of a nightgown. A peek down the neck hole confirmed what he feared: he was completely naked beneath the gown. Even his lucky charm was gone. His heart skipped a few beats. He had never taken off the necklace. Never. The little silver amulet, a snake biting its own tail, had been found in the basket in which his mother had abandoned him. It was his most valuable possession and meant the world to him.

"We don't want to catch a chill, do we?" The matronly nurse pushed him back onto the hard mattress and covered him again.

"What happened? Where's my pendant, and my suitcase? Where are my clothes? And can I have something for the pain, please?" Emmerich tried to come across as embarrassed and friendly.

The nurse seemed immune to his charm, because she just unceremoniously stuck a thermometer in his mouth.

"I asked you something," Emmerich mumbled, grabbing her by the arm. Since he felt too weak to fight, he gave good behavior a try. "Please, it would be most charming of you."

This time she softened. "You can thank your guardian angel," she said, folding her arms across her chest. "You were found in the gutter. Drunk as a skunk, half naked, and with a big bump on the back of your head. You were nearly frozen to death. I don't understand why they don't introduce Prohibition here. Like in America. The devil lives in the bottle."

Someone must have attacked him and robbed him, and he'd been too bleary from liquor to defend himself. Could it really be true? Had he really lost everything all on one day? His new family, his home, his clothes, and his money? He could barely grasp the magnitude of the events.

Emmerich began to explain that he was not a member of the brotherhood of booze but then let it be. He was too depleted to give a lecture, and the nurse wouldn't believe him anyway.

She took the thermometer out of his mouth and looked at it. "Let's see whether your guardian angel also protected you from typhoid."

"Do I look like a typhoid?"

"You don't look like a typhoid, you catch it. But I think you've gotten lucky again. And now bed rest is the thing for you." She expertly straightened out the bedcovers. "Oh yes. . . as far as the pain medication . . . here . . . " She conjured a small glass ampule from her pocket and handed Emmerich two white tablets. "A doctor will look in later, examine you, and take your information."

Emmerich swallowed the pills, closed his eyes, felt a warm cloud slowly envelope his psyche, and laughed involuntarily. Life was and remained a miserable bastard.

Once the woman had finally left the room, he sat back up again. He would have liked to stay in bed, but he didn't want anyone to figure out his identity. A member of the police force picked up in the street half-naked and blithering drunk. Nobody could find out. His job, which he had put at risk the day before, was all he had left.

He looked at the thermometer and declared himself healthy. Thanks to the pain medicine, standing up was no problem, and he tottered around the room on somewhat wobbly legs. They could have left him his socks. If he ever got his hands on whoever was responsible for this . . .

"Where you going?" asked another patient.

The devil didn't live in the bottle, he lived in his nosy fellow men.

"To the lavatory."

"That's what the bedpans are for."

"Too small."

"You can't just leave the room," nagged the irritating fellow, sitting up. "Unless you want to catch your death." He motioned at the thin hospital gown that Emmerich had on.

"What's it to you?"

Emmerich opened the door to the room a crack and hurried out once the coast was clear. The stone floor was ice cold. He opened one door after another until he finally stumbled upon a laundry room. He slipped in but realized there were no civilian clothes stored there, just hospital uniforms. He rummaged through the things, pulled out a few that looked the right size, and ended up putting on a flimsy pair of white pants and a doctor's lab coat. Now he just needed something for his feet. He couldn't find any socks, but there was a pair of boots on the floor.

Emmerich picked them up and muttered. Fate wasn't treating him kindly. Not just because the shoes were too small, but because they were combat boots. Leather was rare, so they'd started to sole shoes with wood. Wooden soles weren't only uncomfortable, they were loud. But what else could he do? He squeezed his frozen feet into the clunky footwear, took off his bandage, and went back out into the hall.

Clack went his boots with every step, *clack, clack, clack*. He put his hands in his pockets and lowered his head.

"*Guten Tag*, Herr Doctor," a nurse rushing past greeted him.

Emmerich hit upon an idea. There was pain medicine here, and he would certainly be able to use some numbing agents in the coming days—for his body and his mind.

He soon found himself in another storeroom where there were crates full of medicine. The stuff the woman had given him seemed good, so he looked for little glass ampules.

"Who have we got here?" he said when he located the right tablets. "Heroin, from Bayer." So that was the name of the wonder drug.

He gulped down another pill and grabbed as much of the stuff as he could. It would have to suffice for now. *Clack, clack, clack* went his boots again as he headed for the exit. The ampules of heroin in his pocket clinked quietly in rhythm.

"Hey, you. Stop!" Emmerich thought about running, but realized that he wouldn't get far with his damaged leg and the too-small combat boots. He sighed and turned around. The man who was standing in front of him—apparently a doctor—looked at Emmerich reproachfully. "Where are you going?"

Emmerich already saw himself dishonorably discharged from duty, fighting over an entry card for the homeless shelter. "Me? I just wanted to step out. Get a breath of fresh air. The sick can be a handful."

The doctor looked him over through his round wire glasses. "You'll have to get used to it," he said finally. "Or opt for a different career." He pointed to a large double door in front of which a group of lab coat wearers had assembled. "The teaching rounds begin," he pulled out a silver-plated pocket watch, " . . . right now."

His severe look reminded Emmerich of some of the commanders he'd served under during the war, and he had to resist clicking his heels together and saluting.

"Yes, sir," he said.

"What are you waiting for? Punctuality is a virtue." His tone left no room for protest.

Emmerich put his hands in his pockets, held the heroin to his body so the bottles wouldn't make any noise as he walked, and joined the group—Chief of Medicine Dr. Klein, thirteen students, and him.

Klein, whose physical presence did justice to his name, spoke at length about the history and the various departments

of the hospital, bored the group with a talk about the preven-
tion of epidemics, and finally went into an encomium about
the war.

"The war, which is cursed by so many, was actually an unexpected and unparalleled opportunity to advance basic medical
research and to gain unique new insights into the human con-
stitution."

I would have happily foregone those insights," mumbled
Emmerich, who was standing between two men with slickly
oiled hair nodding their heads euphorically. They looked at
him with consternation and exchanged knowing glances
between themselves.

"First and foremost the areas of bacteriology and clinical
surgery can without a shadow of a doubt be considered victors
of the war," the Chief of Medicine continued his paean, and
Emmerich was getting itchy.

When the speech was finally over, feverish applause broke
out and Emmerich took a tentative step backwards. *Clack.*

"Where are you going?" asked one of the oily men. "The
teaching rounds are starting now."

"Just to stretch my leg for a moment. It was wounded in the
oh so wonderful war."

The stuck-up bastard looked at Emmerich's leg and took a
disdainful glance at his boots. The guy himself was wearing an
immaculate pair of pants made out of thick wool and ankle-
high leather shoes that seemed to be competing with his hair
to see which could glisten more. His lab coat was flawlessly
clean, and on his ring finger was a thick signet ring that he
managed to move at every possible chance into the field of
vision of whomever he was speaking to.

"Well, then, congratulations. In that case you're already
accustomed to infirmity." The pomaded stallion shoved
Emmerich into the next room hard enough that he nearly stumbled into the Chief of Medicine.

"Since when did they start accepting guys like him into the medical school?" Emmerich heard the guy whisper. "What an embarrassment."

"He's obviously useless," answered the guy's sidekick. "Did you get a look at his hands? He's got the paws of a worker."

Emmerich was standing directly between Dr. Klein and the group of students, and he could feel all eyes on him. "So," he said, trying to sound enthusiastic, "let's go!"

The teaching round was like a stroll through the zoo. The patients were exhibited and gaped at like exotic creatures, and then they were talked about as if they weren't even there.

"Here you can see a typical case of Reiter's Syndrome as a consequence of dysentery," lectured Dr. Klein about a dis-traught, unsettled-looking old man. "Can anyone tell me the classic Reiter triad?"

Emmerich cowered and stared at the floor as arms went up all around him. He'd been able to dodge all the questions up to now, and he prayed that the round would soon be fin-ished.

"Infections in the eye, the urethra, and the joints," called out the oily little smarty-pants looking very proud of himself. After he'd earned a mild nod from Dr. Klein, he turned to Emmerich. "I've been watching you. You don't know anything at all, do you?"

The group wandered to the next bed, and Dr. Klein turned his attention to a young man who at first looked fully healthy. He handed over the patient's file and it made its way around the group.

"Who would like to give it a try?"

"This man hasn't had a turn." Emmerich's new friend pointed at him. "We wouldn't want to leave anyone out. Now that Austria is a democratic republic and everyone has the same rights."

Laughs rung out, and Emmerich, who had gradually worked

his way to the back, was pushed forward again. This was it. His cover was about to be blown.

"What is your diagnosis?" asked Dr. Klein, handing him the file.

Emmerich, who was now the center of all attention, feverishly looked over the paper while trying to think of a way out of his predicament.

"Do you not know, my good man?" called the showboat, grinning hammily.

"The diagnosis, please," Dr. Klein demanded.

Emmerich looked up. "Arthrofibrosis," he said. "The connective tissue in his knee has formed scar tissue as a result of an injury, which has led to painful stiffness."

"Treatment options?"

"In the long run, none. You just try to manage the pain through convalescence and medicine." He patted his pocket.

Dr. Klein nodded. "Exactly right. And with that, the visit is finished. We meet again later in the lecture hall."

"Sorry," Emmerich whispered to the patient and followed the group outside. There he positioned himself directly next to his special friend and showed him his fist. "I hope we meet again soon—in a dark alley."

He was still reveling in the guy's stunned expression when something else suddenly caught his attention. Two paramedics were pushing a man down the hall on a stretcher. Which wasn't particularly unusual in a hospital, but the man's mouth was hanging open and his tongue was stained yellow.

"What's with him?" Emmerich asked the paramedics.

"He was found unconscious in the Kosmos cinema." They pushed the unknown man into the room where Emmerich had woken up that morning and hoisted him into a bed.

"Any details?"

Emmerich went up to the patient and looked into his mouth. His teeth, at least those that were still there, were in exceedingly bad condition. He was obviously no champion of oral hygiene. It was certainly possible, then, that the yellow coloring had been there a while.

One of the paramedics pointed at the man's throat, where a dark red welt was visible. "Somebody obviously tried to strangle him."

"Did anyone see anything? Are there any suspects? And do we know this guy's name?"

The paramedics looked at him with wide eyes. "We're ambulance men, not cops."

"Right, of course." Emmerich cleared his throat and tried to mimic some sort of professional doctor-like gesture. Since nothing occurred to him, he put his hand on the patient's forehead and said, "No fever."

"So, here I am. Sorry you had to wait, but a patient of ours has gone missing." The matronly nurse came in with a bedpan in one hand and a washcloth in the other. "It's like a nuthouse here, and now there's a half-naked alcoholic running around the halls somewhere."

Emmerich lowered his head and made his way toward the door.

"Where are you going?" called the nurse.

"To Dr. Klein," he answered with his face toward the door. "You know what he always says: punctuality is a virtue."

12.

E mmerich wandered aimlessly through the streets of the city. He had no idea where he should go. All the friends he trusted unconditionally had never come back from the war—either killed or missing—and since then Luise had been the only person with whom his life was intertwined.

The thought of her and Xaver transformed the contents of his stomach into a hard lump. He paused, took a few deep breaths, and thought back to his childhood at the orphanage, the years on the street, and his time at the front. He'd certainly experienced plenty of awful things, and he wasn't about to be defeated now.

Emmerich concentrated on the positives, for instance, that he'd not felt so good physically in a long while. He didn't feel cold or hunger or pain, and the curious looks from passersby at his unusual outfit didn't bother him one bit. It must have to do with the heroin, he thought, ruing the fact that he hadn't yet taken any more.

When he couldn't think of any better alternative, he went to the commissariat, the place that seemed the most like a second home to him.

Clack, clack, clack. He entered the main room of the station house, where it was suspiciously calm instead of humming with its usual hectic activity, and clomped across the smooth stone floor.

Hörl, who was reading a file, looked up and furrowed his brow. "Did someone call a doctor?" he shouted into the backroom and then turned to Emmerich. "Good day, Herr Doctor. What brings you—" He suddenly stopped and squinted. "Emmerich? What's with the outfit?"

"I'm learning a new trade so I don't have to see your faces every day." He grinned and went over to Winter's table.

Hörl shook his head. "Trying to understand him is like trying to understand women," he mumbled and then went back to reading his file.

"Where've you been?" Winter stared at his boss with wide eyes. "And why are you wearing . . . " He remembered that there was no point in asking Emmerich too many questions, and he swallowed his curiosity.

"Listen, I need something to put on. You wouldn't happen to have—"

"I don't have any money with me, and my clothes won't fit you, unfortunately." Winter looked around frantically. "You missed your appointment with District Inspector Sander," he whispered.

"Shit," Emmerich spat. He'd completely forgotten that he was supposed to report to the chief. "Was Sander here? Was he upset?"

"EMMERICH!"

This rendered any number of questions superfluous. Emmerich straightened his neck reflexively and turned slowly. In front of him stood Sander with his arms crossed across his chest. He looked as ominous as a force of nature.

"I can explain," Emmerich began, but Sander's rage crashed down unsparingly over him.

"Your impertinence is truly unbelievable. You seem to think you can do anything you like," he growled. "I am going to hammer some obedience into you. And what on earth is with that outfit? Do you think you're funny?"

"I was undercover at the general hospital and found out something important," Emmerich tried to justify himself.

And it did indeed seem to assuage Sander. The color of his face returned to normal, and he took a deep breath. "I'm listening."

"An unconscious man was brought in. Somebody had tried to strangle him. I believe there's a connection to Jost and Zeiner. You know what that means."

"Of course I know."

Emmerich took a deep breath.

"It means that you ignored my instructions. Again." Sander had leaned forward and Emmerich could feel the heat of his breath on his face.

He mustered all of his courage. "It means that I was right and that a murderer is on the loose in the city," he countered.

Sander looked him right in the eye. "Did you take a blow to the head?"

Emmerich reflexively grabbed at the lump on the back of his head, but immediately lowered his hand again. "I don't yet have any proof, but if you let me get after it—"

"Do you really wish to embarrass yourself in front of Dr. Horvat and his men? I've read Wiesegger's report and spoken with Professor Hirschkron. He stands wholly and completely behind the expertise of his assistant. If you can't give me any solid evidence, I will not be responsible for you impugning the reputation of this department."

"But the murders—"

"Write up a report and submit it to me. I'll have a look at it and then decide how to proceed."

Emmerich sighed loudly. Resistance was obviously futile. "Understood," he mumbled.

Sander nodded without a word, didn't dignify him with another glance, and left the room at a marching pace.

"I have an idea how we can find Kolja's stash," said Winter cautiously when Emmerich's attention was directed back to him.

Emmerich frowned and shook his head disbelievingly. "Doesn't anyone care about the dead?" he yelled angrily.

"There are millions of dead scattered across the entire continent," Hörl answered. "Perhaps it would be wiser for you to get over it and stop aggravating Sander. The city council is all over him and he needs to deliver results. If he doesn't, heads are going to roll. And probably not just his."

Winter grabbed Emmerich's arm before he could explode. "If you lose your job, you won't be able to continue trying to clear up the murders, either."

Emmerich wanted to make a counterargument but nothing occurred to him. In the end he had to admit that Winter was right. For once. "Fine, let's hear your idea about Kolja."

"This morning two women were arrested with black-market contraband. I had a look at the stuff, and it occurred to me that it all smelled funny. Sort of musty. Like a damp basement or—"

"The sewer." Why hadn't they thought of it before? As a result of the covering and diverting of the Wien River there was an extensive, subterranean labyrinth whose gangways, catchment basins, and access shafts made perfect hideouts and contraband stashes. You could supply half the city quickly and easily by means of the sewers. The most obvious thing was often the last thing you thought of. "Well done," he said, and Winter grinned from ear to ear.

"How should we proceed?"

Emmerich pulled a set of keys from his desk drawer and pointed to the door. "I have to take care of something real quick. Let's meet in fifteen minutes at Karoline Bridge in the Stadtpark. Bring lanterns."

13

When Emmerich turned up, Winter was already waiting at the bridge.

"Where did you manage to get a change of clothes so quickly?"

With the exception of his shoes, Emmerich was indeed in a completely new outfit: he was wearing warm wool pants, a linen shirt, and a thick brown corduroy jacket.

"We have to climb over that gate over there," he answered, heading off toward it. "If I'm not mistaken, there's an access shaft behind it where we can get down to the bottom of the Wien."

Winter followed him and couldn't believe his eyes. "Oh, my god!" he blurted. "On your back . . . is that blood?" He looked at the stain and ran his finger over it. "Is this a bullet hole?"

"So what if it is."

"Oh, heavens. Is this stuff from the evidence room?" Winter couldn't believe what his boss had done. "Isn't it unlucky to wear a dead man's clothes?"

"Wearing the wrong clothes in these temperatures is unlucky. So is asking too many questions."

They climbed over the gate, behind which stood a so-called tower—a column that hid a spiral staircase that led to the subterranean world. The two detectives descended into the depths, then headed silently off through the Wien River tunnel toward Schwarzenberg Platz.

It was ghostly quiet in the sewers. The noise of the city seemed far away; the pebbles crunching beneath their feet and the burble of the Wien flowing softly next to them were the only sounds. The farther they went from the entrance the darker it got, until—even though it was the middle of the day—they couldn't see their hands before their faces, and they had to light their lanterns.

"Oh, no!" Winter gasped when his lamp illuminated a dead dog and scores of rat cadavers. The sickly sweet smell of decay pressed into his nose, and he turned away. "That's not a good omen."

"Shhh. We have to be quiet," hissed Emmerich. "Lots of vagabonds live down here. Some of them are real savages. You do not want to tangle with them."

"We could get backup," Winter suggested.

"It wouldn't help." Emmerich turned right and they were standing in front of a pipe about a meter in diameter. "Numerical superiority is only an advantage in open spaces."

"No way! You expect me to go in there?" Winter seemed on the verge of quitting and fleeing back to the street above. "That's way too dangerous!"

"War, that was dangerous—this is just a walk in the park by comparison." With no hesitation, Emmerich clambered into the narrow tunnel.

Winter crossed himself and followed. On all fours they crawled through the slightly sloping pipe, which was not such an easy undertaking. Sharp pebbles bored mercilessly into their knees and the palms of their hands, the moist air made breathing difficult, and the claustrophobic confines presented psychological challenges.

"Who would have thought that the starving multitudes would work directly to our advantage, eh?" Emmerich tried to make the best of the situation with a joke.

Winter didn't laugh.

The next few meters were uniquely torturous, and he breathed with relief when they finally emerged into a small catchment basin where they could stand upright. Unfortunately, rainwater had backed up on the floor of the basin, and it slowly soaked through their shoes.

"Great." Winter wiped sweat from his face. "If the smugglers or the vagabonds don't get us, cholera will." Winter continued: "Where are we going? Do you have a plan?" But his boss did the same thing he always did when Winter doggedly asked questions—he ignored him.

"There are rumors," said Emmerich cryptically while shining his light around the walls. "A guy I arrested a while back said that there was a hidden cavern beneath Schwarzenberg Platz that stays dry all year round. The only way to reach it is by a pedestrian bridge that can be retracted at any time. They call the space the Fortress. If Kolja has a warehouse somewhere down here, it'll be there. Why didn't it occur to me earlier?"

"And if we manage to find it, what then?"

"Then we'll go get backup, watch all the entrances, and arrest every sewer rat that goes in or out." Emmerich was satisfied with his plan, and Winter, too, couldn't find anything to object to. "Let's go," announced Emmerich, and they crawled into the next pipe, which led out the back wall of the catchment basin. It was even narrower than the previous one.

As Winter pulled his body through the damp, foul-smelling slush, the makeup of which he didn't want to think about, one horror scenario after the next went through his head. What if they got stuck? What if it began to rain and the sewers flooded? What if the tunnel collapsed? He fought the rising panic and was happy that Emmerich couldn't see the tears welling in his eyes.

When the pipe finally spat them out again—they found themselves in a basement-like, one-and-a-half-meter-high vault—Winter's nerves were shot. "Do we have to go back the same way?" he asked in a quaking voice. "Or is there another way out?"

"No idea." Emmerich continued on, hunched over, until he ran up against a brick wall. "I didn't expect it to be so intricate." He shined his light on the wall from top to bottom, tapped on it, and turned around. "It seems as if we'll have to go back."

A moment later, the dull echo of footsteps rang out. "What was that?" Winter turned around frantically and hit his head. He ignored the pain and stared into the darkness. "Please don't let it be the savages."

Emmerich looked over his shoulder. "Shhh," he whispered. "Maybe they'll go a different way."

Winter nodded, with bated breath. He could feel the adrenaline coursing through his body as the footsteps got closer. "Can we hide someplace?"

Emmerich looked around. "There's a recess in the wall back there. It might work," he said quietly.

They put out their lanterns, crept back, and pressed themselves into the narrow niche.

The footsteps were only a few meters away at that point, then suddenly stopped. Emmerich and Winter stood stock-still and tried to listen in the dark. Silence. Not a sound. Somewhere in the shadows, danger was lying in wait like a spider for an insect.

Keep moving. Keep on moving, prayed Winter silently.

All of a sudden laughter rang out, and bright light blinded the two detectives. Winter raised an arm to shield his eyes.

"So, what have we here?" they heard a deep, raspy voice say. "If it isn't a pair of cops cuddling together like a couple of lovebirds. Come out!" Two broad-shouldered, scarred men stood before them—one had a gas torch in his hand, the other a pistol. "Which one of you lovebirds is August Emmerich?"

"I'm betting it's that one." The man with the piece pointed at Emmerich. "Milquetoast there is too young. Empty your pockets! And no funny business."

The two strangers took everything they had on them.

"Alright, this way," ordered the one with the torch.

They had no other choice but to obey. Winter was astounded that Emmerich didn't seem the slightest bit perturbed. His own heart was beating right out of his chest. This had revealed a whole new side of his boss. Normally he always had a plan. What did this mean? Did it mean they had no shot at escaping? Were they finished?

They all crawled back to the river and waded through the sludgy Wien to the other side of the waterway, which flowed through an artificial concrete bed lined with tall quay walls. Winter looked around frantically, searching for a way out, but they were trapped. The wall was too high and too smooth, and the two smugglers didn't take their eyes off them for so much as a second. There was no escape. They were done for.

Without a hint of resistance, they entered another stinking sewer access and struggled, sweating and wheezing, through another confusing tangle of stairs, plateaus, and tunnels, until there was the muffled sound of running water, which became louder with every further step.

Finally the sewer widened and they found themselves at the edge of an abyss that could be crossed only by a narrow wooden plank.

"They're going to kill us," Winter murmured, wiping the sweat from his brow. "They're going to shoot us, whack us in the head, or drown us like rats. They'd never have showed us the way to the Fortress otherwise."

"Calm down. Save your energy." Emmerich looked into the depths, where roaring water disappeared into a pitch-black chasm. Jumping would have been suicide. "The one who survives is the one who knows when to fight and when not to. We'll wait for the right time and place."

With held breath they crossed the shaky plank and came to another semicircular hall. Winter forgot for a moment the predicament they were in, gave in to the exceedingly strong impulse to stretch, and looked around, awestruck. In the space, which was even more vast than he had imagined from Emmerich's description, were stacks of crates and barrels of all sizes and shapes. Maneuvering among them in the light of gas torches were countless men diligently stacking and hauling, and counting money.

Emmerich looked at the brisk activity. "Unbelievable," he mumbled, "in the middle of the city. Right beneath our feet."

"Who do we have here? Looks like . . . Inspector August Emmerich." A figure emerged from the shadows. Veit Kolja. "Who would have thought that you of all people would end up with the police." Kolja laughed so loudly that the echo of his voice reverberated from the walls. Emmerich narrowed his eyes to try to make out the man's features in the diffuse light.

"Did you search him properly? The good August is a cagey old dog who knows a lot of tricks. You got to watch out for him." The two men nodded and handed over the items they'd confiscated. "You know who I am, don't you?" Kolja, who was at least a head taller than Emmerich, stood right in front of him now and turned his face to the light. "I recognized you straightaway. Out in the Vienna Woods. Did you really think I wouldn't notice the two of you following me?"

Emmerich shot Winter an angry look and then studied the face of the man in front of him. He recognized nothing in Kolja's features, but his voice and the way he spoke seemed familiar.

"Don't keep me in suspense," he said.

The smuggler pointed to a long scar on the underside of his jaw. "You gave me this because I tried to take a sandwich from you. To this day, I have no idea where you had the shiv hidden."

Emmerich's jaw dropped. "Vanja? Vanja Kollberg?" He tried to see in the man before him the slugger who'd made his life so difficult as a child.

"Thirty years and a new name can't change everything." Kolja looked at Winter, whose expression wavered between panic and curiosity. "That's right," said Kolja. "Your boss and me were once friends."

"Let's not exaggerate," Emmerich said.

"We grew up together in an abbey. We were orphans, abandoned like troublesome animals. Speaking of which . . . do you still wear that childish pendant in the hope that you'll find your whore of a mother someday? Is that why you became a cop?"

Emmerich spat on the ground. "Shut your mouth or I'll shut it," he hissed.

"That's how I remember you." Kolja laughed again. "You know . . . The two of us, we're pretty similar."

"You're the only one who believes that." Emmerich was boiling. "We have nothing in common, not a single thing. We're on totally opposite sides."

"You just need to ask yourself which one is the right one. Who do you think is feeding and clothing half the city, since the fancy-pants in city hall are too inept or too greedy to do so? Who do you think is taking care of the elderly and the sick who are too weak to wait for hours in front of the shops only to be sent away with empty hands?"

"Don't act as if you're doing something noble. You're fleecing the people and enriching yourselves by their misery."

Kolja crossed his arms behind his back and began to pace back and forth. "We are risking our lives and our freedom," he lectured. "Everything, just to smuggle food, clothing, and coal across the border. Our job is dangerous, our costs are high. That has to be rewarded. What do you think—"

"What's with the chitchat?" Emmerich interrupted. "Why did you bring us here? If you want to off us, spare us the drivel and get it over with."

"Are you tired of living?" Winter stared at him with his mouth open. "Stop provoking him," he begged.

"You cops are like a Hydra. You cut off one head and two new ones grow back. There's no point in knocking you off."

Winter's breathing became audibly calmer.

"So get to the point. What do you want with us?" Emmerich pressed.

"I want you to stop following my men. Make sure that we can do our business in peace. Make up some story for your bosses. If you're even a tiny bit like you used to be, it won't be hard for you."

Winter nodded and stared longingly at the narrow wooden plank that led to freedom.

Emmerich didn't think for a second about complying with Kolja's request. "And if it does prove hard for me?" he said provocatively.

Kolja grinned, revealing two rows of healthy, gleaming white teeth. "The times are hard. Something could always happen to your pretty girlfriend and her sweet children." He turned to Winter. "And your dear grandmother would be next."

Winter turned pale. "I didn't say anything," he mumbled.

"So? We have a deal?" Kolja held out his hand to Emmerich.

"I guess we'll find out." Emmerich pushed aside the proffered hand and turned toward the wooden plank.

"Wait!" yelled Kolja. "You're just like you used to be. You could never stand losing." He gave him back the heroin tablets. "What's the story with these? This is way more than the legal amount, my friend. You're no knight in shining armor." He patted him on the shoulder.

Emmerich reached for the pills without a word, stuck them

in his pocket, and walked toward the shaky beam. Winter followed him hurriedly.

"Can someone please get poor August a decent pair of shoes and a clean jacket?" called Kolja to his men. "We've got plenty."

"I'd rather walk around naked," Emmerich called back.

He wouldn't willingly admit it, but he was glad to finally get out of the underworld.

14

They went the wrong way several times in the intricate system of tunnels, and it was late afternoon when Emmerich and Winter reemerged into the daylight, completely covered in sludge. A young woman who had just stepped out of a horse-drawn carriage put her hand over her mouth and took flight as soon as she spied them. The two of them paid her no attention because they were too busy stretching their limbs and filling their lungs with fresh air.

"What now?" asked Winter.

Emmerich strolled cavalierly past the lighted rink of the Vienna Skating Club, where well-heeled sons and daughters were going around in circles. After one glance at the two dark figures they all fled to the rear end of the rink.

"You heard what Kolja said. If we keep after him our loved ones will pay the price. I'd say our hands are bound."

"And Sander?"

"We'll hold him off until I figure out a way to get Kolja." In front of the Konzerthaus Emmerich turned into Pestalozzigasse and tromped determinedly toward the tram stop on the line that went to the hospital. "And as long as we have nothing else to do, we might as well take care of the dead men."

"Perhaps we should wash up and change clothes before then," Winter suggested. "We won't be allowed in anywhere like this, and especially not into a hospital."

Emmerich realized that Winter was right and that he himself

had a problem. He thought for a second. "Where do you live anyway?"

"Me? I live out in Währing."

This did not surprise Emmerich. It's what he had always expected. The 18th district, in the northwest, was affluent, bourgeois, and posh. There were lots of grand avenues, well-manicured parks, and lavish villas.

"How many square meters is the place?"

Winter looked puzzled. "No idea. Enough, anyway."

"Wonderful." Emmerich tried to figure out where the closest tram stop was. "Because I need to stay with you for a few days."

He turned away so Winter wouldn't see his grin. Just a shame that he also had to miss the look on Winter's face.

The tram ride proceeded silently. Neither Emmerich nor Winter said a thing. People took stealthy glances at them with wrinkled noses and sat as far away as they could.

"This is it," said Winter finally.

They stepped off in front of a little mansion.

"This place?" Emmerich needed a minute to regain his composure. "And here I was feeling bad for inviting myself over," he mumbled as he followed Winter through a cast-iron gate. "This house is huge. If I'd have snuck in, nobody would even have noticed I was here."

He took in the stone façade adorned with balconies and oriel windows, and the various coats of arms that emblazoned the huge entrance portal.

Despite all the reforms and efforts, the most bitter poverty and deepest misery still existed side by side in the city with prosperity and extravagant wealth. The population of Vienna lived in close quarters and yet in completely different worlds.

"Who else lives here?"

"Aside from me, just my grandmother. But don't expect too much. The appearance is deceptive."

When they entered the villa Emmerich could see what Winter had meant. The walls of the spacious foyer were completely bare, two of the windows were broken, and where a painting had once hung there was only the dusty outline of its former presence. An icy wind whistled in, blowing dust and dirt across the marble floor. Emmerich looked around, amazed.

"I'm afraid the rest is no more homey," said Winter. "In the past few years we've had three break-ins, and anything that was left we sold in order to buy groceries and fuel."

They walked up a curved staircase with a dangerously wobbly bannister, and the clack of Emmerich's shoes echoed through the entry hall. Pain once again shot through his leg.

"What happened to the rest of your family?" he asked.

"Spanish flu," answered Winter tersely, though Emmerich didn't need any additional information to understand.

The horrible epidemic had broken over the city like a wave of death the previous autumn, wiping out over twenty thousand people in less than five months. Emmerich, whose immediate circle had been spared, gulped. He hadn't been fair to Winter, had taken him for nothing more than a pampered child of privilege without ever digging deeper.

"I'm sorry," he said sheepishly.

They went down a broad hallway that was ghostly quiet. Doors led off either side.

"Why don't you rent out rooms?" Emmerich asked. "There's certainly enough space."

"My grandmother doesn't want to. She's stuck in a previous era. The idea of 'simple people'"—Winter held up his hands and made quotation marks—"residing here turns her stomach."

This could get interesting, thought Emmerich. He'd be living in a ghost house with Winter and his snobbish grandmother. While he tried to decide whether he found the situation unpleasant or amusing, he discreetly took a pain tablet as Winter unlocked a large wooden double door. "I have to warn you. My grandmother is fairly peculiar. If you want to stay here, don't say anything bad about the Kaiser, and try to exhibit the best possible manners."

He opened the door. Behind it was a little living area that was more inviting than the rest of the house. It had herringbone parquet floors, the walls were covered with decorative wallpaper, family portraits hung all around. And a large tile stove gave off a pleasant warmth.

"Ferdinand, is that you?" Winter's grandmother, a frail old woman with an aristocratic air, had entered the hallway. She had on a floor-length green silk dress and lace gloves. When she got a look at the two of them she put her hand to her chest and gave a little cry. "Good god, Ferdinand. You look as if you've just crawled out of the gutter." She waved a hand in front of her nose. "And you smell like it, as well."

"I'm sorry, Grandmother, but we were on duty."

She wrinkled her nose. "I ask myself every day why you got into such a filthy, vulgar line of work. Lord knows it's not befitting of our status. It's something for simple people."

"We've already discussed it," he tried to nip the discussion in the bud. "May I introduce my superior, Herr Inspector August Emmerich?"

The hint of a smile flitted across the face of the motionless old woman. "Are you any relation to the von Emmerichs of Bohemia?"

"I'm afraid not. I was named after saints in the orphanage, and Emmerich of Hungary is just one of my titular saints."

Winter's grandmother took a step forward and looked him over. "The sight of you does nothing to increase my sense of security."

"Herr Emmerich will be staying with us for a few nights, and he'll need some of Father's clothes."

"My apartment caught fire," Emmerich lied. "And your grandson was kind enough to offer a roof."

"Is he trustworthy? Can I be sure that he won't slit my throat in the middle of the night? You know that lowly people hate us. They chased the Kaiser out like a mangy dog, abolished the gentry, and stole everything that we held dear."

"Grandmother!" Winter turned red. "Sorry," he said, turning to Emmerich. "She doesn't mean it."

"I most certainly do." She lifted her chin. "If he swears that he's not a communist he can stay for a night as far as I'm concerned. I can do nothing to hinder it." She turned and strode back to her room. "What all I must endure. As if it weren't bad enough that a proletarian party took power—now they're moving in with me," she muttered loudly enough for Emmerich to hear.

"Did your apartment really catch fire?" asked Winter when his grandmother had closed the door loudly behind her.

"I wish," answered Emmerich. "Unfortunately it's little more complicated than that."

15.

After they'd washed and changed, the two detectives went to the general hospital in the hope of determining the identity of the man who'd been brought in unconscious.

Emmerich had on some of Winter's father's things, and though they fit as if tailored just for him he couldn't help but notice that for the second time today he was wearing a dead man's clothes—this time including the shoes. Gloriously soft, warm boots with leather soles. It was as if his feet were in paradise.

"He was in the second-to-last bed on the left," he said, happy that they could finally get back to the investigation.

"Who are you?" It was the patient who'd gotten on Emmerich's nerves early that morning. Apparently he didn't recognize him in the elegant outfit.

"Visiting," Emmerich answered.

"Visitors' hours are over."

It took an effort for Emmerich to resist smacking him one with a bedpan. "Not for us." He reached automatically into his pocket to retrieve his badge only to realize that it must have also been stolen the night before, along with his brass knuckles and his service revolver. Somehow he hadn't thought of it up to then. It would cause him trouble—more trouble than he already had. "Show him your badge, please," he asked Winter.

The Imperial Eagle silenced the nosy man, and they were able to turn their attention to the unknown man, who was sitting upright in bed reading a book. "*Grüß Gott*," said Winter. "How nice that you are conscious again."

The man put the book aside and looked at them over his glasses. "I wasn't—"

"That's not him." Emmerich looked at him. "Where's the patient who was in this bed early this morning? About forty years old, with a yellow tongue and a red mark around his throat."

The man shrugged. "No idea, I've only been here a few hours. Broken rib. My old nag kicked me," he explained, lifting his shirt to show a thick white bandage wound around his rib cage. "The miserable creature—"

"Right, got it," Emmerich swatting his hand in the air dismissively. He began hurrying from bed to bed to see who was in each. "You must know what happened to the man we're looking for," he said, returning to the nosy man.

"He's dead," he said, narrowing his eyes. "Died this afternoon."

"Damn it," Emmerich cursed. "Did he regain consciousness before he died? Did he say who he was?"

"He never woke up. Say . . . do we know each other? You seem so familiar."

"Maybe I arrested you sometime," Emmerich commented, pulling his wool cap further down over his face. "Did you notice anything suspicious?"

The man shook his head. "It's a hospital. People die here."

"Anyone with him?"

"A doctor."

Emmerich, who knew through personal experience how easy it was to pass as a doctor, nodded. "Can you describe him?"

"They all look the same in their white lab coats."

"Do you know where the body was taken?"

"Who here is supposed to be the copper, you or me?"

"Come on, let's go look for the dead man," said Emmerich to Winter, hurrying out.

"I've never been arrested, by the way," called the annoying patient behind them. "We must know each other from somewhere else."

Emmerich and Winter got lucky—the nameless corpse hadn't been taken to the medical examiner yet, but rather was still awaiting transfer in the morgue. They identified themselves as police and let a nurse explain how to get there and then headed for the basement, where the storeroom for the bodies was.

"As if we hadn't spent enough time belowground today already," grumbled Winter. He shivered when the heavy metal door closed behind them and then wrapped his arms around himself.

The well-cooled but poorly lit room was covered floor to ceiling with white tiles. Against the walls were stretchers where the bodies of the dead, covered with sheets, could be made out like apparitions. It smelled both antiseptic and putrid at the same time, and Winter was about to make a comment about the repulsive atmosphere but resisted, not wanting to lose the newly won goodwill of his boss again.

Emmerich, unfazed as always, dashed around lifting the sheets up one at a time to study the cold, pallid faces beneath. "Here," he finally said, waving over his assistant. "This is the guy."

It was the fourth body Winter had seen in the last three days, but he still hadn't gotten accustomed to it. It took quite an effort for him to step up to the stretcher and look at the bluish face of the man without betraying the sense of horror he felt while doing it. His stomach could be heard rebelling.

Luckily Emmerich didn't register his reluctance—he was too busy with the body. "Give me a pair of gloves," he said, motioning to a side table with several pairs on it.

"What are you going to do?" asked Winter while doing what he was told.

"I want to quickly . . . " Emmerich pulled on the gloves and tried to open the stiff lips of the dead man. "Whoops," he said when the jaw finally opened with a loud crack. "What do you think?"

Winter didn't look into the mouth for one second more than was necessary. "Just like Zeiner."

"We have to find out who this man is," said Emmerich. "I worry that Sander will catch wind of it if I call in the records department." He scratched his head.

"I could make a sketch of him. And we could take finger-prints ourselves."

Emmerich looked surprised and nodded approvingly. "Wait here, I'll get a pen and paper. Study his features." He rushed out.

Winter found himself alone in the morgue. "You sure I shouldn't come with you?" he called, but it was too late. The door had already closed behind Emmerich.

He didn't have to wait long by himself in the cabinet of horrors, because Emmerich came back shortly with a piece of paper and a coal briquette.

"Did you know that because of the coal shortage, every patient is asked to bring a briquette to the hospital so the rooms can be heated?" he asked. "The world really is teetering on the edge."

With clammy hands, Winter drew a portrait of the uniden-tified dead man. When he was finished, he presented it to his boss.

Emmerich was visibly amazed. "Not bad. Very realistic. Maybe I underestimated you. It's possible that you're going to be a great asset to the police after all."

Despite the chilly surroundings, Winter was suffused with the warmth of happiness.

They ground up the rest of the coal into fine dust and took fingerprints with it as best they could; then they went back to the station house, where there was a lot of activity.

"The sun has barely set and the scum is already creeping out of the gutter," lamented Hörl. "Half the city does nothing but whoring, boozing, and stealing anymore. And we have to handle it all."

"In that case you're already warmed up and you can take these down to the lab." Emmerich handed him the piece of paper with the fingerprints. "I need these identified as quickly as possible."

Hörl turned and rotated the piece of paper. "What case number should I write on it?"

"I'll give you three guesses."

"Smugglers?"

"What else!" Emmerich winked and held up the sketch Winter had drawn of the dead man. "Ever seen this guy?"

Hörl studied the sketch and shook his head. "And it doesn't look like anybody from missing person reports, either. One of the smugglers, I assume?"

"What else!" repeated Emmerich, waving Winter closer. "We're going to be out in the field again," he told Hörl. "First in the homeless shelter and then in the Chatham Bar. If anything relevant to identifying him comes up, send someone for us."

"Sounds like a great deal. I stay here and handle all the shit while you go drinking at the *Je t'aime* Bar."

"Strictly for work, naturally." Emmerich grinned. "We've got to nab those smugglers somehow."

"But of course," grumbled Hörl, turning back to his work.

At the shelter, the brothers in misery swore up and down that they didn't know the man, and the housemaster as well as the rejected men who were freezing outside in the gray, cold night had nothing more to offer than a shake of the head.

Emmerich carefully rolled up the piece of paper, pulled up the collar of his jacket, and trudged over to 1st district.

Apparently there had been consequences as a result of the incident that had ended with tankard blows to the head, because the entrance was now watched over by a different bouncer, who let the two of them—clean and dressed well this time—pass without objection.

"*Grüß Gott*, gentlemen. Have a wonderful evening."

"Clothes make the man," Emmerich said once they were inside.

He showed the sketch around, but neither the workers nor the customers were of any help.

After the last "sorry, never seen him," Emmerich sat down at a free table and rubbed his tired eyes. All around him people danced, sang, and told jokes. It had been a long and difficult day, and he could tell he needed some time to process everything.

"Here you are." Winter had gotten two beers and handed one to Emmerich.

"I thought we weren't supposed to drink on the job," Emmerich said, taking the cool glass.

"As far as I can tell, we have finished working for the day."

"Do you think I'm fooling myself?" Emmerich stared at the foam atop his beer. "Is it possible that I'm imagining the murders? Are they really just tragic accidents, the kind that happen every day?"

"Let's look at what speaks in favor and what against," Winter suggested.

"Okay." Emmerich took a sip of beer and began to summarize. "Dietrich Jost wasn't in any shape to load a weapon and fire with accuracy, and yet he supposedly shot himself. When we confronted his best friend, Harald Zeiner, with these facts, he stormed off and met with two men in the pub Poldi Tant. There they ate *Kaiserschmarrn*, which was colored with fake egg yolks. A few hours later Zeiner was fished from the Danube canal, dead. It all seems suspicious to me."

"The medical examiner found no evidence of foul play, and there are no other indications of murder. The only argument in favor is Jost's trembling. But the men at the shelter could have exaggerated about that," Winter continued, playing the role of skeptic.

"Less than twenty-four hours later a man whose mouth was stained just like Zeiner's was strangled. That can't be a coincidence."

"If the unidentified man had really been sitting with Zeiner in Poldi Tant, then the murder hypothesis would make sense," Winter admitted.

Emmerich leaned back and looked at his watch. "It's too late to ride out to Nußdorf and ask the woman at Poldi Tant whether she recognizes the sketch. We'll have to take care of it tomorrow." He let his gaze drift off into the distance and disappeared into his own thoughts for a moment. "If we can find the connection between the dead men, everything else will be clear."

Winter took a sip of his beer and winced.

"Something wrong with the swill?"

"The beer's good. I just remember, though, that we still have go back to see the medical examiner about the autopsy of the unidentified body."

"Well, at least Wiesegger can't say it was suicide this time."

"There is that," said Winter, thinking again of Zeiner's open rib cage and the fat corpse covered with frost. He'd been lucky that Emmerich had helped heave the guy into the tub.

They finished their glasses in silence, then stood up and left the bar.

"Okay, see you tomorrow," said Emmerich, heading off automatically in the direction of his home.

"Where are you going?" called Winter. "It's the other way."
Emmerich froze. "Oh right. I completely forgot."

Standing outside, they could hear a song blaring as the bouncer opened the door to the Chatham Bar for a young couple. "*Glücklich ist, wer vergisst, was doch nicht zu ändern ist.*" *He is happiest, who forgets, that which cannot be changed.*

"We'll see about that," said Emmerich, following Winter to the tram stop for the line to Währing.

16.

A knock awoke Emmerich from a deep sleep. "*Guten Morgen.*" It was Winter's voice.

Emmerich rubbed his face, opened his eyes, and fretted. He was once again lying in a strange bed. It took him a moment to orient himself, then he realized where he was, and he let himself think back over the past two days. Luise, Xaver, the night he couldn't remember, the rude awakening in the hospital, his flight from the doctors, Kolja . . . he quickly tried to clear his thoughts.

When he lifted his legs out of bed, the familiar pain shot through his knee, and he suppressed a scream. "I'm coming," he said, hobbled over to his jacket, which was hanging from a chair back, pulled out the heroin, and gulped down a pill. Then he thought for a moment.

It probably wasn't smart to carry the bottles around with him everywhere. First of all they clinked when he walked; also, he could lose them at any moment. He shook a few tablets into his pants pocket and hid the rest in the bottom drawer of a little dresser.

Winter had quartered Emmerich in the dressing room of his grandmother, something the old woman had protested fiercely at first. "Am I supposed to dress and do my hair in my bedroom? How uncouth!" she had said bitterly. "He can stay in the old servants' quarters." Winter had stood up to her, however, and insisted that Emmerich stay in the heated portion of the house. And to Emmerich's surprise, Winter had been able to win the dispute. The young man he had taken for an inept boob was proving to be a useful fellow who was full of surprises.

"*Guten Morgen*," Emmerich greeted his assistant and his grandmother after he had washed and dressed. The two of them were breakfasting in the living room.

"It's scandalous," the old woman said, and it took Emmerich a moment to figure out that she wasn't talking about him, but about an article in the newspaper, which was in her lap.

"Would you like a cup of tea?" asked Winter. "Unfortunately we don't have any coffee, but my grandmother was able to get fresh bread and jam."

"I had to stand in line like a common servant. And then the bloodsucker wanted a fortune for it. This sort of thing wouldn't have been allowed under Kaiser Karl, and certainly not under Kaiser Franz Josef, god rest his soul."

"Tea sounds wonderful." Emmerich sat down as far away as possible from the old lady, on a filigree chair so delicate that it looked as if it would break beneath the smallest weight. "And I wouldn't say no to a piece of bread and jam."

"Do you know the latest crime your government is planning?" She said the word "your" as if Emmerich himself were the founder and chairman of the Social Democratic Workers' Party. Before he could answer, she began to read in a theatrical voice: "In order to raise the foreign currency necessary to acquire essential foodstuffs, it has been decided to sell abroad certain works of art, antiquities, manuscripts, codices, furniture, and so forth that, while of minimal art historical or cultural value to the Republic of Austria, are inherently valuable." She fanned herself with a napkin. "Philistines! Ferdinand, I think I need my heart medication."

"It won't be so bad." Emmerich tried to calm her. "It says it right there, it'll be the objects of minimal value. And nobody's going to get anything out of all that pretty stuff if the people all starve to death."

"You proletarians don't know a thing about art and culture. You can't judge what's valuable and what isn't. And as if that's not enough! The Commission for the Inquiry into Military Breach of Duty requests all persons able to provide information deemed relevant under the circumstances to get in contact," she read from another article. "Now you want to sully the honorable Imperial and Royal Army and our brave war heroes. Nothing's sacred anymore. Ferdinand, where's my medication?"

"Here, Grandmother." Winter handed her a brown bottle. "Herr Emmerich was himself in the Imperial and Royal Army and fought for our country."

She refused to allow herself to be impressed, shook a few drops from the bottle into a glass of water, and drank the mix in one go. "I do not believe that Herr Emmerich can stay with us much longer," she said. "As you know, I need to avoid exertion, and his presence is not conducive to that in my weakened state of health."

"He hasn't done a thing. You're just trying to impose your will again," said Winter.

"We should get to work." Emmerich took his bread and jam and headed for the door. "I'll look in on my old apartment later and see what state it's in. Who knows, maybe I can move back in."

He was in fact harboring a glimmer of hope that Xaver Koch had realized that there was someone else who had captured Luise's heart. Perhaps he had already packed his things and moved on. He hadn't wanted to ask Luise to discuss things so soon, but Winter's grandmother left him no choice. The thought of Luise and the children made his heart beat more quickly. But he had to ignore it. He needed to concentrate fully on his work.

"It's really not necessary," said Winter. "You're my guest and you can stay as long as you like." He gave his grandmother a harsh look. "I wish the Spanish flu had taken her instead of my parents and siblings," he said once they were outside. "But not even the virus wanted anything to do with her."

17

Winter wasn't pleased when Emmerich revealed that they would start their day at the medical examiner's. If he'd known, he wouldn't have eaten breakfast—but it was too late now. The taste of jam, so fresh and sweet on his tongue, would from now on be associated with death and dying and forever lose its effect.

"God damn it!" Emmerich railed, wrinking his nose as he went to enter the dissection room.

Winter feared the worst. He cast a wary glance through the open door and saw, relieved, that Emmerich's displeasure had nothing to do with a particularly mangled corpse but with the fact that Wiesegger was on the job again this morning. Winter was even more pleased to see that there was no body at all to be seen. Wiesegger and his assistant were standing before an empty steel examination table with their faces buried in a file. Paper instead of putrefaction. Winter could barely believe his luck.

"Herr Emmerich, what an . . . "

Wiesegger struggled to find the right word. It was certainly neither an honor nor a pleasure, nor a surprise for that matter, so he left the unfinished sentence hanging in the air and turned his attention back to the file.

"Have you already examined the dead man from the general hospital? The one with the strangulation marks on his neck?" asked Winter.

Wiesegger nodded. "I conducted the autopsy yesterday

evening. We're finishing up the report right now. If you would like, I can have a copy sent to you."

He seemed to be acting more courteous then he had during the previous visit, and Emmerich wondered why.

"You can just tell me what you found out—just don't say you think it was a probable suicide."

Winter didn't hear his answer because his eyes happened to land on the steel tub next to the examination table. What he saw caught him completely off guard. In cloudy water swam hands, feet, arms, legs, and right in the middle of this limb soup the slit-open torso of a woman. His stomach protested, and he ran out of the room holding a hand over his mouth.

"Go look after him," said Wiesegger, and his assistant followed Winter. "Our profession is not one for those with weak nerves." The medical examiner shoved the paperwork aside, pulled on a pair of rubber gloves, fished one limb after another from the tub, and laid them out in front of him on the table. "It's not a problem for you, is it?"

"You don't have to worry about my nerves." Emmerich approached the macabre puzzle and looked over the various parts. "Do we know who she was?"

"Not yet. The head disappeared without a trace, and the rest has yet to reveal any clues to her identity."

"You can tell the investigator that she was rolling butts for a living."

Wiesegger raised his eyebrows. "I'm sorry, rolling butts?"

Emmerich pointed to the hands. "See the calluses on the thumb and middle finger? They're typical of women who work out of their homes rolling cigarettes. To make any kind of living at it you have to produce more than ten thousand a week. That leaves marks."

He would have loved to add a snide remark about how hoity-toity fellows like him didn't have a clue about the horrible living conditions of the working class, but he let it slide. He had evidently risen in the estimation of the medical examiner.

Wiesegger studied the rough skin and nodded approvingly. "Not bad," he mumbled. "Not bad."

"Could we perhaps address my body?"

"Of course." Wiesegger honored Emmerich with a hint of a smile. "This time I must agree with you. It was murder. The strangulation marks and the abrasions on the finger of the dead man leave no doubt that he was choked from behind."

"Are there any clues as to the identity of the victim?"

"You'd have to tell me. You are the identification expert."

Emmerich didn't answer, he just snorted. "Your body lived in rather mean circumstances," said Wiesegger. "His overall condition suggests malnutrition and poor hygiene. He also had nicotine and alcohol habits. His lungs and liver were in poor condition."

Emmerich suppressed a groan. It didn't take an autopsy to ascertain these facts. This had already been obvious to him.

Wiesegger hadn't missed his facial expression. "I did, however, find something else that will be of interest to you," he added solicitously, removing the wet gloves and handing Emmerich a piece of paper. "This is an extract from the autopsy report."

" . . . stomach distended; in same, a large amount of brownish yellow ingestate containing pieces of meat and with an acidic odor. Mucous membrane . . . " Emmerich read aloud, furrowing his brow. "So?" he asked.

Wiesegger didn't answer, instead handing him a piece of paper from another report.

It stated: . . . stomach distended; in same, a large amount of brownish yellow ingestate containing pieces of meat and with an acidic odor. Mucous membrane . . .

"Look at the name on that report," Wiesegger interrupted.

Emmerich did as he was told, and smiled. "Harald Zeiner."

"He and the unidentified dead man ate the same thing before their deaths. The contents of their stomachs were in different stages of digestion, but the composition was the same. I'd guess schnitzel with potato salad and *Kaiserschmarrn*."

"Colored with Dottofix?"

"Dottofix, Dottox, Eggfix or whatever the name. But definitely an egg substitute."

"The men ate dinner together, which suggests there was a connection between them. Which in turn could mean—"

"—That my suicide theory may not be entirely correct."

Wiesegger's discomfort about revising his opinion was obvious to see. Suddenly he no longer seemed so smug; he was just a nice young man who'd made an unfortunate misjudgment.

"There's no shame in that." Emmerich was in a generous mood. "There was no evidence to support my theory, after all. I just had a gut feeling. Something you develop over the years. Comes with experience."

The medical examiner smiled. "I'll send you a copy," he said and turned back to the dismembered woman. "Cigarette roller, eh . . . " he mumbled.

Emmerich said goodbye and went out to where Winter, blanched chalky white, was waiting for him.

"I'm so embarrassed. I was completely overwhelmed. It won't happen again." He wiped his mouth. "How was it with Wiesegger? What did he say?"

Emmerich summarized the conversation and told him about the enlightening analysis. "And speaking of stomach contents, it seems as if yours might need to be refilled. Let's see if we can coax a little more out of the waitress at Poldi Tant."

Winter wasn't sure whether his boss meant food or information. "I'll never be able to eat apricot jam again," he lamented as they left the medical examiner's behind and headed toward Nußdorf.

"No great loss," Emmerich answered. "Plum jelly is much better anyway."

Poldi Tant was packed once again today. Despite the poverty and food shortages, there were apparently still people in the city who could afford to spend their days in cafés or pubs.

The lines of the song, He is happiest, who forgets, that which cannot be changed, shot through Emmerich's head. This could easily be accomplished with the help of beer and wine. And heroin. Whenever he slurped down one of the wonder pills the hours that followed were completely pain-free. He felt strong and healthy. The medicine really earned its heroic name.

"Now that it's clear it was murder, we can turn the case over to *Leib und Leben*," observed Winter.

Emmerich had to concede that he was right. "Trust is good, verification is better," he quoted Sister Erzsebet from the orphanage. "We don't want to leave ourselves open to looking silly in front of Horvat and his men."

Truth be told, it was about more than that to him. Much more. Not just that he didn't want to make a fool of himself— he wanted to make a name for himself. He wanted to solve the case and in so doing prove his skills so as to make the impossible happen—earning a spot in the best police division in the country despite his war wound.

Winter seemed to accept the pretext. "Whoa, steamy," he said as they entered the pub.

The air was so thick that you could cut it. It smelled like a mix of soup, pipe smoke, and alcohol. Laughing, chitchat, and the obligatory Schrammel music filled the room, and soon the buxom waitress came tromping toward them. Like the previous time, her cheeks were red and she had on a green dirndl.

"So, the gentlemen from the food safety division." She put her hands on her hips and glared at them so ferociously that Winter moved behind Emmerich. "Another complaint? Want to try something else? What'll be today? Goulasch? Boiled beef? Or maybe blood sausage and roast potatoes?"

"Do you have any fried chicken?" asked Emmerich.

"Got nothing." She stuck out her chin aggressively. "Hygiene laws, my ass. Sponging my food and wasting my time."

"Where'd you get that idea?" asked Emmerich when he'd found his voice again.

I went to the Margareten commissariat. Looked at the mug shots. Just like you told me to. Your colleague laughed out loud when I asked about the hygiene code you cited."

Emmerich wanted to smack himself. He'd completely forgotten that he'd told her to report to the station house. "You didn't recognize anyone from the pictures?" he tried to distract her.

"Of course not. There probably wasn't even a crime."

Emmerich wanted to contradict her, but was interrupted by a fat bald man. "Stop flirting, Fini, and bring me another glass of wine," he bellowed.

"I have to get back to work, and you lot can kindly piss off or I'll charge you for the other day's schnitzel." She hurried off to the bar and pulled out a magnum bottle of wine from behind it. "What do you want?" she asked gruffly when Emmerich followed her. "Can't you see I have work to do? Upstanding people have to pay for their food by working for a living."

"I'm sorry about the schnitzel." Emmerich put on a penitent face. "But in all truth this isn't about a hygiene code violation, it's about murder, and we need your help. Two of the three men who were here that night are dead. The third is either the murderer or the next victim. Either way I need to find him."

The waitress put down the oversized green bottle and narrowed her eyes. "You're not lying?"

"What would I stand to gain by lying to you?"

This seemed to make sense to her. "But how am I supposed to help? I already told you that I don't know anything."

"People often know more than they realize. Is there someplace we can talk?"

She thought for a second. "Wait in the kitchen," she said, pouring the glass of wine. "I'll check on the customers really quickly, then I'll be there."

"Employees only!" yelled the sweating cook, red-faced from the heat, when Emmerich and Winter stepped into the kitchen. He was stirring a large soup pot, which brought back bad memories for Winter.

"It's alright, Sepp. They're with me." The waitress came in behind them and motioned to a small table at the back of the room, next to the trash cans. "I don't have long. When the cat is away . . . you know how it is. So?" She looked at them quizzically.

"Try to think back to that night," Emmerich suggested. "Probably best if you close your eyes and concentrate."

"You trying to hypnotize me? Like the Indians?"

"Just do what he says, Fini, and then get out of here," the cook called as he tossed some nondescript herbs into the soup. "You have to look after the customers."

"Fine, but god help me if anyone laughs." She closed her eyes and took a deep breath.

"And? Anything?" asked Emmerich.

"Everything's black."

"Think of the table. Think of the men. It was late, there probably weren't many other people still here."

"I remember I was worried about being able to go home. They didn't look like they were concerned about closing time."

"In your line of work, you always have to remember what people order. Your ability to remember things must be fantastic," Emmerich spurred her on. "Think. What did the third man look like? Anything unusual about him?"

"He sat with his back to the room. I only saw him from the front briefly, as he was walking out. Big and broad-shouldered, he was. An attractive man. He looked a little like Emil Jannings . . . " She smiled fawningly. "Only he was older," she continued. "Hard to describe."

"But you would recognize him if you saw him again?"

"Pretty sure. He definitely wasn't among the mug shots."

"Concentrate again, Fini," Emmerich urged her. He needed more. More information, more details, more clues. "Did you happen to hear what the men were talking about? Can you remember any snippets of conversation? You can solve a horrible crime and maybe even save someone's life."

The red of her cheeks was darkening to purple, and she fanned herself with her hand.

"Fini, the customers!" yelled the cook.

"Quiet, Sepp. I've got a responsibility here." She closed her eyes again and lowered her head. "It was about money." She rubbed her nose and furrowed her brow. "Hmm . . . " She looked up again. "Emigrating!" she yelled so loudly and suddenly that Winter jumped up and knocked into one of the trash cans, and its top fell to the tiled floor with a clang. "They were talking about fleeing the country, and about the war."

"Fini! The customers!" The cook looked at them. The fact that he had traded his soup ladle for a fileting knife did nothing to lessen the tension.

"That's it. Can't think of anything else."

Emmerich thanked her. Money, emigrating, war. These were topics half the country were discussing daily. Nothing he could hang an investigation on.

Leaving the kitchen, his gaze fell on the contents of the trash can. "What is that?" he asked, fishing out a hoof.

"What's left of a calf, for veal schnitzel."

"Sure was a big calf. And one that wore horseshoes." He pointed to the row of small holes lining the edges of the hoof.

"First the hygiene police, then murder inspectors, and now veterinarians. You should really decide on one at some point." Fini smoothed out her apron and hurried out into the main room.

"Was that really an old nag the other day?" asked Winter once they were outside.

"Tasted good to me. I've certainly had worse."

Winter wanted to ask what that might have been but stopped himself, looking across the street. "Am I imagining it, or are we being followed?" he whispered.

"Today's not the first day, and there've been several of them."

18.

"Y"ou coming to the Apollo tonight, Emmerich?" asked Hörl, who was standing in front of the commissariat with a few other colleagues, rolling a cigarette. "There's boxing. Afterwards we'll have a look into Ronacher. A certain Claire Bauroff is dancing there." He winked conspiratorially. "Dancing naked, that is."

The other men laughed, and Winter blushed.

"Bauroff came to entertain the troops at the front. Everyone's already seen her endowments." Emmerich snatched the finished cigarette out of Hörl's hand and tucked it behind his own ear.

"What about you, kid? It's virgin territory for you, eh?" Hörl, who was apparently on the day shift today, wouldn't be dissuaded.

Winter felt uncomfortable. "I don't know. I've got a lot to do." He hurried into the commissariat.

Emmerich followed him. Inside he lit the cigarette and took a deep drag. "Don't let them get under your skin," he said. "Bauroff's chest isn't worth it anyway. We're better off taking care of important things."

Tap, tap, tap. Winter was already at his clunky, black typewriter. The sound that the type bar made when it hit the ink ribbon reminded Emmerich of the irritating clack of the combat boots that he fortunately no longer had to wear. *Tap, tap, tap.*

"I've already got the most important material down,"

Winter announced calmly without responding to Emmerich's words.

Emmerich stood behind his assistant and began to dictate the report for Sander.

"The correlation between the stomach contents, as documented by Medical Examiner Wiesegger, allows us to conclude that the two victims were together in the public house Poldi Tant—"

"Wait. Not so fast." Winter shoved the heavy rubber roll that the paper was wrapped around to the right until it clicked into place with a *ping*, then let his fingers hover above the keyboard again like hungry birds.

"That's the colon . . . " Emmerich pressed the key, causing another *tap*. "Isn't that quicker? Wasting time like this drives me nuts." He hated desk work, and tapped on the back of Winter's chair.

"Emmerich!" cried Hörl across the room. "District Inspector Sander wants to know what the story is with the smugglers."

"Yeah, yeah, I'll take care of it."

Emmerich went over to the window and looked out. He'd put the smugglers completely out of his mind. He had to show results. And he couldn't just make up some half-baked theory.

"How should I continue?" asked Winter.

"Come up with something, you were there." Emmerich was fed up with paperwork. He put on his jacket. "I need to take care of a few things. Be back soon."

Tap, tap, tap he heard until he left the building—at that speed Winter would spend the rest of eternity sitting at the typewriter.

The autumn sun was low in the sky and its rays were anemic. Emmerich held his face to the light anyway, trying to warm himself. He buried his hands in the pockets of his jacket, ambled along Margaretenstraße toward the city center, and quietly whistled. *He is happiest, who forgets, that which cannot be changed.*

Just before Pressgasse he sped up, turned right, and then quickly hid in the nearest building entryway. Sure enough, a few seconds later a shadow rushed past him and then stopped in the middle of the block, apparently unsure which way to go.

"Looking for me?" Emmerich asked the scrawny fellow as he looked around frantically.

"Me? You? Why would I be?" the man answered, walking away with exaggerated calm.

"Your shadowing skills leave something to be desired," hissed Emmerich as he followed him. "Next time just introduce yourself and then walk with me. That would at least be polite."

"I don't know what you're talking about." The gaunt man blushed and walked faster.

"Not good at lying, either. I'll have to let Kolja know."

The man stopped, drooped his head, and mumbled something incomprehensible into his beard.

"Tell Kolja I need to talk to him. It's important. I'll wait at Schwarzenberg Platz for him. In front of the Hochstrahl fountain. Now." Emmerich folded his arms and the man scratched his head nervously. "I don't have all day. If you go quickly, maybe I'll forget about telling Kolja how badly you're doing your job."

This seemed to light a fire under the man, and he nodded. "Schwarzenberg Platz. Hochstrahl fountain. Now," he repeated and then hurried off.

"You should take a lesson from your colleague. You could learn a lot from him," Emmerich called after him.

Kolja's henchman stopped and turned toward him. "From who?" he asked, looking genuinely confused.

"The other guy you have tailing me. He's worlds better. I almost didn't notice he was following me."

"What?" The man frowned and shook his head. "There's only me," he said, then ran off.

While Emmerich walked past the Technical College and St. Charles Church on his way to Schwarzenbergplatz, his shadow's words went through his head. *There's only me.* He was sure there was a second. He hadn't seen him yet, but he had a sixth sense for such things. Maybe Kolja hadn't told them about each other? Or was he being watched by someone else who didn't have anything to do with the smugglers? And if so, who? And why?

At the fountain, he sat down on the low wall that skirted it, closed his eyes, and took a deep breath. These were turbulent times he'd found himself in. The steady splashing of the water calmed his soul, and he absentmindedly ran his hand through one of the three hundred and sixty-five little fountains that ringed the enclosure. They symbolized the days of the year. *Panta rhei*—all flows, a wise man once said. If only it would flow a little slower.

A heavy passing cart shook the ground, and Emmerich looked at his feet. Somewhere beneath them was the Fortress. He might even be sitting directly above it, separated from Kolja and his henchmen by only a few meters of concrete and dirt.

"Hey, you! Emmerich . . . " His shadow was suddenly standing next to him.

"Where's Kolja?"

"He's waiting for you at Café Central. You're supposed to go there."

Emmerich took his hand out of the fountain, shook off the water, and snorted. What was Kolja up to? Ordering him around like an errand boy. And of all places the Café Central, such an over-the-top establishment. He was tempted to refuse, but he had to swallow his pride. He needed something from Kolja, after all. Not the other way around.

Central was housed in a former bank and bourse building which had functioned chiefly to represent the Empire in a blaze of glory. Evidently neither the guests nor the staff of the café wished to acknowledge that the Imperial and Royal monarchy had recently fallen, because they celebrated its splendor as if nothing had happened.

In earlier times the intellectual elite had gathered here, but these days it was first and foremost the aristocrats of the finance world, high-ranking officials, and rich merchants bustling among marble-faced columns, golden English wallpaper, and monumental murals. And Kolja.

The smuggler was enthroned at the best table in the house, reading the paper in the middle of the ballroom-like space. He was wearing elegant clothes and putting on such a show of sophisticated manners that it seemed as if he'd always been a member of this select company. Either he'd succeeded in leaving his past behind, or he was a master of deception. Probably the latter.

"August, my friend," he called, gesturing welcomingly to the chair opposite him.

"Here, with the snobs? Really, Vanja? Who are you trying to impress?" Emmerich sat down and surveyed the fine china on the table.

"Nobody. I don't need to." Kolja waved over the waiter. "Two coffees and two apple strudels, please."

"I can order for myself if I want something," Emmerich hissed, but Kolja just ignored him.

With a nod of the head he made clear to the waiter that the order still stood. "To what do I owe the pleasure?" he asked now, wiping his mouth with a cloth napkin and smiling.

Even now, with his features highlighted by a heavy crystal chandelier, he still had nothing in common with the coarse orphan boy Emmerich had battled thirty years before. If it wasn't for the scar on his chin he would never have believed that Veit Kolja and Vanja Kollberg were one and the same person.

"Do you have to talk in that fucked up way?" Emmerich growled at him.

Kolja's face didn't change. "If Sister Erzsebet had heard that she would wash your mouth out with soap and then cane you a few times. Whatever happened to her anyway? Do you know?"

"She's burning in hell."

Kolja nodded contentedly. "Good," he said, and for the first time since they'd met again they were in agreement.

"My boss is putting pressure on." Emmerich came straight to the point. He didn't want to stay any longer than necessary. Among all the Rothschilds, Auerspergs, and whoever else their names were, he felt out of place. And besides, he didn't want to be spotted with Kolja. "I need to deliver results. Give me something. An insignificant stash, a few unimportant middlemen, or an expendable delivery for all I care."

While Kolja thought it over, an exceedingly self-absorbed waiter served the food and drinks. The smell of freshly roasted coffee beans rose to Emmerich's nose, and he had to hold himself back from diving straight into what had just been brought. When was the last time he'd drunk coffee that wasn't made out of acorns, barley, or chicory?

"Please help yourself." Kolja stirred sugar into his coffee and lit a cigar.

Emmerich didn't want to indulge him and resisted. "I'm not here to have a tea party with you. Can you give me something or not?"

Kolja puffed thick white rings of cigar smoke into the air and grinned. "You're being impatient. It's a bad habit, and not the only one, if I recall correctly."

Emmerich began to flush with anger. "Yes or no."

Kolja slowly placed the cigarette down in an ashtray, spooned whipped cream onto his strudel, and took a bite of it.

"Mmmm," he enthused. Although it was difficult, Emmerich maintained his composure. He forced a smile and leaned back in his chair.

"Does the name Wilhelm Querner mean anything to you?" Kolja asked. Emmerich shook his head no. "I thought so. You cops really haven't the slightest idea what's happening in the underground."

Emmerich stared at his counterpart with his lips pressed tightly together, but refused to be provoked. "Don't keep me in suspense."

"Querner is the head of a gang of smugglers who, in the last few months . . . "

"Got it," Emmerich interrupted. "I'm supposed to take care of the competition for you."

"Querner and his men operate in brutal and immoral ways. They're real criminals."

"As opposed to you guys." Emmerich laughed out loud.

"We deal in food, clothing, and medicine that we acquire legally abroad and then smuggle across the border. Querner's men steal, rob, and cheat, and double-cross, wherever they can. They steal from the poor. We're businessmen, they're criminals."

"If distorting the truth were an Olympic sport you'd have a whole crate of medals."

The coffee smelled so good that Emmerich took a quick sip when Kolja looked away to find his lighter. When he'd finally found it, he relit his cigar and took a deep drag.

"Did you know that of the three hundred and forty thousand children who live in Vienna almost three hundred and thirty thousand of them are malnourished? The only reason they haven't starved is because of the American relief organizations' food programs."

Emmerich couldn't really follow the mental leap. "I myself have three . . . " he began, but didn't finish the sentence.

Instead he reached for his cake fork and began to eat the apple strudel.

"In reality Woodrow Wilson is less concerned about the children than about nipping Bolshevism in the bud. But it doesn't matter. So be it. In any event, the Americans have sent over nearly twenty thousand tons of food for children's welfare programs. Condensed milk, rice, beans, sugar, onions, cocoa, and flour. And winter clothes."

"Okay." Emmerich had an idea of what Kolja was driving at.

"All this stuff is in the Schweizertrakt of the Hofburg Palace. Part of it is supposed to be sent to the surrounding states and I'll give you three guesses as to who wants to help himself to it first."

"Querner."

"That's something we would never do, for example. Taking food from children."

Emmerich wasn't sure whether he should really believe this, but he stayed silent.

"I know from a reliable source that the job's going to take place tonight. The gang is going to go in and grab what they can under cover of darkness. We were planning to stop them, but I will allow you the honor." He smiled graciously and waved the waiter over again. "Another round? It's on me, of course."

Emmerich swatted aside the suggestions and stood up. "I'm supposed to do your dirty work for you. You'll owe me for that."

Kolja ordered a cognac and then turned back to Emmerich. "You get Querner out of my way, and in exchange you can make hay out of his arrest. Imagine the headlines! Heroic Vienna police save hundreds of children from starvation. The way I see it, you'd owe *me* something." He took up his cognac. "Sure you don't want one?"

"I'm sure," said Emmerich even though it wasn't true. He could have used a swig of liquor just then.

19.

The Schweizertrakt, in front of which Emmerich, Winter, Hörl, and three other patrolmen in plain-clothes were cooling their heels, was the oldest part of the Vienna Hofburg, the palace that had served as the Kaiser's residence until his abdication. Since the laying of the first stone in the thirteenth century, generations of Hapsburgs had tried to put their stamp on it by adding to it and changing it, so that after six hundred years the complex had grown to nearly two hundred fifty thousand square meters, incorporating many architectural styles.

Since the end of the monarchy there had been much discussion of a democratic use for the complex. There had been suggestions for a pool in the palace garden and a people's hall in the Winter Riding School, and there had been a thought of installing a museum of modern art in the imperial mews. These were all just pipe dreams for now, however, so many of the three thousand rooms stood empty or were handed over for use by relief organizations like the American Relief Administration, a children's aid agency.

"Who would ever have thought," said Hörl, blowing smoke rings, "that condensed milk, rice, and beans would become more coveted than jewels." He motioned toward the entrance to the Imperial Treasury, where the imperial treasures were kept alongside other valuables.

"You can't eat gold and gemstones, and they won't keep you warm, either."

Emmerich watched the simple façade of the inner court-yard, behind which the foodstuffs and winter clothes were stored. The stuff had traveled over five thousand miles, brought here from the United States by steamship, barge, freight car, and automobile in order to ease the misery of Austrian children—as long as Querner and his gang didn't steal it first.

"Where the hell are they?" mumbled Hörl. "I'm cold and I need to go to the bathroom."

"Are you sure the heist is taking place tonight?" asked Winter quietly.

Emmerich looked again at the papers he'd gotten from the responsible administrator. How had the Americans won the war? They were poorly organized and functioned like rank amateurs—they were sitting on the largest haul of treasure in the city and had only one mealy-faced watchman as security.

"The deliveries to the rest of the country are supposed to go out tomorrow." He pointed to the date to confirm. "The next batch doesn't come until next week. So if not tonight, when?"

Doubt began to creep over him. They'd secured the store-rooms and made sure that the only way in was through the Schweizer Gate. Had they missed something? Had Kolja sent him on a wild goose chase? Or had Querner noticed their presence and called off the heist?

All these possibilities were conceivable and they would all further lower Sander's opinion of him. He'd already heard allegations of carelessness and wasting resources. The American administrator had also protested loudly when they sent him away, and there was a good chance that the arrogant pencil pusher would lodge a complaint.

He had to make an arrest.

"Great, now I'm out of smokes," moaned Hörl, wandering over to the steps known as the Ambassadors Stairs that led up to the storerooms. "I'll have a look to see if there are any inside."

"The stuff is for children," Emmerich spat, holding him back. "There's definitely no tobacco."

"Smoking curbs your appetite. I'm sure it works on kids, too." Hörl tried to push past Emmerich.

Emmerich was about to vent his frustration on his colleague when suddenly they heard the hum of engines.

Finally.

In an instant Emmerich's irritation switched to feverish excitement. "Quick," he called to the assembled men. "Take your positions."

The troop sprang into action: Emmerich hurried to the entrance door, Winter rushed to his side, the other police hid in various recesses.

Beyond the red-black Schweizer Gate, two trucks came into view. They were too wide to fit through the narrow gate, so Querner and his men parked them there in the adjoining courtyard.

"Here we go! Hurry!" came a deep voice, and then the doors of the vehicles opened and one man after another emerged.

"There's a lot of them." Winter grew pale.

" . . . Five, six, seven . . . " Emmerich counted, gulping, " . . . eight, nine, ten . . . " So Emmerich and his troop were outnumbered. To make matters worse, Querner's lugs were all big and strong, which couldn't be said of his own.

"Oh, god," Winter whispered as the crooks came toward them with sinister looks on their faces.

They walked purposefully, and in long heavy strides. Their body language displayed confidence. None seemed to have any moral qualms about stealing food from thousands of children.

"Scum."

Emmerich fixed on the man who was leading the group.

The man was a good half a head taller than him, had broad shoulders, and his arms were as thick as some people's thighs. A bloody scar ran from the right corner of his mouth to his ear, giving his face an added look of maliciousness.

This must be Querner.

The ten men stopped in front of Emmerich and Winter, and Querner gave a signal to a bearded giant who could have auditioned anytime for the role of Wotan in Wagner's Ring Cycle.

"Vee kam for de guds," the giant said.

Emmerich, who didn't speak English, didn't know how to answer. "Okay," he finally said, pointing to the Ambassadors Stairs.

Querner turned to his men. "Come on! Get the stuff!"

Emmerich waited until half of them disappeared into the building, then held up his right hand. "Stop!" he ordered in an authoritative tone. He wanted to split up the gang. It would be easier for his own squad to arrest five men at a time.

Querner narrowed his eyes and Emmerich noticed he seemed to suddenly be on alert. The sinews in his neck tightened, a vein on his forehead pulsed, and his left hand reached into his jacket pocket.

"What iz?" asked the giant, frowning so much that his eyebrows nearly touched each other.

"The Ausweis," Emmerich demanded, trying to sound as American as possible.

Much to his surprise, Querner pulled two documents out of his pants pocket and handed them to him. The two items were an Imperial and Royal passport under the name of Rudolf Gruber and a confirmation from the "Amerikan Relief Administration" with an official seal and the signature of Herbert C. Hoover.

Emmerich studied the papers closely but couldn't see any irregularities. The letterhead, the stamps, the photo, and the many entries all seemed aboveboard and completely authentic.

Were these actually genuine? Was this guy not Wilhelm Querner but Rudolf Gruber? Were these men not crooks but the actual drivers who would deliver the aid supplies to the surrounding states? Had they just come a bit early?

What should he do now? He couldn't just arrest them on a wing and a prayer.

Emmerich wiped the sweat from his brow and tried not to betray his uncertainty.

"Achoo," Winter, who was next to Emmerich and had apparently noticed his boss's doubt, sneezed. "Achoo."

"Blez ju," said the giant.

Emmerich didn't understand, and frowned.

Winter held his hand in front of his mouth. "Forgery," he hissed to Emmerich in the form of a cough. "American with a K instead of a C."

Emmerich looked at the seal again and immediately saw what his assistant meant. "Now," he said the next instant, casting a thankful glance at Winter and pulling out his pistol. "You're under arrest."

The crooks reached for their weapons but Emmerich's men were faster and now also superior in numbers. The thugs were handcuffed while uttering a string of curses and insults that would have made a sailor blush.

"So, gentlemen. Who would have thought that a simple C would one day put you behind bars?" Emmerich sighed, relieved. "Quick!" he called to his own men. "Keep your eyes on the Ambassadors Stairs. The others will be out any minute." It wasn't difficult to overpower the rest of the crooks. They emerged from the building carrying heavy sacks and were too surprised to put up any real resistance.

"Can any of you drive one of those?" Emmerich pointed to the two trucks Querner and his henchmen had arrived in.

"I can," said Hörl. "I shuttled the officers around during the war."

"*Wunderbar*. In that case I suggest we load our cargo and take them in. Choose a truck and I'll take the other one."

"Do you know how to drive something like that?" asked Winter.

"No, but it can't be that difficult." Emmerich, his body still pumping with adrenaline, got behind the wheel and turned the ignition key. "What are you waiting for?" he yelled to his sidekick. "Hop in!"

After a short, breakneck ride, they reached the station house. Winter stepped out of the truck, his legs trembling.

"The world can only hope that you can never afford a vehicle like that," he mumbled, staggering to the entrance.

20

G reat job!" District Inspector Sander shook Emmerich's hand and clapped him patronizingly on the shoulder. "In a quarter of an hour I'll be meeting the mayor and representatives of the American children's relief agency. The authorities are relieved and extremely pleased that we've brought these unscrupulous criminals to account."

We, my ass, Emmerich thought. Sander hadn't stood out in the cold for hours, long enough for his legs to take root, and he hadn't risked his life arresting the gang—but now *he* was earning the praise.

"Who's off now and wants a beer?"

Hörl and another officer were carrying two crates of *Ottakringer* into the station house and being met with many hellos. All the officers who had taken part in the arrest of the Querner gang had gathered in the commissariat to celebrate their success together.

Emmerich took a bottle, popped the top with a loud pop, and washed down his irritation. Let his boss dress himself in borrowed plumes—as long as he could pursue the murder case undisturbed, he didn't care.

"No thanks," Sander said when Hörl offered him a beer, too. "I'm about to meet the mayor—I need to show up sober." He straightened his collar and plucked imaginary balls of lint from his immaculately fitted three-piece suit. Emmerich turned to leave the commissariat, but Sander didn't let him go so easily. "Terrific that you got the anonymous tip-off."

Emmerich faked a smile. "Law-abiding citizens are a blessing."

Sander clapped him on the shoulder again. "The arrest of the Querner gang was an important step in the right direction. Next up is Veit Kolja. How are you getting on with that case?"

Emmerich's smile faded. Couldn't Sander leave him in peace for a couple of days at least? He had hoped the Querner sting would placate him for a while and divert his attention from Kolja.

"I'm doing my best," he said, teeth clenched.

"That's what I'm counting on. And not only me. When can I tell the mayor to expect Kolja to be locked up?"

Give him an inch, he'll take a mile. "It will be a while."

Sander didn't even try to hide his displeasure. "As soon as the Querner report is done, please give me a written update on your next steps." He looked at his watch and put on his Homburg. "Have a nice evening."

Emmerich drained his beer and snorted. Nice evening, my ass. He went to look for Winter and found him in an animated conversation with Hörl.

"There you are, boss." Winter's cheeks were red and his eyes were gleaming from all the hubbub. "That was kind of exciting today, eh?"

Emmerich shrugged and stopped himself from making a comparison to the drama of trench warfare and gas attacks. "Can you take care of the paperwork later?" he asked his assistant instead. "Sander wants the Querner report as quickly as possible, and I have to take care of something."

"Yes, of course." Winter looked around conspiratorially. "You are welcome to stay at my place again, by the way. Don't be intimidated by my grandmother."

"Thanks for the offer," said Emmerich, praying he wouldn't have to accept.

136 - ALEX BEER

It was pitch black as Emmerich stood in front of an apartment door that was both familiar and oddly foreign to him. His heart beat so hard that it felt as if it might jump out of his chest. Even the heroin, which had served him so well in the past few days, was unable to calm him. His mouth was dry, his hands were wet, and it took three attempts before he finally managed to knock.

The few seconds before the door was finally opened were the longest of his life.

"August!"

He was immediately relieved when Luise rather than Xaver answered. She stepped out into the hall, pulled the door quietly shut behind her, and wrapped her arms around his neck.

"Where have you been? I was so worried." She pressed her face to his neck and he felt warm tears soaking into his collar.

"I wanted to give you all some time. How are you? How are the children? And what's the story with Xaver?" The tension spreading over him was unbearable.

She pulled herself away and kissed him. "I love you," she said. "More than I ever loved him."

Emmerich felt a great weight fall away from his soul, and something happened that was totally new to him: his eyes filled with tears of joy. "We can help support Xaver," he sputtered as he reached for her hand and put it on his chest. "And he can obviously visit the children whenever he would like. It'll be no problem. You'll see. Everything will be fine."

"No . . . no . . . " Luise began to tremble. She pulled her hand away and took a step backwards so her back was against the wall.

"But why? It's really not a problem for me." He reached for her hands but she pulled them away.

"I love you," she repeated. "but I swore an oath. Before God and the church. In good times and bad, until death do us part. I have to uphold it."

Her words hit him like a punch in the gut; dizziness overcame him. "But . . . you thought he was dead. You started a new life, rightly so."

"But he's not dead." Luise looked at him with red eyes. "What am I supposed to do?"

"You don't have to sacrifice your happiness because of a few words you said years ago." He took her tear-soaked face in his hands. "Luise, we love each other, the children are happy, and I can take care of you. Don't throw it all away for an uncertain future with a stranger. Because that's what he is. The man sitting inside our apartment isn't the Xaver you married, it's a stranger. War and imprisonment change people."

She nodded silently and stared at the floor. "He really is unrecognizable."

"Exactly." Emmerich kissed the top of her head and breathed in the scent of her hair.

"You don't understand." She straightened herself and took a deep breath. "Before God he is my husband despite it all. And in the eyes of the church." To buttress her words she pulled from beneath her shirt the chain with the silver crucifix she never took off.

"God and the church . . . " Emmerich took a step back and felt dizzy again. "What have they ever done for you? Do they give you love? Food? Medicine? Do they make sure the apartment is heated? That the children can go to school?"

"August!" Luise glanced at Frau Ganglberger's door, where the sound of light breathing could be heard.

"She can listen. The whole house can hear us for all I care. You belong to me and not to him. You're my wife, not his. Marriage certificate or not."

"August, please," she begged. "Please don't make this more difficult than it already is."

"Get an annulment. We'll write to the archbishop. If he's really as good a man as you always say, he'll understand our request." He stepped closer to her and took her hand again. "What do you say?"

"Ach, August. Of course I thought of that, but there are no grounds for an annulment. At least none that the church would recognize. I'm so sorry. I'm infinitely sorry."

She said a lot more, speaking with a tear-choked voice, but Emmerich didn't hear her words anymore. The entire world was spinning too fast and he was getting dizzy.

"Got it," he said at some point, pulling a tablet out of his pocket and gulping it down. The compressed white powder stuck in his dry throat and filled his mouth with a bitter taste.

"I'm so sorry!" Luise, paler and more frail than usual, rubbed her face with the sleeves of her shirt.

"Me too." Emmerich, who wasn't good at goodbyes, turned and left without looking back once at the building that had until recently been his happy home.

21.

Emmerich wandered aimlessly through the city. He had a strong desire to drink himself into oblivion. The only thing that held him back was the idea of waking up in the morning naked and disoriented in the hospital again. His life was in a downward spiral that he didn't want to accelerate—the abyss was coming toward him fast enough without his help.

Without thinking and above all without feeling, he roamed the streets until fatigue and hunger became too strong for him to ignore any longer. He'd given up hope that his suitcase would be recovered. Pants, shirts, shoes, his savings . . . everything lost forever. Worst of all was the loss of his pendant. Involuntarily he groped at his chest and felt once again the unfamiliar empty space. Even if he'd never known his mother, the amulet was a sort of remembrance of her—his only connection.

Since he still had no money and couldn't afford a hotel, he had to reconsider Winter's offer, like it or not. Winter's grandmother and her snide remarks were the last thing he needed, but what else could he do?

He went back to the commissariat, where the mood in the last few hours had gone in the completely opposite direction from his own. While he was filled with sadness and emptiness, here everyone was laughing, joking, and drinking.

"August Emmerich, the hero of the hour. Hoist a drink with us," called an officer whose name Emmerich couldn't remember.

"Not now," he said, more gruffly than intended. "Where's Winter?" he asked another colleague.

"He left fifteen minutes ago."

"For home?"

The colleague shrugged. "I don't think so. Hörl took him somewhere to continue celebrating. Said something about boxing and Claire Bauroff."

Emmerich was too tired to look for Winter in the hustle and bustle of the Apollo or the dimly-lit Ronacher. When was the last time he'd rested? And the last time he'd eaten? The heroin had permitted him to ignore all signals from his body, which was now taking a vicious revenge. He felt like a balloon with the air let out. Like he didn't have an ounce of energy left. Everything was suddenly taxing. Breathing, swallowing, life.

"Thanks," he said on his way out.

The laughing and happiness of the men was unbearable, and besides, he badly needed sleep, which was impossible as long as the party was going.

He went back out into the cold night, likely to end for him in an emergency shelter wedged in with a heap of those living on the margins. And tomorrow, for better or worse, he would have to bite the bullet and ask Sander for an advance against his next paycheck.

As he turned the corner, factory workers on their way to the night shift came streaming toward him like ants. Their faces were tired and haggard, the hard work had left marks. Many of them walked awkwardly or bent over, as if a heavy weight were bearing down on them. Emmerich used to be happy that he was not one of them—today he envied them.

"Hello, handsome." A woman had stepped out of the shadows of a building entryway. She was petite and had her blonde hair up. As he drew nearer he could see that a few strands had come loose from the bun and were playfully caressing her pale face. It was tough to guess her age because she had so much makeup on, but she looked young. Too young. "How about it?" she asked, snaking the stole she had on her shoulders more tightly around her emaciated body.

Emmerich wanted to just walk past her but something held him back. She seemed somehow familiar. But he couldn't figure out when and where he'd seen her before.

The young woman, too, seemed to remember him, because when he stepped into the light of a streetlamp her eyes widened and then she looked at the ground. "No offence meant," she mumbled and tried to scurry off.

"Halt. Wait a minute." Emmerich grabbed her arm.

"Please don't," she begged.

He let her go. "I don't want to hurt you . . . I just want to . . . "

He paused as he realized why he recognized her. Hörl had detained her for illegal prostitution, and Emmerich had let her go. In his opinion there was no point to jailing the women—they weren't working this line of work for fun, but because hunger and misery had left them no other choice. They'd been punished enough by life.

She coughed and looked around frantically. "Where's your colleague?"

"I'm alone. Don't worry. Nobody's going to do anything to you."

The street girl seemed to believe him, because her face relaxed noticeably. "You're letting me walk a second time. It's very generous of you." She coughed again. "I can repay the favor if you want," she said in a throaty voice.

Emmerich used a finger to turn her head into the light of the streetlamp. She was unnaturally pale and had dark rings under her eyes. Placing his hand on her forehead, he confirmed what he had already suspected. "You're sick and you shouldn't be standing around out here in the cold."

"I have to earn money."

"The wind is going to pick up again. If you don't take care

of yourself you'll be down for the count for the next few days. It makes more sense to go home now. Do you live nearby?"

"A few streets over, in Favoriten, I have a maid's chamber there."

"Come on, I'll get you home," he said, offering his arm.

Favoriten was a working-class area full of factories and bleak squares. Unlike in the city center or in the rich neighborhoods around the edge of the city, there were no parks or trees for miles around and certainly no lovingly kept flower beds. Everything in Favoriten was strictly functional.

"Here we are." The young woman gestured to a sagging brick shell of a building with old, soot-covered windows. "Thanks for your kindness."

Emmerich buried his hands in his pockets and looked around. "Would you possibly know where the nearest emergency shelter is?"

"On Puchsbaumgasse, I think. All the way at the end. You have to go there for work?"

"I wish," he mumbled, preparing to head off. "Good night and feel better."

"Wait!" called the young woman. "Do you want to come up?" she asked. "I have tea. Not good tea, but it warms you up."

"Love to." He took the invitation with barely a thought. Anything was better than the city's emergency shelters, those smelly, grim sources of disease. He followed her through a narrow entry corridor full of garbage, and then up a creaky wooden staircase. It reeked of piss. "Isn't blocking the corridors against the house rules?"

"Of course, but it hasn't been enforced for years." They were only on the second floor but the woman was already short of breath.

Emmerich detested the wealthy landlords who shamelessly enriched themselves on the plight of others. But he was too tired on this night to get worked up over it.

On the top floor his companion pointed to a low, sooty door at the end of the hall. "I wasn't expecting visitors."

"No worries, I'm used to it, and anyway you've spared me waiting for morning in the stuffy, damp air of the shelter."

"Watch your head."

She opened the door to a windowless room that was so small that Emmerich felt as if he had entered a dollhouse. The pitch of the roof made the room feel even more cramped. To the left was a thin straw mattress, to the right a chair heaped with clothes, and on the back wall was a little shelf next to a brick stove. It was drafty and cold. Emmerich looked in vain for a place to sit down.

The young woman handed him a tattered cushion and motioned to the floor, which was covered with a threadbare carpet. "My name is Minna, by the way."

"August." He sat down and looked at the wall, which was covered with colorful posters, postcards, and sketches. "You seem to be a great admirer of Paraguay."

Minna turned to him and was suddenly a completely different person. Her eyes lit up, her face regained a little color. "It's the country of my dreams," she gushed, reaching for a dented pot and going out to fill it with water from the spigot in the stairwell.

"Tell me about it," Emmerich urged when she returned and set the pot on the stove and lit a fire.

"I don't even know where to start. There are so many wonderful things there."

Minna opened a tin can, spooned crumbled brown leaves into two cups, and stared off dreamily until a quiet bubbling signaled that the water was boiling. She carefully filled the cups and handed one to Emmerich.

He took it gratefully and wrapped his chilly hands around it. "Just start somewhere. I could use a nice story or two."

"Then you're in the right place." She sat down on the

mattress and ran her hands softly, almost tenderly, over a poster showing exotic birds. "Someone once told me that Paraguay is the land of flowers and fruit. It's always warm there, the people are friendly, and there are exotic animals." She smiled and looked for a moment almost like a little girl. She blew cautiously into the steaming brown liquid, took a sip, and started to cough.

"You alright?" asked Emmerich.

She shook her head. "Vienna is making me sick. This apartment is making me sick. The people make me sick. Everything does. I hate this city." Her eyes gleamed again as she ran her hand over the image of the birds once more.

And only now did Emmerich realize. He should have recognized it right away—the deathly pale skin, the drawn cheeks, the cough and the shortness of breath; children died like flies from the same thing back at the orphanage. Minna had what they called the Vienna Disease. She had tuberculosis. She would soon be coughing blood and running a high fever and having convulsions. She'd get thinner and weaker and one day she'd nod off forever. And this day was not far off, nearer in fact than she wanted to admit.

"I'm sorry." He couldn't think of anything else to say.

"I'm not going to die," she said as if reading his thoughts. "The climate in Paraguay can cure me, that's why I'm moving there." She reached under her pillow and pulled out a brochure that was so worn out it must have been read a thousand times already. "Paraguay is distinguished by an extraordinarily healthy climate," she read aloud. "Yellow fever, cholera, typhus, and other enemies of mankind are unknown in the country. Tuberculosis can be completely cured there."

"And how do you plan to get there, if I might ask?"

"With the resettlement company called New Home. They're helping me emigrate. I'll live in an Austrian settlement near Asuncion." She leaned forward and pointed to a picture

hanging behind Emmerich of pretty houses dotting a pictur-
esque river bank. *A jewel among the cities of the earth* was written below the image. "You know what? To mark the occasion
I'm going to heat up the stove." Minna pulled a few small
pieces of wood from a bucket, put them in the brick stove, and
lit them. "Soon I'll be in a place where I'll never need heat
again."

Emmerich just hoped that would be Paraguay and not
Eternity. "You don't need to do it on my account—"

"Yes, I do." She sat down on the mattress again and sipped
her tea while the comforting warmth spread through the tiny
room. "Without you my plans would have died."

Emmerich didn't know what the young woman was talking
about, and just looked at her. Her eyes were clear, her skin was
dry and pale—nothing suggested she had already gone into a
feverish delirium.

She had caught his skeptical look and handed him a piece
of paper with a list written on it. "To Bring" was the title.

"Passport, six photos, certificate of residence," he read
aloud. "Certification from the tax authority that all obligations
have been met up to the date of application. Morality reference."

"You let me go. Only because of you do I have a clean
morality reference. You can't join a settlement without impec-
cable character. From that perspective you saved my dream
and with it my life. A little heat is the least I can do."

Emmerich nodded abstractedly. A thought was crossing his
exhausted mind, something he couldn't grasp in his worn-
down state. Trying to remember, he stared at the list until his
eye stopped at a number: 10,000 crowns. His alertness came
back to life. "The capital investment is that much? That's quite
a sum."

Minna's smile disappeared. "Why do you think I turn
tricks? With what I was making as a maid I'd never have gotten

the money together. But this way . . . I'm young, and some men pay really well. And besides, the woman I was working for before treated me terribly. So this work isn't much worse, really."

"Even so . . . I'd never have guessed that the price was that high."

The heat crept through Emmerich's body like a gentle anesthetic. His eyes grew heavy, and he had difficulty listening attentively.

"It covers transit costs, plus I get a small plot of land and a place to stay in Paraguay. I hadn't expected it to cost so much either, and I nearly signed a contract with a different agency. That one was half the price."

"But?"

He leaned against the wall and closed his eyes for a moment. Just for a second, he thought. Just going to rest for a second.

"A friend of mine wanted to emigrate to America with that agency, to the United States . . . " Minna chattered on without noticing that her guest was slowly fading.

Emmerich heard her words faintly as if from a distance. " . . . put the money aside . . . took off with it . . . vile swindler . . . criminal organization . . . "

Then he fell asleep.

Emigrate!

Emmerich woke with a start and rubbed his face.

In an instant he was wide awake. The men in Poldi Tant had been talking about it, and the men at the homeless shelter had also said that Dietrich Jost wanted to travel to Brazil.

He looked around, still woozy from sleep, and since the familiar pain was creeping up his leg he grabbed his heroin tablets from his pants pocket. There weren't many left. He would have to stop by Winter's later to grab more.

Quickly he popped a pill in his mouth and washed it down with the rest of the tea, which was now ice cold and bitter.

"Minna." He shook the young woman awake. "You have to tell me everything about emigrating. Most importantly about the black sheep."

"First of all, good morning." The young woman coughed. "Can you make tea? I'm freezing."

Emmerich felt her forehead. Her fever had risen. He hoped so badly that she would make it abroad before it was too late. "Here." He handed her one of his tablets. "It's heroin. It's supposed to help with all ailments."

Minna's face brightened. "Thanks." She took the tablet and broke it up with her fingers.

"What are you doing?" asked Emmerich as he looked for the tea, hunched over because he could barely stand up in the tiny room.

"Heroin is supposed to be a wonder drug." She continued to rub the pieces of tablet until it was a nothing more than powder. "I've heard that it works better if you sniff it."

"Interesting. I'll have to try it next time." Emmerich watched as she rolled up a little piece of paper, stuck it into her nose and snorted the white dust while the tea water heated up.

"Ow," she said. "It burns."

He steeped the mysterious brown leaves—she'd probably picked them and dried them herself—and then handed her a cup.

"I feel better already," she said, and her face had in fact regained some color.

"I'm glad." Emmerich sipped on the brew and gave her a second tablet. "For later. And now tell me."

22

H ere," Emmerich tossed a newspaper onto Winter's desk.

He studied the masthead: "*The Emigrant. An independent source for all emigration issues*," he read aloud, then looked at his boss with a frown. "You're not leaving us, are you?"

"Jost wanted to go to Brazil and the men in Poldi Tant were discussing emigration, too." Emmerich leaned against the desk. "These so-called resettlement companies have spread like the plague in the past few months. They promise people a real-life paradise and get paid exorbitantly for their services."

Winter motioned to Emmerich's rumpled pants. "You weren't able to sleep at home."

Emmerich ignored his assistant's observation. "And like everything else, where there's money, there are black sheep in the flock. What if our victims were taken in by swindlers? What if these swindlers fleeced people of their entire life savings and then silenced them?"

"The victims didn't look as though they had much in the way of savings to steal. On the contrary."

Emmerich thought of Minna. "It's usually the poorest of the poor who want to get out of the country. Those who are doing well don't need to leave. And there are many ways to get money."

Winter nodded. "And now?"

"Now we'll take a closer look at these resettlement companies." Emmerich opened up the paper and pointed to a page full of ads.

"Settlement Society, Association for World Business and Migration, New Home Resettlement Society, Society for the Protection of Migrants from the Former Austro-Hungarian Empire, Association of Austrian Emigrants . . . " Winter looked up at Emmerich. "There's a lot of them."

"There are a lot of people who want to get out of this shit hole."

"Not me," Winter said in solidarity with his hometown. "Things will get better soon. Like it used to be, just without the Kaiser. Don't you think so?"

Emmerich thought for a moment. "With or without the Kaiser, life is hard and unfair." He folded the paper and pointed to the information about the publisher, which was on the front page. "I think we should begin there. At the Emigration Aid Society 'Austria Abroad,' 46a Blindengasse."

As they went outside into the street, Winter stopped. "It smells like rain," he said. "Maybe we should take an umbrella."

Emmerich looked up at the clear sky and wondered about his assistant again. "Come on. The sun is shining, and even if it does rain . . . we're not made of sugar."

They went three stops on the tram. The conductor was a pretty blonde woman—a rare picture. During the war years women had filled almost all the positions at the Vienna Transit Authority, but since the end of the war the men had reclaimed their domain to such a degree that women conductors were rarely seen anymore.

"Tickets, please," she said.

"We're with the police detective corps." Winter showed his badge and blushed all the way up to the roots of his hair. "This ride is for professional purposes."

She nodded and moved on to the other customers.

"So, petite blondes, is it?" said Emmerich when they hopped off and turned into Blindengasse. "And speaking of women . . . how was Bauroff yesterday?"

This time Winter blushed even more, if that was possible. "Yeah," he said with feigned nonchalance, pushing open the door to the newspaper office. "Ample breasts for sure."

"Excuse me?" A corpulent woman behind a massive desk was staring at them from over the rim of her glasses.

Winter's head drooped and Emmerich stepped in front of him. "His grandmother needs new blouses."

"Oh." She smiled. "What can I do for you?" Her nameplate identified her as Frau Nöstel. She pointed to a couple of chairs.

Emmerich sat down and put out photos on her desk of Jost, Zeiner, and the unidentified man. "Ever seen them?"

"Are you with the police?"

Emmerich asked Winter to show her his badge. After she had examined it, she picked up each photo and studied the faces closely. As she did, Emmerich looked around the room. Like at Minna's place, the walls were covered with colorful posters, postcards, and pictures except that here they weren't of Paraguay but the United States, Brazil, Argentina, Canada, and other overseas El Dorados. *Welcome to the Garden of Eden, Find your fortune in this blessed country, Wealthy settlements welcome you with open arms . . .* These and the other slogans tried to lure abroad everyone who was struggling with cold and poverty.

"I don't know these two, but this one was here." She pointed to Jost.

"Can you tell us anything about it? Did he sign a contract with you?"

"He wanted to go somewhere warm and sunny. Preferably Brazil."

"And were you able to help him?"

She looked sadly at her hands. "The poor guy was shell-shocked, he trembled. Totally unfit for any type of work." She saw that the detectives didn't seem to be following her logic.

"Relocation companies are there to protect people," she explained. "To give people information and guidance. Many of those who come to us have irrational hopes or a completely false idea of what awaits them."

"So no Garden of Eden?" Emmerich pointed to a poster that showed a happy, attractive, doe-eyed woman standing among exotic fruits.

"That's a part of the reality. Unlike the shady companies, we communicate the other parts, too. Only when I think my clients understand what they're getting into will I finalize a contract."

"And Herr Jost didn't get one."

"The possibility of a pleasant life abroad is predicated on good mental and physical condition. Food doesn't just fall from the trees over there, either. You have to work hard for it. And Herr Jost was clearly in no condition for that. No settlement would have taken him in, and he'd never have made it on his own. Someone like him is better off here. Soup kitchens, emergency shelters, institutions for the less fortunate—you'll look a long time for that kind of thing in South America." She opened a drawer and pulled out a stack of brochures. "Men like you, on the other hand . . ." She handed Emmerich and Winter each a brochure. "Strapping lads are needed everywhere."

"You sent him away?"

"It broke my heart, but anything else would have been irresponsible—ach, what am I saying, it would have been impossible. What else could I do?"

"Could another company have accepted him?"

She snorted. "Certainly not the honorable ones. But there are also shady ones, as I mentioned."

Emmerich paged through the brochure. It looked idyllic overseas. For a moment he thought about what it would be like to start fresh somewhere else. What did he have to lose? Then he got hold of himself again. He had responsibilities. Vienna wasn't a very livable place at the moment, and as a cop he had the chance to change things for the better.

"Could you possibly give us some names?" he asked.

"They change their names every few months. Their scam works like this: people pay and then are supposed to wait until a large enough group has been assembled so that they can all travel together. Of course, they are waiting in vain."

"And then they just change their name, open a new office, and are out of reach. Cunning. Now we just need to know how we can find these con artists."

"Finally, someone is doing something about it." Frau Nöstel pounded resolutely on the desktop. "I can tell this much, that all the companies that advertise in our paper are trustworthy."

"Including the New Home Resettlement Society?"

"Of course. What made you think of them?"

"Ach, no reason," Emmerich brushed aside the question, thinking of Minna. At least in this she got lucky.

"The best thing to do would be to have a look around near the city employment agency. The bastards from the fly-by-night companies go there looking for victims. They promise heaven and earth to strong men and pretty women. Once they get their hooks into someone naïve, they make sure they get hold of their money quickly. I don't even want to think about what the poor people they scam have to do to get the money together."

Emmerich stood up and put the brochure in his pocket. "Thanks very much. You've been very helpful."

Frau Nöstel's round cheeks went red. "If you see poor, poor Herr Jost, give him my best. And tell your grandmother she should try the clothing store called Breier on Mariahilferstraße. A friend of mine works there and they have a large selection of blouses."

23

S tanding in lines had become a fact of everyday life in Vienna. Thousands of people regularly waited in front of businesses and offices in the hope of getting hold of food, clothing, fuel, or—in the case of the city employment agency—work.

"You can't even see the entrance from here," complained the man behind Emmerich and Winter in line. He shoved his hands into his pockets, leaned his head to the side, and drifted off into a state of resignation.

"They won't run out before the end of the day," said another man, looking at Winter, who, well dressed and in good spirits, didn't fit in so well with the crowd of tired, hungry people whose daily battle to survive had sapped them of all their energy.

Emmerich, who had slept in his clothes and was unshaven and unwashed, fit into the milieu better.

"And now?" asked Winter. "Are we supposed to wait the whole day?"

"If we have to. Standing around is real investigative work. You might as well get used to it." He looked around and put up the collar of his jacket. "I'll survey the situation. You can hold our spot in the line in the meantime." Emmerich crossed the street and ambled down the opposite side of the street looking across at the waiting masses. Was one of them a wolf in sheep's clothing? He paused abruptly when a familiar face caught his eye. The man was tall and haggard and was wearing ragged clothes. His long brown hair was unkempt and fell over his face. Where did he know him from? Was he an old army comrade? Someone he'd once arrested? The flash of recognition hit Emmerich like a punch to the gut.

It was Xaver Koch. Luise's husband.

Emmerich knew that one false look from the man, or a hint of pity or triumph from him would make him lose control. He held the brochure from the resettlement company in front of his face and hurried back to Winter.

"Everything okay? You seem agitated."

"What could possibly have happened? I was only gone a few minutes." Emmerich didn't look at his assistant, he couldn't take either his sympathy or his cheerfulness just then. It's not his fault, he thought. Though he wasn't sure if he meant Winter or Koch.

He leaned silently against the wall of the building and watched the line continue to get longer while up front nothing moved. The man who had said they'd still have a chance today had spoken too soon.

The incessant honking of a car suddenly set the lethargic mass of job seekers in motion. One after the other, people took a step to the side so the vehicle could pass. Just before the car reached Emmerich an ear-splitting pop rang out, like a gunshot, which made all the men reflexively duck. The war was still deep in their bones.

"It was just the car backfiring."

Emmerich hadn't ducked, and now his gaze fell on the face of a man a few paces behind him. He wasn't sure how he noticed him. Maybe it was his tense demeanor, the scar running across his right cheek, or just the fact that the man was just as indifferent as he himself.

Before he could think about it more, the other people straightened up again, looked around sheepishly, and returned to their spots in line.

"Cigarette?" A man in a gray sports jacket made from the remnants of old uniform had sidled up to him.

"Sorry, but I don't have any," he brushed off the annoying sponger.

"Would you like a cigarette?" the man reformulated his question. To bolster his words he held out a pack of Nil no filters.

Emmerich, surprised by the unexpected generosity, took one. "Thanks," he said, let the man light it, and relished the taste of the fine Middle Eastern blend.

"You are looking to emigrate?" The man pointed at the brochure Emmerich still had in his hand.

"My young friend and I have thought about it." He pulled Winter over. "But unfortunately we can't afford it."

"Right. We don't have enough cash," said Winter, stating the obvious.

"My friends, today might just be your lucky day." The guy smiled broadly. "The resettlement companies just want to make money. They demand ridiculous sums that bear no relationship to what they are actually offering." He put a hand on Winter's shoulder. "But there are still good and honest men in the world. And the man I work for is one of them."

Emmerich smiled. "Oh yeah?"

"He's a real philanthropist. Doesn't try to get rich off poor folks. On the contrary—he often contributes. He charges half what the cutthroats charge." He took the brochure out of Emmerich's hand, crumpled it up dramatically, and threw it to the ground. "What country were you interested in going to, if you could choose?"

"Brazil," said Emmerich. "Sun, beautiful women and enough work and food for everyone. And your boss really charges half the price?"

"If that." The guy offered Winter a cigarette, too, but he passed. Emmerich grabbed greedily for it and tucked the Nil behind his ear.

"Good that you guys met me. If you really want to get to Brazil, I've just saved you thousands of crowns." He stuck out his hand to shake both of theirs. "I'm Tamás, by the way."

"August." Emmerich shook the proffered hand.

"Ferdinand," said Winter, doing the same.

"Pleasure." Tamás lit a cigarette and began to talk about his boss, a certain Dr. Farkas.

"*Szar!*" he cursed in Hungarian when the bells of a nearby church struck ten. "I have to go." He rummaged in his pockets. "*Szar!*" he swore again. "I don't have any brochures with me. But hey, why don't you just come with me?" He pulled Winter out of the line and motioned for Emmerich to follow him.

"Slow down, slow down. How do you picture this happening?" Emmerich said to the stranger. "Half price is still a whole lot of money, and if we had that kind of loot we wouldn't be standing in this line."

"We can figure something out." Tamás waved Emmerich and Winter closer. "Dr. Farkas also arranges jobs," he whispered. "Good-paying jobs. And you don't have to wait around, like here." He leaned in so close to the two of them that they could smell his bad breath. "Let's be honest. The city employment agency only gives out crummy jobs. Do you really want to hire yourselves out as day laborer, floor sweeper, or shoe repairman for a few miserable pennies? Not to mention that you have to wait ages to get paid. It could be weeks before you see any money. If at all. Brazil will just keep getting farther and farther away." Emmerich acted as if he'd been persuaded. "Come on. If the offer doesn't convince you, you can always come back here and get in line tomorrow."

"Go ahead," snapped the man behind them in line. "It suits us just fine."

Emmerich took the last drag of his cigarette, tossed it to the ground, and stepped on it. "Alright," he said. "Off to Brazil."

"*Maroni*! Hot *maroni*!" yelled a street vendor as the three men walked past him, fanning his grill with a newspaper so the smell of the roasted chestnuts went straight into their noses.

"Mmmm." Winter closed his eyes and relished the smell. "Are there chestnuts in Brazil?"

"They have everything there. Everything your heart could desire . . . " Tamás turned to them and continued on, walking backwards, "and your eyes and your mouths and your . . . " He grabbed his crotch and grinned lasciviously. "You're going to love it."

"Watch it, intersection!" Emmerich seemed totally unimpressed.

Tamás stumbled backwards on the curb and came within a hair of being run over by a passing draft horse. He reached the other side of the street safely only with a lot of luck and dexterity.

"*Faszfej*," he sneered, spitting on the ground. The steady stream of curses from the driver of the cart, who evidently understood the Hungarian curse word, rang in their ears until they reached a run-down building at the end of the street. Here Tamás stopped and opened the door. "*Bienvenido*," he said. "That's Spanish for welcome."

"But they speak Portuguese in Brazil," Winter whispered to Emmerich.

"Then we are definitely in the right place."

They followed their escort down a set of stairs into a poorly-lit basement. "The boss doesn't want to waste his clients' money on expensive overhead," he explained, opening the door to a little office.

Just as in the resettlement company's offices, the walls here, too, were covered with posters and photos depicting happy people and beautiful locations. *Happiness is just a ship ride away*, said a banner hanging above the makeshift desk made of plywood. There was no friendly, buxom woman behind the desk, rather a chunky bald man with muscular arms that seemed to be testing the strength of his shirtsleeves. He smiled and spread his bundles of muscles into a gesture meant to be a welcoming.

"What can I do for you gentlemen?"

"Brazil," said Tamás, bowing and then saying goodbye. "Good luck."

The bald man nodded to him and then turned his attention back to Emmerich and Winter. "The land of the future." He leaned back. "A tropical paradise full of oranges, grapes, meat, and chocolate. And, of course, luscious women. Good choice. I am Dr. Farkas, by the way."

"We heard that you're supposed to be cheaper than the others."

Emmerich looked around. Against the back wall stood a file cabinet and a stack of boxes that, according to their labels, contained imported goods. On one side wall was a shelf displaying taxidermied exotic animals.

"I'm here to help, not to get rich." Farkas pulled a thick cigar out of an ivory case that was sitting in front of him on the desk and lit it. "The situation that has befallen our poor *Vaterland* is hard to bear. Luckily Brazil, a rich and fertile country, has too few residents and greets colonists with open arms." He stood up and went to the file cabinet. Emmerich stared at him with his mouth open. Farkas was a walking mountain of a man who made even the bouncer at the Chatham Bar look like a fragile choirboy. He pulled out two emigration contracts and set them down in front of Emmerich and Winter. "For only five thousand crowns per person, I can take care of the voyage and all the paperwork. And not only that. I'll make sure there's a place to stay and a job waiting for you there, and represent you in any affairs that may arise after your departure from Vienna. All you have to do is sign your name here, here, and here." He handed Emmerich a fountain pen.

"There's just one small problem," said Emmerich, pulling the Nil he'd gotten from Tamás out from behind his ear and looking at the fat cigar in Farkas's hand.

Farkas handed him matches. "The money?"

Emmerich lit his cigarette and nodded. "Tamás said you could get us work. Lucrative work."

Farkas looked at the two of them. "Do you know how to box? I set up boxing matches at Port Freudenau."

"I was at the Apollo yesterday and saw a fight," Winter said. "Hörl showed me a few tricks afterward."

"So the answer is no." Farkas thought for a moment. "What about math? I need a new bookie."

Emmerich resisted asking what happened to the old one. "There's one other thing," he said. "There's actually three of us."

Farkas's face brightened and he pulled another contract out of the file cabinet. "All are welcome."

"Our friend is shell-shocked. Other companies have refused to take him."

Farkas sighed. "That's inhuman. These people need a ray of hope more than anyone." He rubbed his paws together. "Thank god I am here. I'll find something for him, too."

Emmerich smiled. They were in the right place. He could practically smell it. "Many thanks," he said, folding the contract and putting it in his pocket. "We'll think it over."

Farkas was visibly shocked at the abrupt end to the conversation. "But, gentlemen . . . " he began.

Emmerich ignored him and went to the door. "We know where to find you."

As they left the building, Winter asked: "Did you see how big he was?"

"It was impossible not to notice."

It had begun to drizzle, and Winter hunched beneath the collar of his jacket. "An umbrella would have come in handy after all."

Emmerich didn't answer. He remained standing in the entryway and insisted Winter hold the door handle. "Make sure that it doesn't close."

Winter did as he was told while Emmerich ran down the street to a pile of rubble. He fished around in it and returned with a bit of wire and a few thin wood slats.

"Stand in front of me," he told Winter, pushing the latch in and wedging it in with pieces of wood. When he was finished he closed the door and nodded contentedly when it didn't lock.

"Now what?" Winter suspected the worst.

"Now we wait again." Emmerich motioned to the entrance to a courtyard across the street that was blocked by garbage containers.

"My God, what is in these things?" Winter could barely breathe when they got into position.

"It's not a body, anyway. They smell different. So it doesn't matter to us." Emmerich squatted down so he could keep an eye on the entrance to Farkas's office through a gap between the containers while Winter pulled the collar of his shirt over his nose and breathed quietly through his mouth.

They spent a good half hour in this position before the door finally opened and Farkas walked out into the street. He had on a long, warm coat and an elegant hat and marched in long steps toward the city center.

"Mealtime," whispered Emmerich, waiting until the massive man was out of view. "He must be going to lunch. That should give us enough time."

"How are we going to get in?" Winter felt uncomfortable with the idea of breaking in. "I'm sure he didn't leave his office unlocked."

Emmerich didn't answer. He just held up the wire he'd fished from the rubble. "We can get in anywhere with the right tool."

"Is that what you learn as a detective?"

Winter watched Emmerich with fascination as he worked on the lock to the file cabinet. Just as with the office door, it didn't take long before another quiet click confirmed his proficiency as a safecracker.

"It's something you learn in life." Emmerich grabbed a stack of filled-out emigration contracts and other papers from the cabinet and sat down at Farkas's desk. Winter sat opposite him and together they began to look through the documents. "No sign of any contact with foreign countries or shipping companies. The guy's clearly a fraud," Emmerich determined quickly.

"What a rotten piece of—" Winter suddenly paused and waved a contract in the air. "Look what I have here. Dietrich Jost."

Emmerich gave a thumbs-up and went through the rest of the stack. "Nothing else here. Zeiner could still be in your stack."

Winter answered no, and they began again. But they didn't find a contract for Zeiner the second time through either. Emmerich looked in the cabinet again but found only blank forms. "Strange." He looked in the crates of imported goods while Winter examined the shelf of taxidermied animals.

"Nothing else here. Maybe we should beat it. What if he comes back?" He looked at the door.

"Big men have big appetites," Emmerich brushed aside his concern and began to go through the papers a third time. "You make me nervous with your fear."

"I'm not afraid," Winter protested, and then stopped short.

"Shh! Did you hear that?" He went to the door. "Someone's coming."

Emmerich wouldn't be disturbed. "Just a second," he said, feeling beneath the desk.

Winter was getting more nervous. "The windows have bars

and there's no place to hide in here. Let's get out of here." He opened the door a crack, peered out, and turned with shock to Emmerich. "He's coming. Farkas is coming."

Before Emmerich could react, the door was thrown open and Farkas entered his realm. "What the hell is going on? What are you doing in here?" he yelled so loudly that even Emmerich cringed.

"Police. We've come to confiscate your files."

"You're not taking anything." Farkas sent Winter to the floor with a single blow as if he weighed nothing at all.

"Go get backup," yelled Emmerich as Farkas shoved the desk aside and squared up to him—Emmerich barely came up to his collarbone. "Go on!"

Winter gathered himself with a groan and tumbled out of the office.

Emmerich turned in a flash and reached into one of the crates hoping to find something he could use as a weapon. Farkas started to laugh loudly when the inspector threw a chocolate bar at him.

"I'm going to send you to paradise now, ass-face," he sneered. "And I don't mean Brazil." He made a fist and started to swing.

Emmerich ducked and made as if he was going to run to the right but then jumped to the left. His opponent anticipated the feint, grabbed him by the collar, and shoved him up against the wall. Emmerich tried to pull away but Farkas's grip was too strong. The fraudster's fingers closed around his throat like a vise and choked him.

"Let me go, for god's sake. I can't breathe," he rasped.

Farkas was unmoved. "Nobody breaks into my place without being punished," he said, pressing harder on his throat.

Emmerich could feel the blood stopping in his head and kicked at his attacker, flailed about, scratched, and punched, but none of it affected Farkas. He just continued to choke him.

That's it, thought Emmerich, closing his eyes. This time I should have listened to the kid.

He felt sick to his stomach and dizzy. The pain in his throat was unbearable. He'd survived his horrible childhood and the war only to be iced by this wretched scam artist . . . He felt his strength fading, he was losing consciousness. Luise, he thought, as his mind faded. Ach, Luise . . .

A bloodcurdling scream suddenly filled the room, and Emmerich opened his eyes a crack. The scenario that played out in front of him couldn't possibly be real. Winter was standing behind Farkas on the desk; he had his arms up in the air and was screaming as if he were being flayed alive. Farkas turned and Winter threw a handful of sand in his face. Then he kicked him in the crotch. The brawny bald man howled and buckled.

This gave Emmerich the chance to break free. Reflexively he reached for the nearest object—a cigar box made out of wood—and smashed it over Farkas's head as hard as he could. Farkas fell to the ground like a wet sack.

"What the hell was that?" asked Emmerich, gasping, while he removed the shoelaces from the unconscious Farkas and tied up his arms and legs.

"Hörl really did teach me a few things yesterday." Winter stared at his hands, which were shaking uncontrollably. "Step one: frighten," he counted. "Animals achieve this goal by making themselves as big as they can and roaring. Step two: surprise. Step three: strike. Preferably the ears, the larynx, or the crotch. I never thought I'd have to put it to use today."

Emmerich nearly betrayed his appreciation, but then Farkas came to.

"Piece of shit," he groaned. "You goddamn dogs!"

Emmerich held Jost's contract up to his face. "Why did he have to die?"

"He's dead? Shit." Farkas tried to blink the sand from his

eyes. "I didn't bump the poor bastard off. I'd have to be an idiot. He was going to bring the money this week. I guess I can forget that."

"Did you get him a job?"

Farkas shook his head and yanked at the shoelaces. "I can't feel my hands."

"I asked you something." Emmerich kicked him.

"I sent him off to beg, but nobody has any money these days, and even less sympathy. He had to find another way to drum up the money."

"How?"

"He didn't say. He just said he'd come by this week to pay me."

"What about these two?" From his pocket Emmerich pulled the photo of Zeiner and the sketch of the unidentified man. "Were they here, too?"

"What did you put in my eyes? I can barely see." Farkas blinked.

"Sand from the rubble pile."

Emmerich smiled inside. Who would have thought the pile of rubble would prove so useful, he thought. He held the photo and sketch closer to Farkas's face.

"Never seen them."

"You sure?" Emmerich took a handkerchief from Farkas's chest pocket and wiped his eyes.

"Never seen them," he repeated. "And now let me go. I'm no murderer."

Emmerich ignored him, sat down at the desk, and thought for a moment. If Farkas was telling the truth, this was not the place they needed to be. "How was Jost going to get the money?" he asked, picking up the chocolate bar and breaking off a piece. "Mmmm." It hadn't worked as a weapon, but it was unsurpassed as a nutritional delivery system and a luxury food.

"I already said that I have no idea."

"But you know how people make money quick in this town. Spit it out. I wouldn't want to kick you again."

"Moving stolen goods," the tied-up man began. "Prostitution, rigged betting, black market, robbery, extortion, breaking and entering . . . I don't know. You're the experts."

"Anything that required endurance, strength, or dexterity was out of the question for Jost. That leaves only extortion and rigged betting. What about the boxing matches you set up? Are they rigged?"

"No, I'm just sports crazy, and anyway . . . If he bet on anything it would be the ponies. He said that he'd been a zookeeper at the Schönbrunn menagerie before the war."

Emmerich pricked up his ears. "This could be something for us," he said, standing up. "Thank you for your cooperation." He bowed and pointed to the contracts that were still on the desk. "I've written down all the names and information. If they don't find themselves happy and content overseas within one month, you will find yourself in trouble. Big trouble. This little episode today will be nothing by comparison. Got it?" Farkas grunted his assent. "Great, we're in agreement." Emmerich grabbed the cigar box and headed for the door.

"You can't just leave me here like this!" The huge man wriggled like a stranded worm in the rain.

"Why not? Register a complaint against us."

"I'll get you," he yelled after them as they left the building.

"Not if we get you first." Emmerich straightened his cap. "You okay?" he asked his assistant, who was standing on the street next to him breathing deeply.

"That's the second guy this week I knocked out." Winter wavered between pride and amazement.

"Thanks. You saved my skin." Emmerich handed him the cigar box. "Here, you earned it."

"But I don't smoke."

"You don't know what you're missing. And now off to Schönbrunn." Emmerich lit a cigar and put the chocolate bar in Winter's pocket, which made him visibly happy.

In times like these, it was rare to see two men walking down the street looking so satisfied.

24

One thousand five hundred rooms, and still nothing more than a summer residence for the Kaiser," said Emmerich when they arrived in front of Schönbrunn palace. "If that's not decadent, don't ask me what is."

The magnificent baroque structure, the façade of which had lent its name to a color—Schönbrunn yellow—rose as proudly into the sky as if the monarchy were still in full flower.

"Those days are gone." Winter didn't want to hear any of Emmerich's pessimism. "The children's society even got their own wing of it to house war orphans."

"Get out of here, they got eighty-four rooms. Eighty-four out of a thousand five hundred! The rest were snatched by top politicians, government-friendly companies, and the army. Sure, it's called a republic now, not a monarchy, but I don't think it makes much difference to the simple *Volk*."

"Give things a chance." Winter, hopeful as always, put a piece of chocolate in his mouth and turned into the gravel path that ran diagonally through the park surrounding the palace and into the menagerie, as the zoo was called. Low, well-manicured hedges and tall chestnut trees lined the path on both sides and gave the impression that time had stood still. "It's nice here," Winter decided. "Just like it used to be. As if the war never happened."

Before Emmerich could answer they passed a pond where a swarm of small fish were fighting over a few mosquito larvae. He gazed at the frenzy.

"The palace ponds are being used as fish farms now. Heard about it recently. These look like trench fish."

"Leave the fish alone!" A woman with scraggly white hair emerged from a hedge and held a fist in the air.

"Don't worry, we're not going to steal anything." Emmerich started to go but the old lady stepped in front of him and stuck out her hand.

"Spare some change."

"Sorry, but I don't have so much as a *heller*." He tried to slip past her but she wouldn't let him.

"And there went out another horse that was red," she recited from the Book of Revelation. "And power was given to him that sat thereon to take peace from the earth, and that they should kill one another: and there was given unto him a great sword."

"There's nothing I can do about that at this point." Emmerich peered at Winter, who was watching this exchange from a safe distance.

"Spare some change," she repeated. "Please . . . "

Winter reached into his pockets and turned them inside out to show that he really had no money.

"The First Horseman brought conquest, the Second war, the Third famine, and if you don't give me something, the Fourth will soon come."

"For me alone?" Emmerich laughed.

"Indeed. Fear, decline, and . . . " She paused dramatically.

"And?"

" . . . death." She touched Emmerich's stomach with the tips of her fingers. "You will die." The look on her face was so convincing that his laughter fell away. "Or someone close to you will lose his life."

A shiver went through Emmerich's limbs. This old lady was crazy. But he couldn't help thinking of Luise's foreboding and the fact that women often seemed to have a sixth sense.

"Here," he said, quickly pressing a cigar into her hand. "That's all that I can give you." His gut told him it was better not to get into it with the witch.

The woman held the thick brown cheroot up to her nose, sniffed it, and gave him a toothless smile. "Beware the Fourth Horseman! Beware the pale horse!" she shouted and disappeared back into the hedges.

"My god is she scary," whispered Winter, and Emmerich didn't contradict him. They continued on and arrived at a star-shaped plaza with an ornate fountain in the middle—the Western Najadenbecken.

"Let's not stop at this one." Winter walked more quickly. "Don't want another nut jumping out at us."

When the entrance to the zoo finally came into view, Winter couldn't suppress a broad smile.

"Someone's excited."

"When I was little, my nanny brought me here often, and I was allowed to feed the animals bread crumbs. I loved it." He looked around, and his happiness gave way to skepticism. "Strange that nobody's here. Back then you had to wait in line to see the most exciting animals."

I hope you know how much a nice childhood is worth, thought Emmerich, and he thought without meaning to about the fact that he would never be able to marvel at the animals with Luise's children. He quickly swallowed his sadness and rage.

"Probably just the bad weather." He pulled his cap further down over his face.

Winter was visibly upset as he walked around the circular grounds, arranged around the Kaiser pavilion. Thirteen sections fanned out from the pavilion to house various sorts of animals, and some of them seemed completely uninhabited.

"The bears were here, and the lions over here." He pointed to two generous enclosures where gaping emptiness reigned. "And where are the giraffes?"

"Gone," said a passing man whose uniform and the fact that he was carrying a broom left little doubt that he was a zookeeper.

"Gone?" Winter followed him angrily. "What does that mean?"

"Just gone. Sold, given away, fed to other animals, or starved. We ate a few of them ourselves. I mean, didn't you know?"

Winter looked like a child who'd just been told Santa Claus didn't really exist. "You can't be serious, right?"

"Do I look like I'm joking to you?" The keeper ran his hand over his beard. "The critters didn't have anything to eat, what else could you do? We tried everything. Come on, don't look so sad. There're still a few animals left."

"What happened to Lori, Greti, Mizzi, and Pepi, the elephants?"

"I'm sorry. They died. They were all so fussy—except for Mizzi, she's holding on bravely. Luckily the kangaroos aren't so delicate, and there's still a rhesus monkey and a macaque in the ape building. The reptiles are still here."

Winter shook his head in disbelief. "I heard that a soldier tried to shoot a polar bear last year, but I didn't know things had gotten so bad. What's the story with the birds?"

"We sold the exotic birds and let the native ones go. It was beautiful, I'll tell you," the man tried to cheer up Winter. He pointed his broom into the sky. "The birds were overjoyed to finally be free and able to fly."

"The people whose stewpots they landed in must have been pleased, too." Emmerich tipped his cap to the zookeeper.

"I didn't say that," said the keeper as Winter blanched.

"We're with the police and need some information about a former staff member," Emmerich changed the topic to the actual reason for their visit. "Dietrich Jost. He worked here before the war."

"*Ja*, I know who you mean. He was responsible for the

lions, the useless bastard. When that trembler realized his kit-
tens were hungry, he went knocking on Herr Director Kraus's
door to ask if he could feed them my kangaroos. Sacrificing the
weak for the well-being of the strong. What an asshole. Thank
god the director told him to piss off. Those lazy beasts would
never have caught my hoppers anyway. But they ate the horses
and the antelopes. I'd rather have let them go." He put out his
hand, which had droplets of water on it, and looked up at the
sky. "It's about to pour."

Emmerich didn't care. "Could you perhaps answer a few
questions about Jost for me?"

"I barely knew him. I've only been here since last year. But
you should talk to Josef Krenn. He and Jost worked together
before the war."

"And where would we find Herr Krenn?"

"With the big cats." He gestured to an enclosure that
Winter had already noticed was ominously empty. "Go on in.
Don't worry. The kitties won't hurt anyone anymore. Who's so
big and scary now, eh?" He took a bow, ducked his head, and
hurried off. "Good day, gentlemen."

"Please don't . . . " mumbled Winter as they approached
the entrance to the predators' enclosure.

They climbed over a barricade, opened a door, and found
themselves in a completely deserted enclosure. Both the area
for visitors and the area for animals were deserted.

"Herr Krenn?" Emmerich peered through the cage bars.
"Are you here somewhere?"

There was no answer and he searched for another door,
which he quickly found. Surprisingly, it was unlocked, and
Emmerich and Winter found themselves in the open again,
between giant boulders and an extensive pond. The sky had
gotten darker, and thick raindrops splattered down.

"Please don't, please don't . . . " Winter mumbled again.

"Please don't what?"

"Please don't let the big cats be dead."

"I was thinking the opposite."

Emmerich had realized where they were—in the lion's den, in the most literal sense. They were standing in the middle of the outdoor enclosure of the predators, where normally tigers, leopards, and other dangerous beasts played. "If they haven't starved to death they'll gorge themselves on us," he whispered and crept back toward the door.

"Say, have you completely lost your minds? What are you doing here?"

Emmerich and Winter froze in fear.

"Police. Are you Josef Krenn?" Emmerich was the first to regain his wits.

"Yes, what do you want?" asked the man, blowing his nose on a dirty handkerchief.

"We need information about Dietrich Jost. Your colleague from the kangaroos said you knew him." Emmerich saw that the man's eyes were red.

"What happened to Dietrich?"

Emmerich didn't answer and instead looked around. "We were told we didn't need to be afraid of any predators. Is that true?"

Krenn nodded, and his eyes filled with tears. "Let's go inside. It's uncomfortable out here," he said as a cold wind picked up. Emmerich and Winter followed him through a green metal door into a tiled room. "We used to prepare the food for the animals in here," Krenn explained. "But now . . . ," his voice trailed off and he pointed to a lion sprawled lifelessly on the ground not looking even slightly regal anymore.

"Oh no." Winter kneeled next to the cadaver and reached cautiously into the animal's mane. "Is this Kato? I loved him as a kid." He looked at Krenn. "What happened?"

"They didn't get any decent food for months, only rotten horsemeat if anything at all. At first they howled from hunger, but at some point they got too weak for that." He squatted down next to Winter and petted the shrunken lion, under whose dull fur every rib was visible. He rubbed the dead animal's snout tenderly and caressed his paws. "Kato held out the longest."

"Brave soul." Winter, too, was fighting back tears.

Emmerich cleared his throat. He struggled to hold back a caustic remark. When Death had started swinging his scythe in 1914, dying became a part of daily life.

"I'd like to ask my questions now," he said.

"Of course." Krenn stood up and wiped his hands on his pants. "You have to understand. I took care of the lions for years. They were like children to me. Do you have children?"

Emmerich offered Krenn a cigar. He didn't want to answer his question.

"Oh, a good one. That's something." The keeper took one, let Emmerich light it, and puffed thick white rings of smoke into the air. The quality tobacco lifted his spirits, and suddenly he didn't seem so downtrodden.

"Did Jost have any special knowledge of animals that he could have put to use in competitions?" Emmerich got straight to the point. "Would he have been able to manipulate horse races or dogfights, for instance?"

"Where would you come up with something like that?"

"Please just answer the question."

"Dietrich was an animal caretaker for big cats, just like me. He didn't know anything about horses or dogs. And anyway, you can't manipulate animals to win or lose. Unless maybe you gave them some sort of drug."

"Would he have had access to that sort of thing?"

"Definitely not. I don't even have access, and I'm higher in rank. Our veterinarian is very scrupulous."

"Perhaps the vet wanted to help Jost?"

"Herr Hofrat is very proper. He would never do anything

that might harm an animal. Not to mention that I don't think he was terribly fond of Dietrich. Not after the letters."

"What letters?"

"When Dietrich was on the front, he regularly asked about his animals, and I reported everything to him. The food shortages, the hunger, and the illnesses. That the animals weren't doing well. At first he was just sad and worried, then he started to send aggressive letters in which he demanded that other animals be sacrificed for the good of the lions. I was surprised. I'd always known him to be a nice, calm man, but war brings out the worst in people."

That's true, thought Emmerich, but not always. Sometimes the opposite happens. He'd seen it happen to himself. But he didn't utter his thoughts and motioned for Krenn to continue.

"The antelopes, the tapirs, zebras, and kangaroos . . . he would have delivered them all to the slaughter to save his beloved lions. He turned a lot of his fellow zookeepers against him."

"Were some animals actually fed to the lions?"

"Only those that had died already. Herr Director was very strict. He said no living creature is more valuable than any other."

"And Jost? How did he react to that?"

"He was irate. Continued to send letters, and after his discharge he came by a few times. At first he wanted his job back, then he tried to tell the Herr Director how he should run the zoo."

"Did he get violent? Were there any incidents?"

Krenn said no. "Dietrich was done for. Physically and mentally. Everyone felt bad for him. That's why we collected a bit of money for him—not a lot, of course, we barely have enough to live ourselves, after all—and sent him away."

"And he didn't return after that."

"It wasn't good for him to be here. Too many memories.

Too many losses. We've lost two-thirds of our animals, and we lose more every day." He looked at poor Kato, lying stiff on the ground. "The king of the animals had to abdicate just like the Kaiser. These are hard times for monarchs."

Hard times for murder investigations, too, thought Emmerich. The theory about bet rigging had fallen flat. Jost must have found another means to make money. But what was it?

"Perhaps we should wait until the rain lets up," suggested Winter after they'd thanked the zookeeper for the information and made their way outside, where it was raining buckets.

"Why? You want to pet some more dead animals?"

Winter stood under a small awning. "I just don't want to catch a cold, that's all. And if you're honest, you have to admit that the story of the zoo animals is sad."

"They're animals. You know what's sad? There are three dead men and we don't have any leads."

"Maybe we've been focusing too much on Jost." Winter watched the raindrops smack the asphalt and burst. "What if someone else was pulling the strings and he was just a stooge?"

"Keep talking."

"When we asked Farkas how someone could make a quick buck in this town, he also mentioned extortion." Winter turned aside as a gust of wind blew rain into his face. "Zeiner did and saw things in the booths of the Chatham Bar that had better not be made public. Who knows what went on in there . . . "

"In all honesty, I'd rather not know, but we've got no other choice than to find out." Emmerich clapped his assistant on the shoulder. "Good job." Another ice-cold gust of wind made him cringe, and he felt the throbbing in his leg getting stronger. He put his hand in his pocket and remembered that he had just two tablets left and desperately needed to get to his supply. Emmerich looked at his assistant. "If we're going to tack on a night shift at the Chatham Bar, we should take a rest and dry out our things. Can we do that at your place?"

"Of course. My grandmother's been unusually calm since yesterday. Maybe she's finally mellowing with age. There's a good chance she'll leave you alone."

Emmerich crushed the heroin in the palm of his hand and snorted the white powder when Winter looked away. And the effect was indeed faster and more intense, and a wave of calm confidence washed over him.

When the sky finally started to clear up and there was just a trace of rain still in the air, the two policemen headed for Währing.

"That's the way it is in wartime," said Emmerich as Winter cast a last wistful glance back at the zoo. "War stops at nothing."

"Not even for childhood memories."

"At least you have nice ones."

Not for the first time today Emmerich thought about his past and about the present in which Luise's children would have to grow up, and he thanked the pharmaceutical industry for the sense of elation he felt despite it all.

25

Something was different about today, or perhaps more to the point, Winter's grandmother was different. She was notably friendlier than on Emmerich's previous visit, didn't make any derogatory remarks about his rumpled clothes, didn't curse the proletariat, and when Winter told her that Emmerich would be occupying her dressing room for a few hours, she greeted the news with a shrug.

"Just keep your fingers off my sausage. I'm saving that for dinner," was all she said before she disappeared again.

There's something fishy here, thought Emmerich instinctively, because he—unlike Winter—found her behavior more odd than pleasant. "Has the Kaiser returned or something?" he asked.

Winter shook his head. "Not that I'm aware of."

"Maybe we should have a look at the paper later and catch up on the latest political developments." Emmerich nodded to his assistant and closed the door—a moment to rest and recover was just what he needed. That . . . and heroin.

He opened the bottom drawer of the little dresser—and found it empty. Emmerich could have sworn that he'd left the bottles there. Shaking his head he opened the next drawer up, which also proved to be empty.

He looked through drawer after drawer, rummaged through hairpins, handheld mirrors, and powder puffs, but his tablets were nowhere to be found. Where the hell had the pills gone? He knew that memory could play tricks on you, and that the last few days had been confusing, to say the least. So it was certainly possible that he'd mixed something up or misplaced . . . something occurred to him and he went out to the hall.

"I left something here the last time I visited. You wouldn't happen to have found it and put it somewhere, would you?" he asked Winter's grandmother after he tracked her down in the living room drinking tea and embroidering.

"What did you leave? And no, I didn't move anything."

"Are you sure? Please think for a moment. It was a couple of small glass bottles," he tried to jog her memory. "I'd put them in your little dresser."

She looked off into the distance and pursed her lips. "I'm sorry, but I'm afraid I can't help you."

Emmerich looked her directly in the eyes. Her expression didn't change as she held his gaze with her eyebrows raised. There was no proof that she wasn't telling the truth, but Emmerich knew better. Lying was an art form that he'd become proficient in even as a child. Feigning and bluffing—two essential survival skills in an orphanage. He was a master of deception, and he recognized someone of his own kind.

"My dear Frau Winter, I'm genuinely grateful for your hospitality," he began, "but I need those bottles and would be much obliged if you would return them to me."

She calmly continued to work at her embroidery, which depicted a coat of arms. Emmerich wondered whether she was pretending to be hard of hearing or forgetful, or if perhaps she was just unbelievably cold.

"The bottles contain drugs. My leg was wounded on the front. At the battle of Vittorio Veneto. Where I was fighting for God, for Kaiser, and for *Vaterland*," he attempted to appeal to her patriotism.

She smiled and offered him a tea. "Very heroic of you."

Emmerich slowly realized what was going on. She hadn't accidentally misplaced the heroin—she had taken it. And worse still: she had consumed it. He smacked his forehead with the palm of his hand. He should have realized it immediately. Her inexplicable cheerfulness and calm manner weren't the result of her suddenly mellowing with age, they were chemically induced.

"Would you please hand over my pills?" he said not as calmly as before.

"What pills? All I have are drops for my heart. Ask Ferdinand."

She was a good liar; there was no denying it.

"Do you remember when I stayed the night here? You were worried that I might steal something. Ironic, then, that exactly the opposite has happened."

"If only I knew what you were talking about." She sipped tea from her cup, which was fine porcelain. "Sure you don't want any?"

Her audacity left him both awed and outraged. The nerve.

"What else should I expect from an aristocrat? You all take exquisite pleasure in bleeding the common man. And not even the fact that we live in a republic now can stop you."

"Kaiser Charles was exiled and never formally abdicated. He'll be back one day." She smiled sanctimoniously as she continued to stitch her coat of arms.

"We'll make sure that doesn't happen." Emmerich played through all the scenarios in his head but in the end had to admit that his hands were tied. She was an old lady—and even more importantly, she was Winter's grandmother. Violence was out of the question, threats would fall on deaf ears, and turning the house upside down would be pointless as there were just too many possible hiding places.

He went back into the dressing room and hung his damp things up to dry. Then he lay down on the ottoman, hid his last tablet under the pillow, and closed his eyes. His last thought before dozing off was, What has become of the world when a genteel old lady has no compunction about stealing from her fellow man?

When Winter knocked at the door two hours later, it was already dark out. "Shall we be on our way?" he asked through the door.

Emmerich rubbed his eyes. "Be ready in a second," he called, jumping up. His leg still didn't hurt. But how long would that last? The pain would return soon, and all he had was one last pill. That would get him through the night, but he'd have to come up with something after that.

"I've hung fresh clothes on the door for you. Yours were in pretty bad shape, and we don't want to have any trouble with the doorman."

Emmerich thanked him and got dressed. He carefully wrapped the last pill in a handkerchief as if it were a treasure, and stuck it into his pants pocket. Finally he pulled on his cap and clamped the cigar case under his arm. "I'm ready."

"I couldn't sleep, so I read the papers. No mention of the return of the Kaiser." Winter handed Emmerich the newspapers.

"Thanks," he said, taking them, even though he had no intention of reading them—he knew what the story was now.

"Maybe my grandmother really is mellowing with age." Winter smiled so blissfully that Emmerich decided to let him believe it for now. He'd be in for a surprise the day the tablets ran out.

A group of children busied themselves playing hopscotch by the entrance to a building near Schottentor. They'd drawn chalk squares on the damp asphalt and were jumping from one to the next while laughing and singing.

"One, two, buckle my shoe . . . " Almost all of them had on jackets from the American aid agencies.

"Hey, shouldn't you be in bed?" Emmerich asked the little gang, who all hooted when a little girl fell over attempting a difficult hop.

"You're not our father," shot back an unkempt tot who barely came up to Emmerich's hip. "You can't tell us what to do."

"But I can arrest you." He reached mechanically for his badge but realized again he didn't have it.

The children looked at him warily for a moment and then started to laugh when he couldn't make good on his threat.

"You want to play?" asked a girl with long blonde braids. "We're playing Paradise. If you hop the right way you get to heaven."

"But if you fall over or land on the wrong square you go to hell," added the scruffy boy.

Emmerich looked at his leg and then back at the children, who were hopping from box to box with great agility. He'd never make it to heaven. He was destined for hell.

"Let's go," he said to Winter, motioning toward the Schottenstift monastery. "And you lot go home. It's too cold and too late for you to be playing out here."

Once a father, always a father . . . This realization hit him painfully, and he had to revise his previous conclusion: It wasn't that he was destined for hell, he was already in it.

At least they were successful at the Chatham Bar: thanks to Winter's forethought they got past the bouncer with no trouble at all, and inside, too, they got lucky—a little table with a good view of the pass-through to the hidden booths had just freed up.

"Two beers, please," Emmerich ordered.

Winter reached into his pocket to reassure himself. "Shit," he said, shocked. "My money."

"What about it?"

"My grandmother must have taken it. She sometimes has difficulty distinguishing between my things and hers."

"Really?" said Emmerich, hoping his tone wasn't overly sarcastic. "I would never have suspected that of her."

The waiter served their drinks and Emmerich ordered two pairs of sausages with mustard and horseradish. "If we're going to have to run out on the bill we might as well make it worthwhile," he said calmly.

Winter mumbled something incomprehensible that was meant to express displeasure and then stared at the passthrough to the booths. "We're sure there's no rear entrance?"

Emmerich nodded. "This place doesn't exactly conform to the fire safety codes, which in this case works in our favor. Anybody who goes in or out has to go past us."

"And the people? Does it not bother the . . . " he searched for the right word, " . . . the . . . well, you know . . . the johns . . . doesn't it bother them that they can be seen?"

"Have a look around." Emmerich made a sweeping motion with his arm. "The guests are so busy dancing, drinking; and shutting out reality that nobody cares about the booths."

And it was true that the star pianist, Robert Rakowianu, playing the hits on the grand piano, was far more interesting than the men slinking toward the pass-through.

> *Auf den Straßen heutzutage das Getös,*
> *macht nervös.*
> *Darum ruft empört der Antilärmverein:*
> *'S darf nicht sein! Dies Geratter, dies Geknatter, dies Geknall*
> *überall.*
> *Namentlich die Aut'mobile*
> *machen einen Mordskrawall.*
> *Wie das tönt—tut, tut,*
> *wie das dröhnt . . .*

On the streets today the cacophony,
makes us all so jittery.

To which says the anti-noise brigade:
'Tis an outrage! The rattling, clattering, banging,
from all else distracted.
The automobile makes a murderous racket.
How it sounds, toot, toot,
how it resounds . . .

"*TOOT, TOOT*," the guests sang along. They raised their
mugs and bellowed so enthusiastically that the piano was
barely audible.

Nicht so laut, nicht so laut,
nicht so laut musst du sein.
Dein Benzin macht dich bemerkbar,
also brauchst du nicht zu schrei'n!
Nicht so laut, nicht so laut,
ein Trost bleibt dir immer noch:
Wenn die Leut' dich auch nicht hören,
riechen tun sie dich ja doch.

Not so loud, not so loud,
you need not be, not so loud.
No need for all the uproar
when your gas makes such a cloud.
Not so loud, not so loud,
there's still a consolation:
even if the people hear you not,
they'll smell your exhalation.

Winter swayed back and forth to the rhythm while
Emmerich grabbed the arriving plates of sausages.
"I've had worse surveillance jobs," he said, putting one of
the plates down in front of Winter.
"You can eat mine, too." He looked at the door. "The fact

that they're stolen takes away my appetite." He pushed his beer away as well.

"We haven't stolen anything yet. Maybe we'll think of something." Emmerich ate both plates of food and washed them down with a large gulp of beer. "Now a fine cigar and the night can begin." He lit one just as a loud clattering rang out.

A tipsy woman had swung her leg a little too wildly while dancing and had knocked into a table, causing the beers on it to fall to the floor. Emmerich's gaze involuntarily shifted toward the source of the noise, and as it did he noticed a man with a scar across his right cheek. Was that the same guy he'd noticed earlier in front of the employment agency?

When the man realized Emmerich was looking at him he quickly turned away.

"Hey, you!" Emmerich jumped up, but the man was faster.

He disappeared among the dancing and singing guests. Emmerich couldn't do anything but watch as he fled out the door of the bar.

"One of Kolja's men?" asked Winter when his boss returned to the table.

"Who else would be tailing us?"

Winter grabbed the beer he had just pushed away and gulped down half of it. "It doesn't feel right," he said. "We're the ones who are supposed to follow people and spy on them. Not the other way around. It's like we've gone from hunters to the hunted. And, by the way . . . " He stopped speaking.

"And by the way what?"

" . . . I can't stop thinking about the scary old lady in the hedges at the palace. I lied. I actually had a few *hellers* but I didn't want to give them to her. What if something really does happen now?"

"Beware the pale horse," Emmerich imitated the woman and grinned when he was able to coax a tentative smile out of his assistant.

"You recognize him?" He turned Winter's attention to an older gentleman who was slinking toward the pass-through with his head down.

"He's no bigwig."

"How do you know?"

"When I worked in the telegraph correspondence office I came to recognize almost all the important politicians and businessmen. And, also, my grandmother reads the tabloids." He gestured to a blonde woman brimming with energy who was making her way around the room. "That's Lona Schmidt, the actress. She plays the lead in the movie *Der Narr seines Herzens*. It's in cinemas at the moment. And the fat man next to the piano who keeps looking down her dress is Viktor Melius, the director of Unter Bank."

He went on to identify a theater actor and a member of the city council, and Emmerich was amazed all over again about how different life could be. While some people froze and starved, others could drink the finest liquors and entertain themselves in whatever way they wished. Reality was a many-faceted thing.

"None of them are going to the back," whispered Winter.

"Not everyone is here because of the booths, and besides, the night is young. The rush to the dens of iniquity will start soon enough." Emmerich puffed aromatic smoke into the air while Rakowianu started into another hit song, earning frenetic applause.

Wiener Blut, Wiener Blut!
Eig'ner Saft, voller Kraft, voller Glut.
Wiener Blut, selt'nes Gut,
du erhebst, du belebst unsern Mut!

Vienna blood, Vienna blood!
Our own sap, full of power, full of fire.

Vienna blood, unusually good,
you lift us up, our courage you inspire!

"Anything else?" yelled the waiter above the deafening din, and Emmerich ordered another round of beer.

"And two shots of schnapps," he called after the man.

"From hunters to the hunted. From law enforcers to law-breakers . . ." Winter was not pleased about the increasing size of their bill.

"Right and just are not always the same thing."

Emmerich narrowed his eyes and tried to wave away the cloud of smoke in front of him as a woman in a red dress who looked vaguely familiar to him entered the place. She sat down at the bar.

"He's a former judge. Maximilian . . . something with N."

"What?" Emmerich didn't understand what his assistant was talking about.

"The man you were just staring at. He's a former judge and chairman of the war crimes commission that my grandmother was so upset about yesterday. His name is Maximilian . . . Neubert, I think."

Emmerich figured out that Winter was talking about a man he hadn't even registered, who was accompanying the woman. Neubert was big, broad-shouldered, and had a full head of dark hair streaked with gray. Even though he was no longer young, he was handsome.

A champagne cork popped, glasses were filled, and the woman in the red dress turned so that Emmerich was able to see her in profile. Minna.

The cut of her dress made her look fuller, and the low light flattered her complexion. She looked like a beautiful young woman rather than a deathly ill prostitute.

"See and be seen . . ." Emmerich stood up and pushed his way toward the bar.

When Minna saw him, her expression was a mix of surprise, happiness, and unease. "August . . . "

"What are you doing here?"

She looked around frantically. "What do you think?" she whispered in his ear.

"You work here?"

"Twice a week. Please don't mess it up for me. It's warm, the johns are nicer than on the street, and they pay better."

He thought for a second. "I need to talk to you."

"Can't it wait? I'm busy."

"*Don't let us sing anymore about war, just let us sing of love!*" sang a drunk in Emmerich's ear, putting his arm around him.

"Don't you know they're one and the same?" Emmerich shoved the man away and then pointed to the door. "You can't even hear yourself in here. It's important, and it won't take long." He waved Winter over.

Minna whispered a few sentences into the ear of her companion and followed the two detectives out into the cold.

"Winter, Minna. Minna, Winter," Emmerich introduced the two to each other and led them to the next corner.

"Quickly. Please." Minna wrapped her arms around her thin body.

"Does the name Harald Zeiner mean anything to you?" asked Emmerich. He looked on dumbfounded as Winter took off his jacket and placed it on the young woman's shoulders.

"Yes, as a matter of fact. What happened to him? Is he doing okay?"

"He's not doing badly." Emmerich didn't feel like giving a long explanation. "Listen, you have to tell me everything you know about him. It's important. Was he acting somehow strange of late? Abnormal? Did he possibly have big plans?" He spoke so fast that his words practically tumbled over each other.

He'd been negligent, had failed to recognize Minna as a potential informant, and had lost time as a result. Valuable time. Every minute counted in a murder investigation.

"Abnormal? What is normal anyway . . . " It wasn't clear whether this was a question or a statement. "The past few years didn't just kill fifty million people, they killed normality. And to answer your question: Harri was the same as always." She coughed and put her hand to her chest. "Damn it," she murmured. "It's starting again. You wouldn't happen to have another tablet for me, would you?"

"Unfortunately not. Has he ever mentioned a Dietrich Jost? Or a plan to get money?" he asked quickly in order to move away from the subject of heroin.

She pulled the jacket more tightly around herself. "He was pretty despondent last week. When I asked him what was going on he said he was worried about a friend—a certain Didi. Maybe he meant this Jost guy."

Emmerich felt a twinge in his gut. They were finally making headway. "Go on," he urged excitedly. "Why was he worried?"

"This Didi had gotten involved with the wrong people."

"With him?" Emmerich pulled out the sketch of the unidentified dead man.

She held it toward the light of a streetlamp and shook her head. "No, that's Anatol. He's a hustler, sure, but not somebody you'd need to be afraid of."

Emmerich wanted to slap himself. If only he'd been more deliberate and not gotten distracted by his leg and the whole thing with Luise . . .

"Anatol? Last name?"

"I think it's Czernin. He's a friend of Harri's." She coughed again and looked at the hand she'd held in front of her mouth.

Emmerich didn't need to look. Her expression told him everything. She had coughed up blood. "You know anything else about him? Where he lived maybe?"

"He lived in the Beehive, I don't know anything more. Really. About any of the three of them. And I don't know who they had trouble with." Lost in thought she wiped her hand on Winter's jacket and gave it back to him. "I have to get back inside. My customer is waiting, and I'll catch my death out here in this cold."

Emmerich let her know with a nod that she could go. "Thanks," he said. "Take care of yourself."

After Minna disappeared back inside, he turned to his assistant. "Anatol Czernin. We finally have a name."

Winter looked at his jacket and shook it out with a fearful look. "Is she seriously ill, Minna?"

"She'll survive." Emmerich hoped he was right. "What is it?" he asked when Winter suddenly turned chalk white. Before Winter could answer, someone grabbed him by the shoulder from behind.

"So there you are. I was worried you might try to skip out on your bill." It was the waiter who'd served them. He gave them a wary look.

"Not at all, definitely not. It was just so loud inside and we needed to discuss something," Emmerich played for time. "Don't worry, we're coming right back in."

"I'd like to settle the bill anyway."

Emmerich knew that there was no point in running, and they couldn't beat up yet another person. "Might I be able to pay in kind?"

Winter's eyes opened wide with shock, and the waiter grimaced in disgust. "Do I look like one of those perverts? I work in the front of the house, not in the booths in the back." He spat at Emmerich's feet and waved to the bouncer.

"Halt!" Emmerich held out the box of cigars. "I meant this."

The waiter opened the container, took out a cigar, and sniffed it. Apparently he liked what he had in his hands, because he visibly relaxed. "Works for me," he said finally. "But next time I want to see crowns or else you'll be banned."

Emmerich rolled his eyes and looked wistfully after his little box of treasure. "A terrible shame," he mumbled.

26

E veryone in the city knew the infamous guesthouse on Schimmelgasse that a journalist from the *Worker's Daily* had recently called a family prison. More than a thousand people lived in the building's two hundred tiny one-room apartments that got virtually no sunlight. Electricity was something people there had only heard about, and according to rumor there was only a single water faucet in the whole place. Nobody lived there willingly and those who did moved out at their first opportunity. The constant coming and going earned the building its name: the Beehive.

"It's already late," Winter said when Emmerich suggested they go visit the home of the dead man straightaway. "Most of the residents are probably asleep."

"The timing couldn't be better. Everyone's home at this hour, and we can question as many people as we need to."

Winter sighed quietly to himself realizing that resistance was pointless.

The façade of the dirty, four-story guesthouse had seen better days. Above the main entrance, which didn't exactly look inviting, wind and weather had made illegible a written motto of some sort. Nobody had bothered to refurbish the letters.

"Ready?" Emmerich opened the unlocked door without waiting for an answer.

"It really does look like a prison," Winter declared when he saw the long, dark hallway off which were scores of doors. "We visited one during police training. It was—" He didn't manage to finish his sentence because the infernal stench of the place suddenly took his breath away. "God in heaven." He pulled the sleeve of his jacket over his hand and covered his nose and mouth with it.

"It's the toilets. They're in the hallways, they have no windows, and if it's true what they say, each one serves at least thirty people."

"And a few rats," added Winter as a particularly fat specimen shot across the floor ahead of them. He shivered with revulsion. "No wonder this place is rife with diseases. How can people live like this?"

"You wouldn't believe what you can get used to."

"Not this."

"Let's talk again in an hour."

"An hour? In this disease factory?" Beads of sweat were forming on Winter's forehead.

Emmerich ignored him and knocked on the nearest door. When nothing happened he knocked on the next one. The faster they got out of here the better, he agreed with that much.

"Yes?" A cockeyed boy opened the door. The overwhelming smell of onions escaping the apartment made Winter recoil.

"We're looking for this man." Emmerich held the image of Czernin up to the child. "He lives here, right?"

The boy grinned insolently. "Maybe," he said, putting out his dirty little hand. "What do I get out of it?"

Emmerich, whose only possession was his last heroin tablet, looked to his assistant. "You have anything on you?"

Winter patted his pockets. "Here. It's all I have." From his coat pocket he pulled out something wrapped in shiny tinfoil. "The last piece of chocolate."

"We should have taken more of that from Farkas's office." Emmerich handed the sweet to the boy.

The kid ripped it out of his hand. "Third floor, second-to-last apartment on the right-hand side," he said and then slammed the door shut.

"Certainly is a strange generation coming up," remarked Emmerich as he started up the well-worn steps. "It's really going to be something in ten or twenty years." Since Winter was conspicuously quiet, Emmerich turned around to look at him. As he suspected, his assistant was concentrating fully on not touching anything. Not the greasy handrail to his right or the scratched and smeared wall to his left. "What is it? You didn't act like this in the homeless shelter or the sewers."

"There was air in the sewers and at the shelter on Blattgasse there was a disinfection room they all had to pass through. But today . . . first Minna, who coughed on me and befouled my jacket, and now this."

"It'll be better the higher we go," Emmerich lied, knowing full well that the conditions were equally awful on every floor.

When they arrived at Czernin's door, Winter sniffed. "I don't smell any difference up here."

Emmerich ignored the observation that he knew was coming, and knocked with his fist on the thin wooden door.

"What?"

An emaciated woman with an infant on her arm threw open the door and stared at the strangers with hazy eyes. Her skin was pale and her hair dull. She had on a blue apron dress and brown wool stockings. It was difficult to guess her age—she could have been the mother or the grandmother of the child.

"I'm August Emmerich, and this is Ferdinand Winter. We're police detectives. I hope we haven't woken you."

"Do I look like I can afford a luxury like sleep?"

Emmerich would have liked to tell her she looked good, but spared himself the lie. "Are you the wife of Anatol Czernin?" he said, getting straight to the point instead.

"What did he do?" she snapped. "Where is he?" She

pressed the baby tightly to her sagging breast and narrowed her eyes.

"Could we possibly come in for a moment?"

"Did you . . . did you throw him in jail?" Her voice was trembling. "You can't do that. We need his income. Who's going to feed the children if he's locked up?"

"Please calm down." Emmerich took her by the arm and pushed her gently into the apartment.

As he had feared, inside they encountered the most miserable squalor. The dwelling—this form of lodging didn't deserve the name home—was a dark hole with barely any air to breathe. Passing through the musty kitchen, its walls covered with mold, they entered a room that served as the living room, bedroom, and work space. It was perhaps four strides across, six strides long, and dimly lit by a flickering petroleum lamp. That was it. No other space.

Along each of the two side walls was a battered wooden bed with a tattered mattress. On the far wall, opposite the door, stood a warped dresser next to a small window onto the dark courtyard. The rest of the space was taken up by a shabby table covered with piles of shoes.

Winter cringed when suddenly a heart-rending cough rang out, followed by labored breathing. In one of the beds lay two girls who were so small and emaciated that their bodies barely made a bulge in the thin bedcover.

"One of them is always sick." Czernin's wife sat down at the table. "They take turns. But what can I do?" She put the baby in her lap, picked up a shoe, and began to sew beads onto the top. With deft fingers she attached one colorful bead after the next until a star-shaped ornament had taken shape.

"How many children do you have?" Emmerich sat down next to her.

"This one here makes five." She motioned to the infant, who didn't make a sound.

Emmerich knew kids like these. They'd learned that screaming didn't get you anything so you might as well save your energy.

"Nobody thought we'd manage with all of them," she said strangely, almost apologetically.

"Where are the other two?"

"Working," she said tersely, without elaborating on what sort of work they did.

One of the sick girls shook again with a fit of coughing, and Winter, who was now as pale as Frau Czernin, discreetly opened the window.

"What do the little ones have, anyway?" he asked.

Since Emmerich knew what had happened to Winter's family, he didn't protest his fear of germs.

"How should I know. Doctors are only for rich people. So spit it out already. Where's Anatol?" She placed the embroidered shoe to the side but didn't pick up a new one, instead lifting the baby and holding him in front of her like a shield.

"Unfortunately I have to inform you that your husband was murdered," whispered Emmerich so the children wouldn't hear.

He waited for a reaction, but nothing came. Czernin's wife sat stock-still on the chair, holding the infant as if he were a burning log, never changing her facial expression.

"Dead? He's . . . dead? And how's it supposed to work for us now?" she asked after what seemed an eternity.

"There's an array of charity groups. I can write down a few names for you."

"Pfff," she waved dismissively. "Me, kiss up to some condescending noblewoman as a supplicant? So she can look down on me when she gives me her old clothes? Not a chance. I might not have much, but I still have my pride."

"Your pride won't keep the children fed or healthy."

"That's not your problem."

Emmerich had to admit she was right. "I need to ask you a

few questions about your husband," he said, getting back to the point of their visit. "May I? Do you feel up to giving me a few answers?"

Anatol Czernin's widow looked at Emmerich with dark eyes. "What else can I do?" she replied.

Emmerich nodded. "Do the names Dietrich Jost and Harald Zeiner mean anything to you?"

"Never heard of them."

"Can you tell me where your husband spent the past few nights?"

"Not here. I assumed he was at a bar, pissing away our money on booze."

"Did your husband have any enemies?"

She shrugged, and Emmerich could tell he wouldn't get far this way.

"If we find your husband's murderer, you may be able to sue for compensation," he said, trying to get her attention.

"I've really never heard those names, but my Anatol never told me much. He's been strange since the war. Solitary. Quiet. Drank a lot and gallivanted about. It's certainly possible he knew the two of them. And as far as enemies . . . a few people have claimed he robbed them. No idea whether it's true." She furrowed her brow and thought for a moment, but nothing more seemed to occur to her. "Is that enough?"

"Can I possibly have a look at your husband's things?"

"Fine by me." The woman laid the infant carelessly in a bed and pulled an old cardboard suitcase out from beneath it. "There's not much, but if it will help, be my guest."

Emmerich stood up, and the old familiar pain immediately shot through his leg. He gritted his teeth, hobbled over to the bed, and opened the suitcase. Cautiously, he examined the contents: old shoes, a shaving brush, suspenders, a pair of rusty cuff links, and a knife. Nothing that would help them.

"Anything else of Anatol's in the apartment?"

Czernin's widow thought. "Not that I know of," she said finally, and Emmerich, disappointed, shoved the suitcase back in its place.

For the third time since they'd been in the apartment of the Czernin family, one of the sick girls suffered a coughing fit. Winter stuck his head out the window, and Emmerich nearly sent him out, letting it go in the end. What didn't kill his assistant would make him stronger. Winter could use a bit of hardening up if he was going to make something of himself as a detective.

"What's in the dresser?" asked Emmerich, hoping not to leave empty-handed.

Bedclothes, diapers, and the children's clothes. Knock yourself out."

The widow turned back to her work. With what she made in a month embroidering shoes she probably couldn't afford a pair herself. Of course, she had more pressing needs.

Emmerich was pondering whether it made any sense to rummage through the dresser, or whether he should just leave the poor woman and her woeful children in peace, when there was suddenly a loud crack.

"I'm so sorry!" Winter jerked around. "I'll repair it or pay for the damage. I promise."

It took a minute for Emmerich to realize what had happened—his assistant had leaned against the dilapidated windowsill and it had broken. Now he was trying to figure out a makeshift way to reaffix the rotting piece of wood, but it wouldn't stay in place.

"No! Nothing but trouble with the likes of you." Frau Czernin examined the damage with a worried face. "As if life isn't punishing me enough, you have to demolish my apartment on top of it all." For the first time since Emmerich had delivered the bad news, tears welled in her eyes.

"Woodworms were into it." Winter pointed to the edge of the breakage, which was riddled with little holes.

"You still have to take responsibility," said the woman. "Otherwise I'll get into big trouble with the landlord."

Winter wasn't listening to her. "Just a second," he said, and bent over to painstakingly examine the damage, or at least that's what Emmerich initially thought. But then he looked more closely. Winter had found something—a hollowed-out space that had been hidden beneath the windowsill.

"What do we have here?" asked Emmerich. His pulse quickened as he cautiously reached into the dark hole. "Did you know about this, Frau Czernin?" He pulled out a golden pocket watch with an engraving: *In recognition of 25 years of loyal service to the district association of Josefstadt.* Frau Czernin shook her head. "I don't believe this belongs to you or your husband." Emmerich handed it to Winter and reached into the hole again. Again and again he pulled things out, a silver lighter and a matching cigarette case, two rings, a brooch, a chain and pendant. Looking at the stolen goods made him think of his amulet again, and he felt rage toward the robber boiling up. "Someone is dearly missing each of these things," he said brusquely.

"I swear that I didn't know about it." Frau Czernin looked at the jewelry incredulously. "We're starving and freezing, and those things have been in there all along. Good that Anatol is already dead or I'd kill him myself." She stomped her foot and looked so upset that Emmerich believed her.

He stuck his hand into the hole one more time and felt around. "I think that's it," he said, then paused. "Wait, there's something else." He carefully pulled out an object that was wrapped in a dirty handkerchief and tied up with string.

Emmerich sat down at the table, cut the cords with his pocketknife, and pulled the petroleum lamp closer. With Winter and Frau Czernin looking on expectantly, Emmerich pulled the kerchief aside.

To all of their surprise the bundle didn't contain any valuables, but rather a photo that had been damaged by moisture. It took concentration to make out what was in the picture: ten men in Imperial and Royal army uniforms standing in a forest clearing. All of them had Steyr M95 rifles in their hands and looked at the viewer with serious but not unfriendly faces. On the back was the date July 28, 1915.

"That's Anatol." Frau Czernin pointed to a man in the middle. "He was still young and slender." A touch of melancholy had slipped into her voice.

But another face in the photo stood out to Emmerich, a face that seemed oddly familiar, a man standing to Czernin's right. He was smoking a pipe. "Is that . . . ?" He covered the man's mustache with his finger and looked at Winter, who stooped over the photo.

"Harald Zeiner. And that guy . . . " Winter pointed to the man on the far left. "That could be Dietrich Jost."

Emmerich nodded euphorically. They'd finally figured out the connection they'd been looking for. Sander would finally have to take them seriously. He held the photo close to his face and studied every last detail: the eyes of the men, their body language, and the place they were standing.

"Was this done on purpose, or do you think it's from the way it was stored?" He pointed to a figure on the right side of the photo whose face had been scratched beyond recognition.

"Either is possible," said Winter after examining the damage. "The picture must have been through a lot. Just like the soldiers."

Emmerich agreed. "You recognize anyone else?" he asked, turning to the widow. "Did you husband ever talk about his comrades?"

Frau Czernin held the photo closer to the light and squinted. "I don't recognize any of them, and Anatol never talked about the war. What's done is done, he always said, and he didn't want to think about those awful times."

Emmerich nodded. Men often clammed up about their experiences. "Can you at least tell us where your husband was stationed?"

"On the eastern front. His company was moved several times. I don't know any more than that." She looked over at the two girls, who were coughing again.

Emmerich could tell there wasn't any more information to be gained there. "Let's go," he said, putting the photo in his pocket.

The recovered goods were on the table. "This is for the children. Don't get caught selling it, and don't rip anybody off. Then go get medicine and something decent for them to eat."

Frau Czernin quickly put the things in her apron pocket. "Thanks," she whispered before closing the door behind them.

Outside on the street, Winter took such deep breaths that Emmerich was worried he would hyperventilate.

"A few germs aren't going to hurt a strong young guy like you," he tried to calm him.

"You have no idea how bad they can be."

Emmerich could tell Winter needed a break. "I'll go back to the commissariat and have a look at the evidence given the latest developments—maybe I can figure something more out about the identity of the other men. You can go home. It's been a long enough day."

Winter nodded gratefully. "You should feel free to come over later to sleep. Don't worry about my grandmother, just ring the bell."

"Will do. Thanks."

"By the way . . . " Winter looked at him shyly. "Nice that you let Frau Czernin keep those things."

"Like I said: right and just aren't always the same thing."

Emmerich ground up and snorted his final tablet. He could feel the heroin's effects after just a few steps, and his entire being was enveloped in a soft, warm cloud that absorbed all physical and psychological pain. All his cares and fears dissipated. *If you really look at it, though, my situation's not so tragic. I could be much worse off,* he thought.

He felt so good, in fact, that he thought for a moment of walking over to where the children had been playing hopscotch to try his luck at the chalk squares. But they'd probably long since gone to bed. Minna was right. The heroin got into your system faster and was more intense when you snorted it. It was almost intoxicating. Too good to be true.

For the first time, Emmerich worried. Should he have informed himself about what he was taking? Were there perhaps side effects or limits on how much you could take?

"Ach, who cares," he mumbled, motioning with his hand to swat away the troublesome thoughts.

Heroin was being promoted everywhere as a wonder drug. It was even in cough syrup for kids. He should be thankful not skeptical, and enjoy the benevolent view of the world the drug gave him.

And as if to confirm this thought, an advertising pillar appeared before him. Until recently spaces like these had been dominated by conscription orders, war dispatches, and casualty lists, but now the pillars displayed positive things—notices about charity benefit events and theater performances, ads hawking new products. Maybe Winter's unshakeable optimism wasn't so totally unwarranted.

Emmerich had reached the commissariat and opened the door.

"Emmerich! Where've you been hiding? We missed you yesterday evening." Hörl's face betrayed the aftereffects of the carousing.

"I guess it was for the best; otherwise I'd look the way you do."

"Which would be a marked improvement."

"Ha," snapped Emmerich. "Somebody thinks he's a comedian."

The overnight man struggled to keep his eyes open.

"What are you doing here anyway? You're not on duty tonight. Or are you?"

"I'm always on duty."

Officially, Emmerich's day had ended hours ago, but he didn't know where to go. He had no apartment to go home to, no money for a pub or hotel, and he had no desire to be around Winter's thieving grandmother. The commissariat was the only place left.

Emmerich went into the back room where the file cabinet was with mug shots of missing persons and criminals. He compared one photo after another to the men in Czernin's photo, trying to imagine away the mustaches and add the changes that came with age. But try as hard as he might, he found no match.

"Let me know if you need help," Hörl offered when Emmerich returned to the main room. "I don't really have anything else to do tonight."

"Thanks a lot. But you should have told me," Emmerich looked at the big grandfather clock ticking away in an adjoining room, " . . . a few hours ago."

He rubbed his burning eyes and yawned. What should he do now? The best thing would be to write the outstanding report for Sander. It was unavoidable anyway. He expanded Winter's Querner report with a few extra details and then made up a fantastical plan to catch Veit Kolja and added that. At the end of the report he swallowed his pride and asked for an advance against his next paycheck. He thought for a moment about whether he should tack on the latest developments in the murder cases but decided against it. In the end, Sander would end up getting all the credit for that, too.

After he'd finished the report he went back to looking at the photo of the men.

Who were these men, and what was their story? Would more of them die, or would he be able to stop that from happening?

"Damn, old man, you look tired," said Hörl, whose shift was ending, which seemed to give him new energy. "Don't you want to go home?"

"Soon. I just need to relax for a minute."

Emmerich put his head down on the table and closed his eyes. He didn't notice how uncomfortable it was, or how hard the table was, because Hörl had barely left the room before he was asleep.

What a beautiful morning. How wonderful life could be! Josephine Bauer strolled with a smile on her face across Schlachthaus Bridge toward Prater, letting the autumn sun warm her rosy cheeks.

It was her day off, and she was enjoying every minute of it. She'd gotten up early, bought a candy apple from a street vendor, and bought a ticket from the lotto dealer. She was too worried that her number would be drawn the one day she didn't play. 7-11-73-42-66. Her birth date, her street address, and her apartment number. One day the orphans who drew five numbers every Tuesday and Friday from a drum holding ninety balls would pull hers. Maybe even soon. Josephine just knew it, which is why she'd bought a full share rather than her usual quarter share.

As she walked past the Hoffourage depot, a six-story building that had been converted after the war from a granary into a carriage works, she let her imagination run wild, picturing what she would do with the winnings. She would definitely open her own pub. A nice small one. Comfy and familiar. Just a few tables, a changing weekly menu, and lots of regulars. If there was any money left over she'd get some new clothes and perhaps a season ticket to the theater.

It felt great to be an independent woman. It had been just fine with Josephine that typhoid had taken her ill-tempered tyrant, Adolf, during the fourth year of the war—it had made her the happiest widow around. The whole world yammered on about the consequences of the war, but she was enjoying all the opportunities and advantages it had opened up for her. It had become socially acceptable for women to work, women's rights organizations had formed, and it was no longer a scandal to be single and independent.

And that's exactly what she was—she was in a better situation, able to provide for herself better than all the men she knew. Her wages allowed her to take care of her living expenses without any trouble, and she also had her garden plot, to which she was walking now—it was the one sensible thing that idiot Adolf had ever acquired. The little plot yielded enough fruit and vegetables to fill her up daily, and she was able to sell produce to relatives and acquaintances to bring in a little extra money. At this time of year, she had parsnips, rutabagas, and celery root, and she was looking forward to making a hearty stew.

Josephine crossed Schlachthausbrückenallee and turned right into the extensive grounds of the Wasserwiese park. The former parade ground had been converted into garden plots in 1916 by Kaiser Franz Josef in order to help relieve shortages, though it came to look more like a military exclusion zone than a green paradise. Out of fear of looters, the owners of the plots ringed them with barbed wire fences and metal gates, transforming their properties into impregnable fortresses.

Josephine's parcel was near the middle of the grounds and thus well protected, but you could never be sure . . . Which is why she exhaled with relief each time she arrived and found her little empire untouched. Like today.

She unlocked the three locks that secured the head-high fence around her plot, put the basket she'd brought down on the little path that separated the garden beds, and pulled out a trowel, a tin can, and a loud-ticking alarm clock. Hungry thieves weren't the only ones after her vegetables. Voles wanted to feast on them, too. The noise of the clock was supposed to keep away the miserable rodents. Forever. Because she didn't want to lose a thing.

"Time to say goodbye," she mumbled, kneeling down and jabbing the trowel into the dirt.

"So it is."

Josephine grabbed her chest, startled, when she looked up to see a pair of black boots worn by a man she didn't recognize. She had relocked the gate behind her, she was sure of it, and he couldn't have climbed over the barbed wire fence.

"H . . . h . . . how did you . . . ?" She couldn't get anything else out as her voice broke with panic.

"There are ways." The man showed no emotion. In fact he spoke in the sort of calm tone he might use to strike up a friendly conversation. As she got over her initial shock and stood up to face the intruder, the man kicked her leg so forcefully that she fell back to the ground. "Stay down." His tone was still friendly, but she could tell by the look in his eyes that she was dealing with a dangerous man.

"Help!" she screamed. "Somebody help me!"

"I'd stop that if I were you." He reached behind his back and pulled a pistol from the waistband of his pants, which he aimed at her head. "First of all, there's nobody around. And second, you've sealed off your garden so well that nobody could get in to help you anyway."

"Here," she said, pushing the basket toward him. "Take whatever you want. I also have a little money saved up. I'll give it to you."

"This isn't about money," snapped the stranger. "It's about our country's honor."

Josephine Bauer lifted her head and stared at the man with her mouth open. Was she dealing with some poor lunatic who'd lost his mind, not his life, in the war? There were certainly enough people like that running around the city these days. But he didn't look like one of them. His gaze was untroubled, and he seemed clear of mind.

"Our country's honor? But . . . but . . . what do I have to do with that?"

"For God, for Kaiser, and for Vaterland," he said and pulled the trigger.

28

Must be trouble on the home front." Hörl's voice entered Emmerich's consciousness as if through a thick fog.

"I think they had a fire," Winter said.

August Emmerich slowly opened his eyes and stared at the wood grain of the table surface. "What time is it?" he asked, rubbing his face.

"Eight," Winter said. "Our shift just started."

Emmerich sat up and suppressed a groan. His neck was so stiff he could barely move it, and his lower back was tense with pain.

"If you can somehow manage to find me a proper cup of coffee somewhere, then let me urge you to go do so immediately," he said to Winter.

"Coffee . . . Where would I possibly get a cup of real coffee?" Winter's mind raced.

"Forget it." Emmerich stood up and ran his hand over the stubble on his chin. "I'll see if I can scare one up myself."

Without another word, he pulled on his jacket, put on his cap, and went outside, where the autumn sun smiled down at him mockingly. He didn't actually care about the coffee. What he really needed was pain medicine. He wouldn't get through the next few days without it.

The nearest pharmacy was one that had already refused to help him a few days before—he could forget that place. He had no choice but to go further afield in search of another one.

Emmerich walked as slowly as a doddering old man. He felt like strangling Winter's grandmother. The nerve of that old aristocrat.

"Wait, please, wait a moment." A woman wearing a red scarf on her head, fingerless gloves, and several layers of skirts on top of each other reached for Emmerich's hand and looked without asking at his palm. "Oh, no, no, no. Not good. Not good at all." Emmerich pulled away angrily and limped off, but the old lady wouldn't be so easily deterred. She walked along with him, her skirts rustling. "Can I look into your future, gracious sir?" she pleaded in the typical Bohemian accent that could be heard on every street corner at the moment. "For a few crowns I can give you all the information you'll need to avoid the great tragedies that are written on your palm."

"Get out of here." Emmerich was in no mood to chat. "You're too late. The great tragedy has already happened."

"More coming. More tragedy's coming."

Emmerich rolled his eyes and sped up despite the pain. He'd had enough of crazy old ladies.

The woman was right about one thing, though: more tragedy did come. When he finally reached the pharmacy a note in the window said it was closed indefinitely. The note didn't say why, but Emmerich could guess—shortages of supplies. You couldn't sell something you didn't have.

What should he do now? He had no energy and no time to wander the surrounding streets in the hope of finding an open pharmacy. After quickly weighing his options he decided to try Wiesegger again. Their last interaction hadn't been so unpleasant at all, so perhaps the medical examiner would help this time.

He walked to the next tram stop, got rid of the fortune-teller before she could ask him for money a second time, and rode to Spitalgasse.

Along the way he looked at the people on the street. You never know, maybe I'll see the man with the scar again, he thought. "Who is he, and what does he want from me?" he said aloud, earning an annoyed glance from a elegantly dressed young woman. There was a fine line between normality and life as a crazy old man.

When he finally made it to the medical examiner's complex, he realized it was calmer than usual. No hectic activity, no agitated students, no corpses being shifted here and there. Was Death taking a breather?

Since he found the door to the institute locked and nobody responded to his calls, he shielded his eyes and peered through the window.

"There's nobody in there but the dead," said a young man who rushed past him while studying a folder. "Professor Hirschkron is at a conference and Professor Meixner is still out sick," he explained without looking up.

"What about Wiesegger?"

"You just missed him. He had to go to a crime scene. A woman was shot."

Emmerich cursed silently to himself. This day was starting out great. "Wait! I have a few questions!" he called after the young man, but he was gone.

"More tragedy's coming," he muttered, and since there was nothing else to do he headed back to the commissariat.

"Must have gone an awful long way for that coffee," said Hörl when Emmerich entered.

"And unfortunately without success. But perhaps we can find one along the way, Winter."

"Along the way to where?" his assistant wanted to know.

"The war archive. We have to find out who these other men are, and the easiest way to do that is to figure out what company they were serving in."

Winter quickly threw on his jacket. "Why didn't you come to our place?" he asked. "You really didn't have to sleep here."

"A different bed every night, that seems to be my curse. I'm already curious to see where I end up tonight." Emmerich groaned. The pain in his leg had grown stronger.

"Everything okay with you?" Winter looked at his boss with a worried look.

"Fine." Emmerich grimaced and shooed him aside. "My back's just stiff from sleeping awkwardly." Hopefully his assistant would know not to ask any more questions.

They left the commissariat silently, walked through the streets, passing long lines, wounded veterans begging, and elegant women strolling through the city in their finery. They passed beautifully decorated shopwindows, playing children, and shouting newspaper boys. But Emmerich barely cast a glance at anyone or anything. He just trudged along, one step after the next, gritting his teeth, trying to block out any thoughts.

"We have to go in here," said Winter when Emmerich nearly walked by the war archive.

"Ah . . . like I said . . . " he mumbled, willing his way up the steps and across the marble lobby before bracing himself on the inquiries desk to take the weight off his leg.

"Yeah, yeah, yeah, I'm coming," they heard a voice calling after Emmerich rang the reception bell several times. Shortly thereafter a little round man came shuffling around the corner. He had very little hair left on his head but he did have a spectacular Kaiser Wilhelm mustache that was parted in the middle and turned up at the ends in an exhibition that left the former German regent in the dust. "What can I do for the gentlemen?" he asked, visibly indignant.

Emmerich looked at the man so angrily that Winter hurriedly took the initiative.

"*Grüß Gott*, we're from the police detective corps and need any information you can provide about the soldiers in this photo." He showed him his badge and took the photo from

Emmerich and put it on the desk. "Names, ranks, deployments, etc, etc . . . "

The bureaucrat put a pince-nez on his nose and took down a few notes. "It could take a while."

"We'll wait." Emmerich crossed his arms and looked around for someplace to sit.

"Whatever you'd like, but don't say I didn't warn you." With these words he disappeared through the same swing door through which he'd entered.

"It can't be so difficult to dig up a bit of information." Emmerich sat down on a narrow wooden bench next to the inquiries desk, stretched out his legs, and closed his eyes.

A full hour later Emmerich rang the reception bell anew. "What a state of affairs! No wonder we lost the war," he snarled when the bureaucrat came shuffling out again.

"Maybe you are unaware, but a lot has happened in the last few years. The monarchy fell and we have to organize and administer all the files of the dissolved Royal and Imperial army units. And when I say all, I mean all," the man justified himself, dabbing at his bare head with a handkerchief.

"At least find out where the men were stationed and what company they served in."

The bureaucrat motioned to the door behind him. "Do you have any idea how many unsorted documents there are in our subterranean storage vault? Can you imagine the level of chaos that the war and the collapse of the empire has caused? You are more than welcome to have a look with your own eyes and help us sort through everything." He was sweating so profusely that the pince-nez slipped off his nose.

"We need the information for a murder investigation. Because of you, more people may die."

The bureaucrat stooped down, picked up his tiny glasses, and wedged them back into place. He looked indignantly at the two detectives. "I would if I could, but I'm no magician." He deliberately ignored Emmerich and handed Winter a form. "Fill this out. Your request will receive top priority. I'll send notice to you at the commissariat as soon as I've found the records. There's nothing more I can do." In order to emphasize his words, he crossed his arms.

Like it or not, Emmerich had to accept defeat.

"How long is it going to take to get those records?" asked Winter when they arrived back at the commissariat.

"No idea. Given the incompetence of the Austrian bureaucracy it could be a cold day in hell before we see anything." Emmerich tapped his fingers on the desk. "We can't lose too much time, but I can't think of any other way."

"Are you really alright?" Looking at his boss seemed to cause Winter to worry. "You're pale, and your eyes are glazed. I hope you didn't catch something from Minna. Or in the Beehive. Germs are . . . "

"EMMERICH!" Sander's voice boomed through the room.

Emmerich cringed. What had he done now? He couldn't think of anything he'd done wrong, or at least not that Sander knew about.

He gathered himself and smoothed out his pants. Then he turned slowly around, feverishly trying to dream up an excuse that could explain his unkempt appearance.

"*Guten Morgen*, Herr District Inspector. Did you receive my report?" he said, suddenly stopping and furrowing his brow.

Something was different this morning. Sander, who seemed even stiffer than usual, had two uniformed patrolmen with him, flanking him like massive watchtowers.

It was so quiet in the room that the tick of the grandfather clock in the next room was clearly audible. *Tick tock* went the seconds, as if counting down to some ominous moment, and

Emmerich suddenly felt thrown back in time. Back in a trench, just before battle, knowing full well that something horrible was about to happen but completely in the dark as to the details. It was the famous calm before the storm. *Tick tock. Tick tock. Tick tock.*

"What did you think of my report?" He couldn't bear the silence any longer.

"Your plans for the seizure of Veit Kolja aren't exactly a stroke of genius. But that doesn't matter. I'm going to hand the case over to someone else anyway."

"Who?" Emmerich stared at him, stunned. "But . . . "

"No buts!" Sander held up his hand, and dead silence overtook the room again.

And then he finally said why.

29

A ugust Emmerich, you are under arrest for the murder of Josephine Bauer."

Tick tock. Tick tock. Tick tock.

By all appearances, those present had been robbed of their voices. Winter and Hörl stared at Sander with incredulity, the two patrolmen stood there silently with stony faces, and Emmerich wasn't sure if he was awake or dreaming. A surreal, grotesque dream.

"Who . . . who is Josephine Bauer?" he heard himself mumble.

Instead of answering, Sander nodded to the pair of uniformed men and they grabbed Emmerich by the arm on either side.

"I'm sorry, Emmerich." Sander stood before him and put a hand on his shoulder. "I don't like this any more than you do, believe me." He sighed and looked at the floor. "Search him," he said quietly.

Emmerich felt someone pat him down roughly while someone else rummaged through his pockets.

He allowed the humiliating procedure to happen without resistance. "Who is Josephine Bauer?" he repeated while he was cuffed and shoved outside. "I didn't do anything to anyone. I didn't murder anyone, and certainly not a woman I've never even heard of."

"The whole thing is just a misunderstanding." Winter had followed him and watched incredulously as Sander got into an elegant black car while the patrolmen bundled Emmerich toward a green Heinrich. The multi-axle, windowless wooden wagon pulled by two horses was used exclusively for the transport of detainees, which was why a clutch of curious onlookers had gathered to witness what they hoped would be lurid events.

"It's one of them," called a red-cheeked gossipmonger. "One of the cops." Practically salivating, she turned to the other onlookers. "Look, they're locking up one of their own."

"Corrupt rabble!" A toothless man raised his fist in the air.

"Piss off, there's nothing to see here!"

One of the uniformed officers shoved a gawker so hard that she stumbled backwards onto the sidewalk and knocked over Winter, who was standing behind them.

When he saw his assistant on the ground, Emmerich finally awoke from his trance. He kicked the uniformed man in the shin, causing him to let go, and leaned out the still-open door of the wagon

"Don't worry! It's just a stupid mix-up. I'll be back at work by afternoon at the latest."

Winter stood up and clapped the dust from his clothes. "Good," he called as the uniformed officers pulled Emmerich back inside the wagon and knocked him to the floor. The door of the wagon was slammed shut, the coachman shook the reins, and the prisoner transport wagon headed off.

"See you later," Emmerich heard Winter call after him. "See you later, boss. I'll get you out!"

Through a narrow slit in the rear wall of the wagon, Emmerich was able to see where they were going, though his head hit the side wall every time they turned a corner: Maximilianplatz, Universitätsstraße, Landesgerichtsstraße . . . It was no surprise to him where they were headed.

"Here we are," one of the patrolmen stated the obvious

after the green Heinrich came to a standstill in front of a large, gray building complex.

"Thanks for the information. I'd never have figured it out on my own."

"Shut your mouth. Out with you." The officer ripped open the door and kicked Emmerich in the back so he fell out onto the cobblestone street.

"Been a real pleasure," he mumbled, looking at his scraped palms and examining his leg before finally looking up.

The regional court, also called the Landl, loomed over him, huge and menacing, but Emmerich didn't let himself be intimidated by the imperious-looking building. He'd been through the green door and the long, dark hallways often enough before to attend an interrogation or to accompany a suspect. The institution was so familiar to him that he forgot for a moment that he was on the wrong side of the law on this morning. It was only when he was led to the court officers at registration, where a bureaucrat took his personal information with an indifferent look on his face, that reality began to dawn on him: he was suspected of murder.

"Listen, I'm innocent. I didn't do anything."

"If I had a crown for every time I heard that, I'd be richer than the Kaiser. You must have done something. Nobody's here for nothing."

Emmerich realized there was no point discussing it with the man. "I wish to speak with Herr District Inspector Sander. Please have him brought here."

The bureaucrat remained unfazed. "Yeah, yeah," he said, dipping his fountain pen in an inkwell and giving a sign to two strong men who'd been sitting unobtrusively in the corner.

The two of them got up, and while one of them held him, the other, red-faced and muscle-bound, searched him.

"Shoelaces, underpants, waistband," dictated the one searching him, confiscating the items mentioned.

"What's the meaning of this? You can't just take my things," Emmerich protested, but his words fell on deaf ears.

"Suspenders, handkerchief," the muscle-bound man continued. "Take it easy. It's for your own protection," he said when Emmerich began to squirm.

"I'm not going to hang myself, and definitely not with a snotty handkerchief."

"Rules are rules," was the only answer.

Next Emmerich was photographed, fingerprinted, and finally a morose officer took him for a medical examination. There's one silver lining, thought Emmerich, I can ask for pain medication and something to give me a boost.

He felt so dog tired, he was dizzy, and there was cold sweat on his brow. How was he going to get through the coming hours?

Dr. Stranner, the prison doctor, showed much more interest in the newspaper he had open on his desk than in his patient.

"Undress," he barked without dignifying Emmerich with so much as a look.

"You don't need to examine me. I'm not sick. My only problem is a war wound. Just give me some pain medicine."

"Undress," the doctor repeated, showing just as little interest as the bureaucrat at the registration desk.

"I just said . . . "

Stranner looked at him with a raised eyebrow. "Either you undress yourself or a guard will take care of it for you. Whatever you want." The guard removed his cuffs. Emmerich grudgingly removed his clothes. He got through the humiliating exam with his teeth gritted. "All clear," said Stranner when he was finished, sitting back down with his paper.

"What does 'all clear' mean?" Emmerich got dressed, then stepped toward the doctor. He was immediately grabbed by the guard. He quickly put Emmerich's cuffs back on. "I'm not all clear! Can't you see this? Look!" He stuck out his leg and began to pull up his pant leg, which was no easy task with his hands bound.

"No bugs. No infectious diseases." Stranner's words weren't directed at Emmerich but at the guard. "Take him away."

"You're a doctor. You swore an oath. You have to help me. Please give me something. Anything."

"If you don't stop carrying on right this second you'll get something—a punch in the face." The guard opened the door.

Emmerich started to protest but it was quickly ended when two strong arms lifted him by the armpits.

"You can bring in the next one," was the last thing he heard out of the prison doctor before he was dragged away.

No sympathy, no help, no medicine.

Emmerich knew the room he was taken to next all too well. It was an interrogation room, a small greenish chamber with a metal table fixed to the floor in the middle of it—a massive bulwark representing the line between good and evil. Emmerich was taken to the back side, the one for the villains, and now sat in the same spot as thousands of scam artists, thieves, and murderers had sat before him. He was cold, he was thirsty, and his leg hurt more and more.

"Can someone bring me something to drink? And perhaps a cigarette?"

He tapped his fingers on the table and hoped this insanity would soon be over. He wanted out as quickly as possible.

In all the years he'd been going in and out of the Landl he'd never noticed how meager the rooms were and how awful the air was. It stank of cold sweat. Emmerich felt as if the walls were closing in on him every minute.

Finally the door opened, and it wasn't a guard who entered but Sander. "Damn it, Emmerich, what the hell did you do?" he fumed, his face red.

"Nothing," Emmerich replied. "I didn't do anything, and I especially didn't murder anyone."

"To have to arrest one of my own men . . . Do you have any idea what this will do to the reputation of the department? Ach, what am I saying. To the reputation of the entire Vienna police force."

"I'm innocent," Emmerich insisted, looking at his superior imploringly. "I don't even know who Josephine Bauer is."

Sander looked him over and twisted the end of his bushy mustache. "If you did it, at least confess," he said, with a touch of doubt in his tone.

"There is nothing to confess. It wasn't me. Either someone is trying to frame me or it's a stupid mix-up. What exactly happened?"

Sander sighed. "I don't know the details myself. I was just given orders from above to arrest you for murder. Normally such orders are based on accurate information."

"Then I'm the exception that proves the rule."

Sander snorted and then nodded. "You're a disobedient malcontent, but you're no murderer."

Emmerich was so happy that tears nearly filled his eyes. "Thank you, Herr District Inspector."

Leopold Sander patted him on the shoulder. "Hang in there. This confusing situation will be cleared up soon, I hope. I'll see what I can do." He said goodbye and left the room.

Shortly thereafter the door opened again, and a man in a perfectly-fitted dark-gray suit—probably custom made— entered the room. His full black hair was combed back with pomade, and he was engulfed in a cloud of expensive after-shave.

"I'm Chief Inspector Carl Horvat." He sat down opposite Emmerich.

"I know."

Emmerich's stomach cramped. The somewhat better mood he'd been put into from Sander's visit immediately dissipated. Here he was sitting with the man he'd wanted to meet and impress for years, but instead of shining, he was doing exactly the opposite. He was disgraced, exhausted, and suspected of murder. If it was true that first impressions count, he might as well put to rest his longtime dream of working for the *Leib und Leben* division.

"Your name is August Emmerich?" Horvat's voice showed no emotion, and his facial expression was also neutral.

Emmerich gritted his teeth and sat up straight. "Could I possibly find out what happened and why exactly I'm a suspect—"

"Just answer my questions," interrupted Horvat. "Is your name August Emmerich, and are you an inspector first class in service of the police corps?" He took a thin folder from his briefcase, which was on the floor next to him, and put it down, lined up perfectly with the edge of the table.

"Yes and yes." Emmerich found it difficult to hide his uncertainty and maintain his composure.

"Is this your service weapon?" Horvat opened the folder, took out a photo of a Steyr repeater pistol, and pushed it across the table.

Emmerich became hot and cold at the same time when he realized what must have happened . . . Someone had killed Josephine Bauer with his gun. "I . . . I can explain." He hid his sweaty hands below the table because they had begun to shake uncontrollably. "My service weapon was stolen. I was jumped and robbed. Here, look."

He bent his head down so Horvat could see the lump, which was still somewhat swollen. Horvat didn't dignify his pitiable condition with a look.

"Did you report the loss?" Horvat made a few notes and then put the paper and pen back down, again flush with the edge of the table.

"No, it was . . . " Emmerich searched for the right words. "It was complicated."

"I'm listening."

Emmerich wrestled with himself, playing out the various scenarios in his head, but he couldn't come up with any credible excuse.

"I'm listening," repeated Horvat, looking at Emmerich coolly.

It suddenly occurred to Emmerich that the Chief Inspector had two different colored eyes. One was gray, the other blue, and together they gave him a piercing gaze, one that left no doubt that Horvat could see through any lies.

There was nothing left but the truth. "The husband of my woman, who we thought had died in the war, showed up out of the blue, back from a prisoner of war camp. That led to me drinking in Beppo's Bar and waking up the next day in the hospital. At some point between I must have been attacked and robbed," Emmerich summarized the events.

"When was this exactly?"

"Four days ago."

"And what kept you from reporting the incident?"

Emmerich stammered. "Well, to be honest . . . District Inspector Sander and I . . . there were a few disagreements between us. I didn't want to give him a reason to demote me."

"Are there witnesses to the attack?"

"Not that I know of."

"And at the hospital? Were you checked in and registered officially?

Emmerich sighed. "No."

Horvat, who'd been taking notes nonstop, looked up. "Ach . . . " Before Emmerich could explain himself, he continued with the questioning. "Where were you this morning?"

Emmerich ran his hand through his hair. The handcuffs, which made this move awkward, just further reminded him of how miserable his situation was. "This morning?" Horvat leaned back and made a show of looking at his watch.

Emmerich rubbed his nose. Fatigue and pain were hindering his ability to think. Normally he worked well under pressure, but this situation was different. "I was in the commissariat until about eight," he remembered finally. "After that I went for a walk. Maybe an hour . . . Then I made a detour to the medical examiner's office to speak to Alberlin Wiesegger, Professor Hirschkron's assistant, about something."

"Can Herr Wiesegger confirm this?"

Emmerich felt ice-cold sweat running down his brow and wiped it away with his cuffed hands. "He wasn't there. He'd been called to a crime scene. I . . . " He paused as something clicked in his head. "I suspect it was the scene of this Josephine Bauer's murder."

Horvat didn't offer his assessment of things. "Before that, you said, you were walking around. Can you be more specific?"

"I wanted a coffee. My assistant and Constable Hörl can confirm that."

"You spent an hour getting a cup of coffee? You don't really expect me to believe that, do you?"

"Don't you ever just go walking to clear your head? There's so much going on right now. The smugglers Querner and Kolja . . . and then there are the murders that—"

"Murders?" Something flashed in Horvat's eyes, but Emmerich couldn't read what it meant. "Murder isn't within your purview."

"I know, but—"

"No buts. I can see . . . that what I've heard about you is true."

"What? What have you heard?" Emmerich was on the verge of losing control. He'd always assumed Horvat was competent, not so ignorant. Where was his supposedly superior insight into human nature? Couldn't he tell he was dealing with an innocent man?

"I'm the one asking questions here." Horvat looked at his watch again, which annoyed Emmerich. "Let's go back to your walk. What route did you take?"

Emmerich pressed his lips together. "I can't remember . . . Margaretenstraße, Kettenbrückengasse . . . " he said. His face suddenly lit up. "I just remembered . . . on Wienzeile a fortune-teller accosted me. She can confirm that I was there."

More tragedy coming . . . her words came back to him. Maybe he should learn to listen to women more, regardless of how crazy they seemed.

"Are you serious? A fortune-teller?"

"Go find her! She had a red kerchief on her head and spoke with a Bohemian accent."

"No, really, in all seriousness, Emmerich: a fortune-teller is supposed to be your alibi?" Horvat folded his hands.

Emmerich couldn't bear his counterpart's airs of superiority any longer, and he was suddenly overcome with immeasurable rage. "At least try! I'm innocent, god damn it!" He banged on the table. "I don't know Josephine Bauer. Never heard her name before. What is my motive supposed to have been?"

Horvat didn't show the slightest reaction. Was nobody in this building capable of human emotion?

"Your motive? The oldest one in the world: money."

"Money?" Emmerich's mouth was getting dryer as the situation became increasingly surreal.

"You need money badly. Why else did you ask your superior for an advance on your wages? And your affinity for alcohol and prostitutes is an open secret."

"What?" Emmerich wondered how Horvat could have come up with something so absurd. "I enjoy a beer now and then at the end of the day, and as far as prostitutes are concerned . . . I am understanding about their predicament, but—"

"And looking at you, it's obvious that you're also fighting a drug problem." Horvat hadn't listened to Emmerich. "Let me guess: morphine?" Emmerich stared at him with his mouth open. "Lying is pointless. I can see your withdrawal symptoms—unnaturally pale, trembling, sweating, trouble concentrating. A blood test would confirm my suspicions."

"I don't shoot morphine," Emmerich protested, laying his arms out on the table. "I only took a little heroin. Which is totally legal."

"Ach . . ." This exclamation, which was actually harmless, sounded in Horvat's mouth like a conviction with the force of law. "So the heroin was prescribed? Why do you need medicine anyway?"

Emmerich took a deep breath and weighed all his options. He wasn't going to get a position in *Leib und Leben* division anyway. Might as well stick with the truth, he thought.

"Because of a war wound," he confessed.

"There's nothing in your file about a wound."

Emmerich felt as if he were caught in a fatal downward spiral that was taking him further and further down by the minute. "I never revealed it because until recently it hadn't been a problem. If someone had found out, I might have been transferred to desk work. And I didn't want that. I needed the hardship pay for the children."

"Children? There's nothing about children in your file either."

"They're not mine. I already mentioned the woman I was living with, whose husband was supposedly killed in action . . ." He stopped midsentence. The more he talked, the worse it got. "I know, it all looks a bit funny right now . . ." He started to try to explain again.

Horvat packed up his things and stood up. "It doesn't look funny at all. On the contrary. As far as I'm concerned, it all adds up to a clear picture."

Shivers went up Emmerich's spine. He wanted to justify himself, wanted to protect his name and show Horvat that he was a good man and an even better police officer. He struggled to find the words, but none came.

"In order to finance your alcohol and drug habits and your visits to prostitutes, you attacked the widow Josephine Bauer in her garden plot this morning. But you hadn't reckoned with the possibility that the brave woman would fight back." He gestured to Emmerich's arms, which were covered with scratches.

"I had to crawl through the sewers and exchange blows with a scam artist. Obviously those sorts of things leave marks. And besides . . . Do you really think I'd be so stupid as to shoot someone with my own service weapon and leave it at the crime scene?"

"Your nerves are shot. Heroin and alcohol affect your psychological makeup. Maybe you can plead reduced legal culpability. That way you won't spend your whole life in the clink, only a part of it. A confession would help you." Horvat shoved a piece of paper and a pen across the table.

Emmerich finally lost his composure. He jumped up, sending his chair to the floor with a loud clatter, and banged so hard on the table with his still-cuffed hands that it shook.

"I'm innocent!" he shouted. "I'm not going to let you frame me!"

Horvat didn't bat an eye during the outburst, he stood there expressionless. "Intemperate and short-fused. Not that it surprises me." He tucked his briefcase under his arm. "Guard!" he called, at which point the door opened and he left the room. "Take him away."

Emmerich stood there dumbfounded. No matter how he tried to juggle things in his head, it all looked bad for him. Very bad.

30

A court officer handed Emmerich a nightgown and a tin cup and led him through endless, light-green hallways to the prison wing where he'd been assigned. They passed hundreds of identical doors until they reached cell 398, which would be his new home until further notice. There were already five men on the wooden bunks that were arrayed against the sidewalls of the dark hole—there was no other way to describe the place.

"Don't make any trouble, inmate 420," said the guard, taking off his cuffs and shoving him into the cell.

Emmerich could no longer ignore reality once he stepped past the heavy iron door, and he had to muster all his remaining strength not to break down. How could he have sunk so low? A week earlier he'd been an up-and-coming detective and a happy man who thought he'd found the love of his life, whose children had found a home in his heart. And now . . .

"Oh no, another one," grunted a haggard man with a cleft lip. He was in the bottom of the triple bunk on the right. "As if it doesn't already stink enough in here. You better not have crabs." With these words he turned to the wall and mumbled something incomprehensible.

"Forget that piece of trash" said a short man on the middle bunk on the left. "Welcome to Irongate Hotel, inmate 420. The facilities are shit, and the service even worse. But the place is always full anyway. How long will you be gracing us with your presence?"

Emmerich climbed up to the top bunk on the right and flopped onto the filthy sack of straw that served as a mattress. His quarters stank, but he was too tired to care.

"If it's up to them, for life."

He let his eyes wander around the cell. Would he have to spend years here, or even decades? The toilet consisted of a stinking bucket behind a rotting wooden screen; next to that were a washing table and a shelf with six narrow compartments, and above the shelf were nails to hang clothes. To call the surroundings depressing would have been a euphemism. There was no word capable of describing the place.

"What a bunch of shit."

The prisoners sighed and all agreed. "Dirty system . . . fucking judiciary . . . paragon of injustice . . . " Whether they meant Emmerich's situation or their own wasn't clear.

"To your first day." The man on the bunk beneath Emmerich offered him a cigarette.

Emmerich took it gratefully, lit it, and inhaled the smoke, which not only banished the horrible smell of the straw mattress but also calmed his nerves. Was this his future? Locked up in a cold, dark, smelly hole? Corralled with criminals? And with vermin, as he realized from a biting sensation in his crotch. A glance down at the bedcover confirmed what he feared. Bugs. The insolence with which they feasted on him left no doubt that these cells were their domain. He was no longer a man but a worthless object barely good enough to be sucked dry by bugs.

Later, after a horrid dinner of peas and potatoes that was no better than the food in a homeless shelter, a guard made the rounds.

"Curfew!" he yelled, banging on the cell doors. "Quiet down, you scum."

At the same time, a gas lamp on the ceiling went on. When

the harsh light bore mercilessly through Emmerich's eyelids he pulled the stinking pillow over his eyes.

"Can someone turn that off?" he complained, shivering. "I feel sick and need to sleep." The pain in his leg was worse than ever, and he would have given anything for a heroin tablet.

"You can't turn it off," said one of the other men, laughing. "The night watchman wants to be able to see us at all times." He pointed to the small window in the cell door. "But don't worry. In three or four weeks you'll get used to it."

"Can you ever get used to a night without darkness?"

"Stop bitching," cursed the ill-tempered man with the cleft lip.

"You'll have to get used to a lot of things. A life without freedom or women, to name a few," said the small man before whistling a sad melody.

"And without happiness," said a quiet voice from the lower left bunk.

"Curfew, god damn it!" the night watchman growled into the cell, and the men went silent.

Emmerich had barely closed his eyes before day broke outside and the courthouse bells began to ring. "What time is it?" he asked as the men crawled out of their bunks, groaning.

"Six thirty. The morning soup'll be served soon."

As if this were a code word, the prisoners ripped open a hatch in the door they called a Judas hole and a worker handed in tin bowls filled with a soup made of watered-down roux.

"You have to eat something," said the little guy when Emmerich set his portion down on the floor with disgust. "Eating and drinking keep your body and your mind together. How do you expect to get through a trial and fight the system if you're half-starved?"

Emmerich nodded sadly. The man was right. What good would it do him to get weaker and weaker? He began to choke down the soup.

"I need pain medication," he said. "Is there any way to get something?"

"I don't want to be a killjoy, but you might as well save yourself the trouble of going to the doctor. The only thing he'll give you is some gray powder."

"I don't care what it is as long as it helps."

"You don't get it." The man handed Emmerich a piece of dry bread. "There's no medicine. Not for us. I've been here many times. All prisoners here at the Landl get the same thing, no matter what they have. Headache, fever, or congestion. The powder is nothing but shit. Probably ground-up chalk or something like that. If you take it, you just count yourself lucky not to get even sicker."

Emmerich understood. The scum of society, they were nothing more than that. Parasites, living off the state. Nobody had any interest in making their lives any easier, or even saving their lives, for that matter.

"420," barked a guard through the hatch, and it took a moment before Emmerich realized that meant him. "420. Out."

"Get out of here," sneered the man with the cleft lip. "Hopefully forever."

"If only it were that easy." Emmerich went out into the hall, where he was handcuffed again.

"I heard you were one of us," said the guard, exposing two rows of rotting teeth as he smiled. "That made the rounds quick. A cop, doing time. There's a few folks who are looking forward to seeing you."

Emmerich could only imagine. Most of the prison workers were men who had been rejected for service as police officers and were envious of members of the corps.

"At least someone is looking forward to seeing me. Nobody could say the same about you."

The guard repaid Emmerich's comment with a shot to his kidneys, causing him to fall to his knees.

"You won't be cracking jokes for long. Just wait until you're out of pretrial detention and transferred to a long-term cell. You won't be so quick to open your trap then. If you even can." He smoothed out his uniform, hoisted Emmerich to his feet, and shoved him along to the courtyard, which ran alongside a wing of the building that fronted the street. The prisoners called that wing of the Landl Freedom Alley because it was the way out of the complex. A direction only a few of them would ever go.

Freedom Alley was exceedingly crowded, full of witnesses, lawyers, journalists, and police officers all talking and arguing loudly. Emmerich sank his head—he didn't want to be recognized and cause himself further humiliation.

The guard took him to a dark brown wooden door with gold letters on it stating Regional Court Counsel Dr. Josef Schaupp.

"Wait, the investigative judge? I'm not prepared and I don't have a lawyer yet."

The guard punched him in the back of the neck. "Don't piss your pants, 420. You have a visitor. Conversations always take place in the presence of a judge so you scum don't try to set up any funny business." He knocked at the door and shook his head. "And to think the likes of you managed to get accepted to the police corps."

"Yes?" came from behind the door.

The guard opened it and pushed Emmerich into the office.

Emmerich felt as if he'd landed in a parallel universe. Whereas just moments before he'd been surrounded by brutality and misery, now he was standing amid elegant furniture upholstered in warm colors. He smelled freshly brewed coffee, and a gramophone was playing classical music. Something soothing. Bach or Brahms.

"Thanks," said Judge Schaupp, an older gentleman with ample muttonchops. "You can go now," he told the guard, who had positioned himself by the door.

"But the prisoner is violent."

"First of all, he's wearing handcuffs. Second, I'm armed. And third, the man doesn't really look as if he poses a danger to me."

The guard grunted in response. "I'll pick him up in fifteen minutes," he said, going out and closing the door.

How bad he must in fact look became clear to Emmerich when his visitor, none other than Winter, turned and looked at him so aghast that it was as if he'd just seen a ghost.

"Heaven above!" Winter nearly jumped out of his chair.

"Don't worry about it." Emmerich gestured for him to stay seated. "I'm fine."

"You look sick. Really sick. You must have caught something bad—from Minna or Czernin's children."

"The prison doctor said I was good." Emmerich greeted the judge and sat down next to Winter. "Still, I could do with some pain medicine."

Schaupp acted as though he wasn't listening.

"Are they at least treating you well?" Winter's voice quavered.

"I can't complain." Emmerich tried to put on a happy face for his assistant.

"What happened?"

"Somebody killed this Frau Bauer with my service weapon, and they want to pin it on me. I don't know any more than that. I'd hoped that you might have found something out."

Judge Schaupp turned off the gramophone. "I'm just a neutral observer," he said. "Act as if I'm not here." He pointed to a clock. "And whatever you need to talk about, do it quickly. Fifteen minutes will be up before you know it."

"At first we thought we didn't know this Josephine Bauer, but it turns out we do." Winter spoke so fast that his words tumbled over each other. "She's the waitress from Poldi Tant."

"Fini?" mumbled Emmerich. Now he was more mystified than ever.

Winter nodded. "She had a bit of money, and they are saying she was attacked because of that. To . . . to pay for alcohol and . . . visits to prostitutes." Winter's voice cracked. "They say you had a bad childhood and developed bad character as a result. Obviously I said otherwise, but nobody listens to me."

Emmerich looked touched. "I can't tell whether this is a series of unlucky coincidences or whether somebody is trying to frame me."

"But who? And why? Do you have such serious enemies?"

Emmerich brooded. "It must have to do with the case . . . or with the second man who's been following us, the man with the scar . . . or both," he thought out loud. "Any news from the war archive?"

"The files were sent over to me last night. I spent the night going through them to identify all the soldiers in the photo. Which I was able to do, with the exception of the one on the far right, whose face is scratched out." Winter pulled out a nicely folded piece of paper from his chest pocket and began to read from it. "Aside from the three dead men—Jost, Zeiner, and Czernin—they are Peter Boos, Richard Teschner, and corporal Georg Oberwieser. The other three, Ladislaus Riml, Alois von Hohenrecht, and Jaroslav von Scheure, all died in action."

"And where were they serving?"

"In eastern Galicia. Near Lemberg. They were part of the 13th Company, which was in turn part of the 11th Infantry Division."

"A company is usually made up of four platoons of sixty men each," Emmerich said. "These can be divided into squads. Those ten men probably made up a squad," he mused. "Something must have happened . . . But what? You have to find the survivors and question them. Can you do that?"

"Sander has assigned every available officer to Kolja, but I can look into it after hours. I've already found the addresses where they're currently registered."

Emmerich was about to praise his assistant but was interrupted by a knock at the door.

"Visiting time is over." Schaupp clapped his hands together.

"Can I send food and pain medicine to Herr Emmerich?" asked Winter.

The judge shook his head. "No packages. No gifts. The rules are unambiguous. As a police officer you should know that. The prisoners are taken care of well enough."

"*Auf Wiedersehen.*" Winter wrapped his arms around a stunned Emmerich and squeezed him so hard that he couldn't breathe.

"Away from him!" commanded Schaupp. "Bodily contact is strictly forbidden."

"Excuse me." Winter let go, went to the door with his head drooping, and disappeared out the door.

Emmerich watched him leave the room. He would have sold his soul to be able to follow his assistant.

"We'll see each other at the pretrial conference, Emmerich."

Schaupp went to the gramophone, waited until Emmerich had opened the door, and then shifted his attention to his collection of records.

"Is he finally available?" A young man with panicky blotches on his face stood next to the door hopping nervously from one foot to the other. Judging by his outfit, he was a newly minted lawyer. "I need to talk to him about the case as soon as possible."

Emmerich looked left and right—the guard was nowhere to be seen. Apparently this young man had knocked, not the guard. The fifteen minutes weren't yet up. "Sorry. He's still busy. He'll be ready in ten minutes," he heard himself say. And then everything happened very quickly: the young man hustled off and Emmerich, without thinking, as if being moved by an invisible hand, took Schnaupp's coat from a coatrack in front of the door, threw it over his own shoulders—which, in hand-cuffs, wasn't so easy to do—put on a hat that was sitting atop a nearby bookshelf, and headed for the exit.

Unhurried and completely unchallenged, he strolled toward freedom while Wagner's "Ride of the Valkyries" boomed from Schaupp's office.

31

In a flash, Emmerich found himself outside on Landes-gerichtsstraße. Had he really had the impudence to just stroll right out of prison? And, even harder to believe, had his breakout really gone so smoothly? Nobody noticed him—nobody had even said a word to him.

What now? Should he go back? Maybe nobody had noticed yet that he was gone. He could still sneak back in and wait in front of Schaupp's door to be taken back to his cell. He was in no condition to escape. But on the other hand he didn't feel up to a trial and prison term, either. He'd had a taste of what it was like to be locked up in Landl—and that was only pretrial detention.

He didn't want to put his trust in a trial because he'd been all but found guilty in advance—that much was clear. His belief in the justice system had been deeply shaken. He pulled the hat further down over his face. Going underground was his only chance. If he couldn't prove his own innocence and clear his name, nobody else would.

He slowly limped off.

"Watch it! You tired of living?"

The green Heinrich wagon came racing around the corner so quickly that the escapee was nearly trampled by the horses.

"Sorry."

Emmerich looked down and waited until the prison transporter was out of view again. Then he let his intuition guide him and turned into Grillparzenstraße toward the center of town.

What he needed was a hideout. Someplace he could get his strength back. But where would he find that? Who could he expect to take him in? An escaped prisoner, whose body and mind were both shot? Since he didn't want to drag Winter, Luise, or Minna into the whole thing, there was only one person left . . .

"August, my friend. You can't live without me anymore."

A great sense of relief washed over Emmerich when he found Kolja at Café Central, which wasn't far from the Landl. Just as last time, the smuggler was sitting at the best table and smoking a thick cigar.

"Coffee? Or would you prefer a cognac? By the look of you, I'd say you could use one."

"What I need is a hideout. And fast." Emmerich opened the coat enough for Kolja to see the handcuffs.

The smile on Kolja's face froze and he shooed the waiter away despite just having beckoned to him. "So it's true then, what people have been saying. You shot a woman," he whispered.

"The hell I did. Someone's trying to frame me."

"And your friends on the force? Can't they help you?"

"They're the ones who threw me in jail."

Kolja, who was just about to take a sip of coffee, took the cup away from his mouth and coughed. "And you just split from the Landl?"

"Pretty much."

"I don't believe it." Kolja snorted and slapped himself on the thigh. His genteel façade had cracked, and little Vanja Kollberg peeked out.

Emmerich looked around and saw that the other guests were staring at them. "Can you help me or not? Make up your mind. Fast. There'll be a hundred men out looking for me soon. If they're not already . . . "

238 - ALEX BEER

Kolja wiped his mouth and calmly took a sip of coffee. "None of them will think you've got the chutzpah to just waltz into Café Central. A cunning move, my friend."

"Yes or no."

"Could I leave an old fellow sufferer high and dry?" Kolja spread his arms and smiled. "We orphans need to stick together."

Emmerich knew Kolja's friendliness didn't come without other thoughts. He'd have to pay a steep price at some point, but he didn't care at the moment.

"Shall we?"

Kolja tossed a note on the table. "Keep the change," he called toward the waiter and strolled to the door as if helping a wanted murderer go into hiding was the most normal thing in the world. "Nice hat, by the way. I assume it's not yours."

"You assume correctly." Emmerich was too tense for banter. "Where are we going? Is it far?"

When they emerged onto the sidewalk, sirens were audible in the distance, and Emmerich winced.

"We're already there." Kolja gestured to a *Gründerzeit* building across the street. They crossed the road and he unlocked the door. "Be my guest."

Emmerich slipped in the door and followed Kolja to the first floor, where he led him into an expansive, multiroom apartment.

"Relax. You're safe here." Kolja took Emmerich into a parlor that was at least twice as big as the entire apartment he had shared with Luise and the children, maneuvered him into a brown Biedermeier sofa, and pressed a glass of amber liquid into his hand.

"Who else lives here?" Emmerich emptied the glass in a single gulp.

"Nobody. Ever since the orphanage days I've had a distinct need for space and a peaceful environment." Kolja reached for the bottle. "More?"

Instead of answering, Emmerich reached out his glass. "Now what?"

"Now we'll do what you do in a situation like this. Hide, wait, bargain." Kolja was a picture of calm. He refilled his guest's glass, and then went to the window and looked out. "Cheers." He whistled through his teeth. "The last time I saw so many uniforms in one place was during the battle of Zborow."

Emmerich leaned back and wrapped his fingers around the glass. "I should have stayed in the Landl and gone through with the trial. Maybe I would have been exonerated."

"Bullshit," Kolja said dismissively. "Justice, that blind cow, would be better depicted holding dice than a scale." He put his hand on Emmerich's shoulder. "If you want justice in this country you have to fight for it yourself." He looked at him and squinted. "But for that you'll need other clothes, a new haircut, and you should grow a beard."

Emmerich felt his stubbly chin.

"Most importantly, though, we have to get rid of those." Kolja pointed to the handcuffs that were still on Emmerich's wrists. He left the room, came back shortly with a toolbox, and looked closely at the chain. "This old garbage. Can't Father State afford any decent equipment?" Only a few seconds later there was a click and Emmerich was rubbing his sore wrists with a relieved groan.

Kolja refilled the glass, sat down next to Emmerich, and put his feet up. "Any idea who the son of a bitch is who wants to frame you?"

"If I knew that, you and I wouldn't be sitting on the sofa like an old married couple." The alcohol was having an effect, and Emmerich was beginning to feel better. "Say, how many people did you have tailing me and my assistant?"

"One. Why?"

"Because a second person was following me. Wiry guy.

Agile and fast. Fairly nondescript except for a scar on his right cheek."

"Not one of mine. But I'll see what I can find out. My boys are wired in—they have information the cops can only dream of."

"Then ask about the following names: Dietrich Jost, Harald Zeiner, Anatol Czernin," Emmerich rattled off. "They served in Galicia. Somewhere near Lemberg. Together with a Peter Boos, a Richard . . . " he frowned as he tried to recall what Winter had told him. " . . . Teschner," he remembered. "They were all infantrymen. And then there was a corporal named, I think, Oberwieser. I forget his first name. They were part of the 13th Company of the 11th Infantry Division."

"What do they have to do with it?" Kolja gestured to the cuffs, sitting on the floor in front of them.

"No idea. To be honest, I don't really know anything anymore. The last few days were pretty . . . " he searched for the right word. "Stressful." Emmerich no longer bothered to put the liquor in his glass, he drank directly from the bottle. An enjoyable tingle went through his body, erasing the pain.

"Relax for a while. We can talk more when you're feeling better." Kolja stood up.

"Hey, can you possibly get hold of some pain medicine for me?" Emmerich let himself slump over and then stretched out on the sofa.

"There's nothing I can't get hold of."

"Then I'd love a bottle of heroin and the real murderer of Josephine Bauer."

"I'll see what I can do."

"Thanks, Vanja," mumbled Emmerich. He was asleep the next instant.

"We'll get you back on the police force." Kolja slowly closed the door. "What good are you to me in prison? You wouldn't be able to repay me the huge favor you owe me."

The first thing Emmerich saw when he awoke was a dark splotch of saliva on ocher-brown silk cloth.

He had no idea where he was, but that didn't frighten him. He'd gotten used to waking up every morning in a strange place.

After a while he remembered that he was lying on the sofa of none other than Veit Kolja, and he sat up.

"Crazy new world," he mumbled, wiping spittle from the corner of his mouth.

His gaze fell on the coffee table. A set of fine clothes was laid out there, folded neatly. There was also a ham sandwich and a glass bottle of tablets. Heroin, the label said.

Emmerich sighed. The presence of the pills alone revived his spirits. He crushed a pill and snorted it. The pain-dulling, invigorating effect kicked in immediately, and he looked to the future with new mettle. He'd clear everything up, and then he'd be owed a few apologies and a promotion.

"Someone's come back from the dead." Kolja entered the room and looked at the array of gifts on the coffee table with satisfaction.

Back from the dead . . . Emmerich thought automatically of Xaver Koch. "Seems to be a thing these days." He took a bite of the ham sandwich, convinced he'd never had anything quite so good in his entire life.

"No idea what you're talking about." Kolja raised an eyebrow and looked at Emmerich skeptically. "Maria!" he called so loudly that Emmerich almost choked on his food.

A moment later an older woman appeared in the doorway behind the smuggler. "Don't godda yell. I'm not *gluchy*," she sneered. Beneath her black dress she had an ample Rubens-like figure and her eyes were lined with black kohl, giving her an exotic look.

"This is August," Kolja said slowly. "Draw him a bath and then do his hair over. Black. The same way you do yours." He pointed to her hair and pressed a banknote into her hand. The woman grabbed her hair and cast an indignant look at Kolja before disappearing out of the room. Kolja rolled his eyes. "She thinks I don't know she dyes her hair. She's at least sixty and doesn't have a single white hair. I'm not stupid."

"Is she your wife?"

Kolja's face displayed a mix of amusement and disbelief. "That old hag? She's my housekeeper. I took her over along with the apartment. Barely speaks German, but she cooks and cleans like nobody else. It also suits me just fine that she doesn't understand everything." He pointed to the clothes on the table in front of Emmerich, then turned up his nose. "Maybe you should wash up first. Those are expensive things. Finest quality available at the moment. The bathtub is in the kitchen."

"You have your own bathtub?"

His chest stuck out with pride, Kolja pointed to the correct door. "With a built-in coal stove that heats the water. Have a look."

Emmerich, who, like everyone he knew, washed up with a sponge and water from the shared faucet, had never before seen a private bathtub. Once in a while he had visited the public baths where, for a modest fee, you could stand in a warm shower bath together with hundreds of others—it had never occurred to him that there were luxurious ways to clean yourself.

His initial irritation at bathing alone and without a bathing apron—they had to be worn at the public baths for the sake of decency—disappeared the moment his body slipped into the warm water. My god, it was good.

It took a long time to scrub the moldiness of the Landl from his pores, and if Frau Maria hadn't come in, without knocking first, he'd have probably stayed in the tub until evening.

"Do hair now," she said.

"Can I just dry off and throw on some underpants . . . "

"Now." With rough tugs, she brushed his hair and then smeared a horrible-smelling black paste through it. She also put some of the mixture on his stubble, and it smelled vaguely like shoe polish.

"Wait," she said. "Not touch." She folded her arms and then, after a few minutes, rinsed the stuff out again, parted his hair and then looked at her work with satisfaction. "Good," she said, then left.

Emmerich got out of the tub, dried himself off, slipped into the new clothes, and was happily surprised when he caught a glimpse of himself in the mirror next to the coat closet in the hall. Was that elegant, dark-haired gentleman really him?

"Like new!" Kolja had come up beside him, put a monocle in his right eye, and plopped a hat on his head. "Not even your own mother would recognize you now."

"She wouldn't anyway."

"It's just a figure of speech. But as long as we're on the topic . . . " He stuck out his fist toward Emmerich. "This is yours, isn't it?" He opened his hand to reveal a silver snake that was biting its own tail.

Emmerich was speechless. "Where . . . where did you get . . . my amulet?" He took the piece of jewelry and looked at Kolja with glistening eyes. He had no idea why he was so attached to an object whose primary value lay in reminding him of a mother who had abandoned him like a mangy dog. Emmerich wasn't a sentimental person, and certainly not a naïve dreamer. He understood that the woman who had given birth to him didn't have noble justifications for getting rid of him, and that she had never come looking for him. Even so . . . despite all logic and against his better instincts, part of him still clung to the idea that she had loved him and hadn't willingly abandoned him. He'd never know the truth . . . or would he? "Where'd you get that? Tell me!" he pressed.

"While you were sleeping off your booze I sent my people out searching."

Kolja handed Emmerich a walking stick and stepped back to have a look at his handiwork. What he saw apparently pleased him, and he nodded approvingly.

"And your men figured out who robbed me that quickly?" He turned in front of the mirror and was shocked anew at how different he looked. He particularly liked the cape. Clothes really did make the man.

"I already told you I'm more connected than the police could ever hope to be."

Emmerich really had underestimated the power and influence of the smuggler—a mistake that he wouldn't make in the future.

"So? Who was it?"

Kolja laughed. "If you were hoping for a muscle-bound ruffian, I'm afraid I'll have to disappoint you. These guys were harmless dilettantes. Two malnourished little shits who found you passed out in the gutter. You were so drunk that you tripped and knocked yourself out."

"And the suitcase with my things? My badge? My gun?"

"All sold on the black market, except for your pendant. Shoes, clothing, and pistols are highly desirable items. Not to mention a police badge. But hardly anyone can afford jewelry these days."

"Luckily." Emmerich was so happy to have his keepsake back that he would have liked to hug Kolja. But he didn't want to be too nice. Kolja was, and remained, a crook. Emmerich stuck the amulet in his chest pocket. The fact that he'd so unexpectedly recovered something he thought surely lost gave him butterflies in his stomach. "And these two little street hoods . . . Did they know who they pawned my gun to?"

Kolja grinned. "After my men jogged their memory, they remembered that it was a man with a scar on his cheek."

"So he's been out to get me from the start. But why?"

Kolja plucked a wooden box from the hat rack, opened it to reveal a semiautomatic pistol, and handed the weapon to Emmerich. "Here, for protection. The man who set you up is dangerous. He's a real pro. That's the reason we haven't managed to drag up any info on him so far." He pointed to the door of the salon. "But we do know a bit about the men in the photo—and you're not going to like what we found out."

Emmerich vacillated between respect and concern. Kolja was good. Too good.

In order to stay out of the Landl he'd made a deal with the devil, but the day would come when they were once again on opposite sides—a fact that now made him more uneasy than in the past. When it came to that, he would never again be able to make the mistake of misjudging his opponent.

The haggard man who had followed Emmerich so amateurishly was out in the parlor. The fresh scrapes on his knuckles suggested he'd recently been in a fight, and the untouched state of his face meant he had come out of the confrontation victorious. Apparently he had more talent at fighting than shadowing.

"This is Simon. You already know each other." Kolja poured cognac for everyone. "Tell Herr Emmerich what you found out."

The young smuggler, who appeared visibly uncomfortable in the private realm of his boss, sat perfectly straight on a chair and kneaded his cap. "My cousin's wife had a brother who was stationed in Galicia. He lost an eye there, and half his nose. He wears a horrible prosthetic now."

"The guy's history is of no interest to us. Get to the point," Kolja encouraged.

Simon took a sip of cognac and looked at Kolja, surprised. "Good stuff."

"You're here to report, not to drink. So . . . "

Simon paused and took a deep breath. "So . . . " he began. "The brother of my cousin's wife said there were rumors floating around about atrocities. Bad stuff. A group of Royal and Imperial soldiers supposedly massacred civilians. Women, children, the elderly. Even babies. They were supposed to have done things so brutal it would have shocked Beelzebub. One of the soldiers was so bad they called him the Beast of Lemberg. Apparently even his comrades were scared of him. He loved to slit women's stomachs open . . . "

"And the men in the photo . . . " Emmerich was beginning to understand what Simon was getting at.

" . . . it was them." Simon emptied his glass. "Can I leave now? I need to go. There's another delivery waiting."

Kolja nodded, and Simon went to leave, but Emmerich stopped him. "Which one?" he asked. "Which one of the men was the beast?" It was dawning on him why one face had been rendered unrecognizable.

Simon shrugged, and before Kolja or Emmerich could say anything, he left.

Emmerich, who felt overwhelmed, took a deep breath. War criminals. The men he'd taken for unfortunate victims and risked his neck for were war criminals. It was a twist he had not anticipated.

"Sometimes the good guys turn out to be the bad guys, and vice versa," said Kolja.

"It's only a rumor at this point. Nothing more."

"But nothing less, either." Kolja lit a cigar and crossed his legs. "I don't understand why you look so shocked. Did you really think the reports of civilian massacres were enemy propaganda? Why did you think the press is censored?" Before Emmerich could answer, Kolja continued. "I can tell you why—so the people don't learn about what our army did in enemy territory. Self-defense, my ass. You were on the front and saw what men are capable of. Why not the ones in the photo?"

Emmerich didn't know why he bristled at these suggestions. Because he didn't want to give up his belief in the honor
of soldiers? Because he couldn't accept that everything he had
sacrificed so much for was tarnished? Because he was slowly
but surely losing his ability to distinguish good from bad?

"Innocent until proven guilty," he said, grasping at straws.
"We have to find the other men and warn them. There's only
three still alive."

"Warn them of what?"

"About a killer who's administering vigilante justice."

Kolja bent forward and looked Emmerich in the eyes. "If
these guys killed women and children, they deserve to die."

"That's something for a real judge to decide, not a self-
appointed one. What if they are innocent? I am too, after all."

Kolja rolled his eyes. "See how well your beloved system
works? No wonder people take the law into their own hands."

"Just because you do, you don't need to generalize."
Emmerich suppressed any further commentary. He didn't
want to fight with Kolja. He needed to save his energy to find
the man with the scar and to keep him from inflicting any more
damage. And he had to figure out what role he himself was
playing in the whole thing.

32.

Emmerich stood in the shadows of a collapsing building entryway, his heart pounding, waiting for Winter, who normally passed this way after his shift.

He didn't feel comfortable out in the open like this . . .

"You!" a voice shot through the silence, and Emmerich's heart nearly stopped. In front of him was Officer Ruprecht, one of the patrolmen who had assisted him in the arrest of Wilhelm Querner—and now he was about to try to arrest him.

What should he do? Beat up poor Ruprecht? Threaten him with his gun? Try to convince him of his innocence? His right hand glided under his cape and rested on the hard rubber grip of Kolja's Bayard pistol as his eyes scanned the immediate surroundings. Did Ruprecht have any backup, and if so, how many men?

The officer reached into his pocket and Emmerich's entire body tensed, ready to tangle with his opponent. What was he waiting for?

"Got a light?" asked Ruprecht as he pulled a pack of cigarettes from his uniform jacket.

Emmerich handed him matches without a word.

"I'm cold, too," said Ruprecht, motioning to Emmerich's trembling hand. "And I don't have such a warm outfit as yours." He lit the cigarette and tipped his cap. "Thanks, have a nice night." With that he was on his way, and Emmerich stepped a little further back into the entryway so as not to risk being approached again.

Where the hell was Winter? A glance at the clock on a nearby church confirmed that his assistant's shift should have long since ended. Hopefully he hadn't gone the other way in order to run into the blonde train conductor, thought Emmerich. But his worries proved unfounded. A few minutes later Winter appeared at the end of the street. He hurried past with his head hanging.

"Psst. Over here."

Winter stopped, looked at him, frowned, and then kept going.

"Winter." Emmerich grabbed his shoulder from behind.

Winter jerked himself free and turned, his fist raised. "What do you want?"

"It's me." Emmerich let the monocle drop, took off his hat, and turned his face into the moonlight.

Winter put his hands in front of his face and looked around frantically. "My god," he hissed, shoving Emmerich through an entryway into a decrepit courtyard. "What are you thinking? Everyone's looking for you. They've even printed up wanted posters. Things are really heating up. You need to get out of the city." He looked up at the building, scanning the windows, and pushed Emmerich against a moss-covered wall.

"Somebody here's going to call the police in a second because they think we're up to no good. Try to act normal." Emmerich freed himself from Winter's grip and patted the dirt from the wall off his cape.

"Normal? Since I became your assistant I don't even know what that means anymore."

Emmerich resisted giving Winter a speech about the fact that he still had his badge, his home, and his freedom. "I can't just leave. Where would I go? No, I have to find the real murderer. It's the only chance I have."

"How do you intend to do that? It would be hard enough even if the entire city wasn't looking for you."

They heard the sound of clopping hooves getting closer.

Winter cringed, peered around the corner, and exhaled only when the horse team was out of sight.

"I've found something out. The men in the photo are suspected of having committed war crimes. It's quite possible that they're being killed in an act of vigilante justice. I think maybe one of the survivors has come to Vienna, sought them out, and is taking revenge."

"But what has it all got to do with you?"

"I don't know yet. I guess we got too close to the perpetrator. That's why Josephine Bauer had to die, too—she was the only one who could have identified the killer, after all. He must have been the man who was with Zeiner and Czernin that night at Poldi Tant. He probably lured them under false pretenses. Killing Bauer with my gun was a clever move. He managed to kill two birds with one stone that way."

"But how would he know that we . . . " A bang made both of them jump, and Winter looked around nervously.

"Just the wind," Emmerich tried to calm him. "Blew over a garbage can."

Winter held his breath and relaxed only when a cloud obscured the moon, leaving the courtyard pitch black. "How would the perpetrator have known that we were closing in on him?" he asked.

"He was probably waiting around at the spot where Zeiner's body was found and saw us sniffing around there. When he realized that we were questioning potential witnesses, he must have figured out that we weren't buying it as a suicide. And then he began to follow us."

"You think the man with the scar is the murderer?"

"He's definitely the one who bought my service weapon on the black market."

"How do you know that? And . . . " Winter rubbed the fabric of Emmerich's cape between his fingers. "Where'd you get these nice things?"

"It's better if you don't know. I don't want to drag you too deep into things. Unless it's completely unavoidable, I don't want to ask you for any help, either."

"Anything you need," said Winter immediately, and Emmerich was overcome with a mix of emotion and remorse.

When had his nightmarish rookie turned into the best assistant he could possibly have hoped for?

"You said that the man with Minna at the Chatham Bar, Maximilian Neubert, was the head of the war crimes commission. Could you find him and talk to him?" Winter nodded, but didn't fully understand what Emmerich wanted. "I need whatever files exist about the case. I need to know who the men killed, who turned them in, and whether there are any survivors."

Winter grew uneasy again as the moon reemerged from the clouds and the courtyard was once again bathed in cool, blue light. "I can take care of that," he said.

Emmerich was surprised at himself when he spontaneously reached out and hugged Winter. "I'll be on my way then," he said, slightly embarrassed. He let Winter go again and looked up at the sky. "I have to warn the other men before it's too late."

"That's not a good idea. Have you forgotten that every available officer is out looking for you? Let me do it."

"The wanted posters aren't up yet, and anyway, I'm well disguised. Even you didn't recognize me."

"Go back into hiding and let me handle everything. Better safe than sorry."

Emmerich shook his head. "It's too dangerous. What if Hörl or Sander figure it out? I'd never forgive myself if you lost your job because of me. Or worse—if you were jailed for aiding and abetting."

"Peter Boos lives right near my grandmother. I have to go that way anyway," Winter insisted stubbornly.

"Fine," said Emmerich. "But I'm going to handle Taschner and Oberwieser. Give me their addresses again."

After Winter gave him their registered places of residence, Emmerich put his hand on his shoulder. "I'm indebted to you."

"I'm happy to help. How can I find you if I have something to report?"

"I'll find you." Emmerich put his monocle back in, pulled up the collar of his cape, and looked cautiously around the corner, out onto the street. "Until then . . . take care of yourself!"

He disappeared into the dark night, silently thanking the city council for its plan to save on street lighting.

Emmerich had borrowed money from Kolja, and was able to ride in a luxurious hired car to Leopoldstadt, where Teschner apparently lived.

Nobody would ever think for a second to look for him in a nice car. The police were searching for a down-and-out fugitive, not a gentleman in a fine threads being driven through the streets by a white-gloved chauffeur. As the motorcar roared loudly through the streets, Emmerich leaned back, breathed in the scent of the leather upholstery, and enjoyed the stress-free atmosphere. He was becoming more and more aware of the fact that he considered peace and sufficient space the most desirable luxuries of all, and he envied Kolja for that very reason. Rich food, nice clothes, and expensive cigars were wonderful things, but he found the possibility of having time and space to yourself far more enticing. Privacy is what the rich called it.

"Where would you like me to let you out?" the driver interrupted his ruminations as they turned into Brigittenauer Lände.

Emmerich looked out the window. "Just up here on the left."

He pointed to a nightclub with a seedy reputation. Better to be safe. The driver wouldn't connect him to Teschner this way, and besides, this destination would explain his odd demeanor during the ride. He'd continuously pulled his cap down over his face, kept his head down, and barely said a word.

"Very well, sir. Whatever you like." The chauffeur brought the car to a stop with a knowing grin on his face, and Emmerich handed him a banknote.

"Keep the change."

He stepped out and acted as if he were going toward the club, out of which wild music was blaring. Only after the gleaming automobile was out of sight did he change direction, walk to Obere Donaustraße, and stop in front of an apartment building with a freshly-painted façade.

The name Teschner was indeed next to one of the door-bells. Emmerich rang, but nothing happened. Even after ringing a second, third, and fourth time, nobody opened the door.

He thought for a moment and then dropped his monocle to the ground and stepped on it. "Was only a bother anyway," he mumbled as he knocked the glass out of the frame and then bent it into a lock pick. This was about life and death, after all, so any means were acceptable.

The door to the building was easy to open. Emmerich listened. Not a peep in the hall, which was lit by a gas lamp. He studied the names on the doors and found Teschner on the ground floor. When his knocks once again elicited no response, he employed his lock-picking tool again.

"Herr Teschner? Are you here?" he called into the darkness.

No answer. Emmerich listened in the silence. He heard the honk of an automobile in the distance and a couple arguing somewhere in the building, but there wasn't a sound inside the apartment.

His eyes slowly adjusted to the dark, and he was able to

recognize the outlines of some shapes. Teschner lived in a garçonnière, a studio flat, furnished with a narrow bed, a dresser, a kitchen niche, and two chairs. There was a carpet on the floor, and curtains hung to the floor on either side of the small window.

Emmerich seemed to be alone.

He felt for a light switch, turned the knob in a clockwise direction, and the room lit up. Electricity was really something.

Less impressive was the view that was now illuminated for him: the doors of a wardrobe stood open, there were shoes, clothes, and papers strewn everywhere, a cup lay broken on the floor, and a dried blood fleck on the wall boded ill.

Emmerich surveyed the chaos and wondered what had happened. A hurried departure? A kidnapping? A break-in? And if it was the latter, what had the intruder been after? Valuables or Teschner himself?

He examined various objects and looked into all the corners and cracks—but nothing revealed any evidence of what might have happened or where Teschner was.

He left the building with an uneasy feeling. The avenger had probably beaten him there. But if Teschner was dead, where was his body? If it had been found, Winter would have known and told him. The perpetrator must have dumped it somewhere. But where?

The quiet burble of the Danube canal put a thought in his head. After all, the murderer had already gotten rid of Zeiner's body in the river. He crossed the street, walked through the narrow strip of greenery on the other side, and went down the steep embankment.

Fear shot through him when he saw two men squatting at the water's edge. But in the next instant he saw that they were holding long wooden sticks into the canal, and he exhaled with relief. They were *Fettfischer*, fishing for bones, meat scraps,

and fat from the wastewater with homemade tools. They
would dry their pickings and sell them to the soap industry.

"*Servus*," he greeted them. "Any luck today?"

They nodded silently, looked at each other and then back at
him.

"You here a lot?"

"Most every night."

The older of the two men looked him up and down while
the younger, perhaps his son, got into a crouch. A predator
ready to pounce.

Only now did Emmerich remember that he wasn't clothed
in his normal manner, and instead had on things that could be
sold for enough money to keep the two men in brandy and
food for a month. If he wasn't careful, he could end up being
the next one in the canal—naked.

He reached into his pocket and pulled out a couple of
banknotes. Kolja called this amount of money piddling, but for
a couple of *Fettfischer* it was a small fortune.

"This is all I have with me. It's yours if you just answer a few
questions."

"Well, well, I'm certainly curious about the questions," said
the older man as the younger one stared in awe at the bills.

"Over there, in the house across the street," Emmerich
began, "something happened. A break-in, a kidnapping,
maybe even a murder. Did you notice anything? Was there a
fight, or did you see anyone who didn't belong here?"

While the two of them thought for a moment and whispered between themselves, Emmerich looked at the calm,
black current flowing slowly but surely eastward. What had
happened in Galicia in 1915?

"There was somebody," said the younger of the men without ever taking his eyes off the banknotes. "He was prowling
around yesterday. We noticed him because we were afraid he
wanted to *fettfischen*, too. We get little enough as it is. If

someone else came along we might as well jump in the water. Better to drown quickly than slowly starve to death."

"What did he look like?"

"Small, but tough. And agile. I followed him. Just wanted to make sure he wasn't putting out a net upstream of us. I could barely keep up with him."

"Must have been in the military," the older one added.

"Who wasn't?"

"No, a professional. Not one of the poor bastards that they conscripted."

The son gestured to the notes and stuck out his hand.

"One more question," said Emmerich. "Did the man happen to have scar on his cheek?"

"Not sure. His face was always hidden."

"Not the whole time. He looked at the water. From up there, looking eastward. Like you did a minute ago." The old man turned his head to the side and drew a line from his ear to the corner of his mouth using his pointer finger.

So he had been here. The man with the scar. "Did you happen to notice anything else?"

"Nope, that's it."

"Once we were sure he hadn't thrown out a net, we paid no more attention to him, and at some stage he was gone."

Emmerich handed the money to the men, who quickly hid it under their clothes and climbed up the embankment.

So Richard Teschner had also fallen victim to the man with the scar. Hopefully Winter would have more luck with Peter Boos.

33.

Ferdinand Winter walked past the single-nave, late baroque Ägydius church, which was in dire need of renovation, and turned into Hockegasse, where Peter Boos not only had a barber shop but also lived, together with his family.

Since it was already late, nearly midnight, it took some work to convince himself to knock on the door of the former carriage house. Waking people was impolite, his grandmother had always preached, and he found it difficult to violate manners that had been instilled in him.

It was about life and death, he reminded himself and banged on the door until a pair of windows directly above him were thrown open so forcefully that they slammed against the wall.

"What is it?"

Winter looked up and saw the face of a chubby-cheeked woman illuminated in the moonlight. Her red hair was tousled and sticking out from her head at odd angles. "Frau Boos?"

"Who wants to know?"

"My name is Winter, and I need to talk to your husband. It's an emergency."

"What kind of emergency?" She looked him over. "It better not be about a shave, junior."

Winter reflexively touched his cheeks. "It's something confidential."

She glared at him so angrily that he took a few steps back—he didn't want her to empty her chamber pot on his head.

"My husband went for a walk," she said finally. "He can't sleep at night. He's probably sitting somewhere in the palace gardens looking at the trees."

"The palace gardens? That's private property."

"Owned by someone who doesn't take care of it."

"Do you know where exactly? The gardens are pretty extensive."

"Try near the first pond. And now, goodnight."

She pulled the windows closed so hard that the panes rattled.

The 18th-century English-style Pötzleinsdorfer palace gardens had long been a favorite meeting place of the Viennese elite.

Winter's grandmother had often talked of the grotto, the Greek temple, the "singing quartet"—four statues from the burnt-out Ring Theater, that now stood here—and the glittering festivals at the *Lusthaus*, and rhapsodized colorfully about the rambling woods and the exotic plants around the two ponds. He himself had never had a chance to take in all the splendor, because after the last owner went bankrupt no more events had been held there. Nobody had looked after the 300,000-square-meter grounds and it had gone to seed.

Winter went along Schafberggasse to a narrow drive that led to a gate in the high wall that surrounded the grounds. He pushed on the cast-iron gate and found it locked. Shaking it accomplished nothing because, as he quickly realized, it was held shut by an iron chain. If Boos was really here, he must have climbed in.

He sized up the gate and with a sigh started to climb it. He hoped his boss knew the lengths he was going to for him. At the top, Winter positioned one of his feet between the spikes, grabbed a crossbar, and swung his other leg over. A loud rip and burning pain on his thigh signaled that he had just suffered his first duty-related injury.

But was this really duty-related? Better not to think about it too much. If he had learned anything in the last few days, it was that. With gritted teeth, Winter climbed down and jumped onto the narrow leaf-strewn path that led into the gardens. As he hadn't prepared for this sort of expedition, he had no lamp, and since there were no lights in the neglected gardens, he had to depend entirely on the meager light of the moon.

More stumbling than walking, he fought his way through the blackness and was nearly frightened to death when a little owl emerged from a nearby stand of trees and flew past him screeching.

Bird of death, he thought, and it took all his courage not to turn around and run home. "For Emmerich," he mumbled, "You're doing this for Emmerich." The sound of his voice calmed him down a little. He had to find Boos before anyone else did.

"Try near the first pond," he repeated Frau Boos's words and walked past the ruins of the palace, which were looming ghostlike off to his right. Was it haunted?

Don't think, just keep going.

He ignored the goblin faces grinning at him from gnarled tree trunks and blocked out the odd noises caused by the wind.

"Herr Boos," he called in order to drown out the eerie rustling coming from the underbrush. "Herr Boos, are you here?"

When he came to a fork in the path he chose to go to the right. It took him between tall sequoias, which screened the moonlight such that he couldn't see his hand in front of his face. Winter took a few hesitant steps and was enveloped in darkness.

"Who are you?"

Winter turned and stared in the direction of the voice, but

he couldn't see anything. His heart beat so quickly and loudly that it must have been audible from a kilometer away.

"I'm Ferdinand Winter. Who are you?"

"Do we know each other?"

"How should I know, if you won't tell me your name." Winter squatted down and felt around for a rock, a stick, or anything else he could use as a weapon. If only he had a service revolver.

"You called my name. I'm Peter Boos."

Winter stood back up. What was he thinking? What had gotten into him?

"You were stationed in Galicia four years ago and served in the 13th Company of the 11th Infantry Division together with Dietrich Jost, Harald Zeiner, and Anatol Czernin," he said, his voice trembling. "Right?"

What if Boos really was a war criminal? He should never have come to these godforsaken gardens alone and unarmed.

Boos didn't answer. There was only the sound of his strained breathing. "What do you want with me?" His tone had changed. Curiosity and mistrust had given way to something else. Horror might best describe it.

"I'm here to warn you. Somebody has killed your comrades, and we think this person is after you as well."

Boos took a quick breath, and then there were no more sounds.

"Herr Boos?"

A match lit with a hiss and a moment later the area was bathed in the flickering light of a gas lantern.

Finally Winter could see the man's face. Boos was about the same size as he was, but extremely gaunt. His pale face was caved in and creased with deep lines. He had dark rings under his eyes. He looked as if he hadn't slept in years.

"Thanks." Boos turned and headed toward the gate.

Winter, completely surprised by this unexpected reaction,

initially stood there as if planted in the dirt before then following after the light. "What are you doing? Where are you going?" he called, tripping and falling over a root. Boos continued on without a word, unconcerned about him. He got up with a groan and hobbled after the lantern. "Who is after you?" he called when he got to the gate.

Boos, who was already on the other side, looked at him through the iron bars. "Does that matter?"

"Of course."

"Not for me."

Winter had to look twice, but he wasn't seeing things—Boos was smiling.

"I always knew the day would come when someone would take revenge. It doesn't matter who. I've earned it and will not resist my fate." With these words he walked off toward Schafberggasse.

"Wait a minute!" Winter climbed the gate, this time managing not to snag himself on the spikes atop it. "If you know anything, you have to tell me. Your life isn't the only one at stake here!" He hurried after Boos, and when he finally reached the alley, which was lit by gas lamps and lined with single-story buildings, he exhaled. He was finally back in civilization. He was finally safe.

"Wait," he repeated, but his words were drowned out by the noise from an automobile that raced past him.

And then everything happened quickly.

The car swerved. Boos turned and opened his mouth, but his voice was drowned out by the sound of the impact when the car hit him. His body was catapulted up, swirled around like a leaf in the wind, and then flopped to the ground.

"Jesus!" Winter, frozen in shock at first, quickly snapped out of it and ran to the injured man, who lay unnaturally contorted on the side of the road, quietly gasping for breath. "Hang in there." He knelt down and held his hands against a gaping wound on Boos's neck. "Help!" he yelled. He realized with horror that blood was trickling between his fingers. "We need a doctor!"

"Not . . . " rasped Boos, " . . . revenge."

"Don't talk." Winter was relieved to see lights go on in the nearby houses. "Help is on the way. Just hold on a little longer."

Boos shook his head nearly imperceptibly. "Beast . . . Lemberg . . . " he stammered, and with great effort lifted a hand to Winter's cheek. "Scar . . . "

"Is that who ran you over? The man with the scar?"

Boos closed his eyes. "Sleep . . . finally . . . sleep . . . " he managed before a gurgling sound escaped his throat.

"Don't die," begged Winter. Why wasn't anyone coming to help?

When he saw two headlights coming, he lifted his arm and waved. "Here!" he yelled. "We're here!" He took Boos's limp hand in his own and squeezed it. "Help is coming. Stay with me."

When he looked up again, the lights were still coming at him full speed. Had the driver not seen them? They were directly beneath a streetlamp. "Stop!" he yelled, jumping up. "Stop!"

The automobile sped up, and Winter could suddenly see that it was a sedan, gleaming light gray in the moonlight. This realization hit him like a lightning bolt: light gray.

Pale.

Beware the Fourth Horseman. Beware the pale horse.

He leapt to the side to try to reach safety, but the car also swerved, and before he could react he was hit and sent catapulting into the air.

Bird of death, he thought as an owl flew over him hooting quietly.

And then he thought no more.

34.

Emmerich lingered in a doorway on Berggasse, very near the building where the renowned psychoanalyst Sigmund Freud practiced. A human being is so miserable when all he wants is to stay alive, he was supposed to have said. A wise man, who had a lot of work ahead of him.

Just as with Teschner, Oberwieser didn't answer the doorbell, and since the lock couldn't be picked Emmerich had been waiting for more than half an hour for an opportunity to get into the building.

Even though he was wearing warm clothes, the moist cold air of the southeasterly wind was creeping into his bones. You could no longer ignore the fact that the hardest time of the year was upon them. Many people wouldn't live through it.

Uns're Linke an dem Schwerte,
in der Rechten einen Spieß,
kämpfen wir so weit die Erde,
bald für das und bald für dies.

With our left hand on our cutlass,
our right around our spear,
we'll fight to the ends of the atlas,
whether far or whether near.

A group of men, all wearing military-style armbands and apparently deep into their cups, stopped in front of the building across the street.

"See you tomorrow, comrades," said one of them after the final verse of the song had been sung.

The rest of them clicked their heels, saluted, and marched onward while the man who was apparently their leader came across the street and opened the door where Emmerich was waiting. Georg Oberwieser.

He looks exactly as he did in the photo, thought Emmerich. Proud, agile, and full of energy. As if the war years hadn't left a mark.

"Herr Oberwieser? I need to talk to you."

Georg Oberwieser didn't seem irritated at being addressed by a stranger in the middle of the night. He didn't look surprised or skeptical—on the contrary, his mouth formed a smile.

"You want to join the Heritage Association. Theo already told me he was sending someone to me. You're late, but come on in, my good man." His breath smelled of schnapps, and his eyes gleamed.

For the moment, Emmerich let the man believe he was an aspiring member and followed him to the third floor of the building, where they entered a generous two-room apartment. "I hope I'm not intruding," he said as he looked around: medals, flags, pennants and other reverential objects related to the war and the monarchy had transformed the scrupulously clean rooms into a sort of museum to the glory of the Imperial and Royal Army.

"Where did you serve, Herr . . . ?" Oberwieser motioned to a chair and set two bottles of beer out on a table.

"Italy."

Emmerich felt both strange and at home amid the mementos. It was easy to glorify the past in light of the current political chaos and the humiliation of the Treaty of Saint-Germain-en-Laye, which had turned Austria into a miserable pile of shards that nobody wanted.

"Isonzo?"

Emmerich nodded and washed down his misty-eyed senti-mentality with a swig of beer.

"And how do you know Theo, Herr . . . ?"

Emmerich once again left the request for his name unan-swered. "To be honest, I don't know this Theo. And I don't want to join your Heritage Association."

Oberwieser took in this news with a stoic look but casually moved his hand to his waistband.

"Not necessary." Emmerich sat down and put his hands in plain view. "I'm not here to do anything to you. Just the oppo-site. I've come to warn you."

He reached purposefully slowly into the inner pocket of his cape, pulled out with two fingers the gun Kolja had given him, and placed it on the table.

"Warn me about whom?"

Oberwieser loosened his grip on his own pistol. He'd begun to perspire and was giving off the unpleasant smell of alcohol-infused sweat.

"I don't know his name, but I know it's about the things that happened during the war."

Oberwieser didn't betray any emotion. "A lot happened during the war." Without ever taking his eyes off Emmerich, he took a sip of beer.

"It's about the people that you murdered."

The corner of Oberwieser's mouth curled upward. "The people I murdered . . . ," he repeated, laughing. "Did you not kill anyone in Italy?"

"Of course. Men fit for action in the course of battle. Not women and children. Not the old or the infirm."

"Are you from that goddamn commission? Those traitors?" Oberwieser's neck and face were now covered with red blotches and his fingers gripped the beer bottle so tightly that Emmerich thought it might break. "They want to make villains out of us heroes. Make us into criminals who have to justify ourselves. What would make you want to destroy the honor of the army and drag the reputation of its soldiers through the mud?"

"I'm not from the commission, and I don't want to drag anyone through the mud. For me, it's about protecting your life. But to do that I need your help. Do you understand? I need to ask you a few questions."

The red splotches grew darker. "Do I look like an idiot? This is obviously a trap. Nothing is sacred to you socialist pigs." He pulled the pistol out of his waistband and pointed it at Emmerich.

Emmerich held up his hands. "Dietrich Jost was found shot in the woods," he began to explain. "Harald Zeiner was fished out of the Danube canal, dead. Anatol Czernin was strangled at the movies, and Richard Teschner has disappeared without a trace. I wanted to try to keep you from being the next victim. But if you don't want . . . "

Oberwieser turned as white as a sheet. "There was nothing about that in the papers."

"The perpetrator is clever, makes his murders look like suicides, accidents, or organized criminal activity. A real·pro. Go over to the nearest commissariat and ask. They'll confirm everything."

Oberwieser wiped the sweat from his brow and thought for a moment. Finally he put his pistol back into his waistband. "What do you want to know?"

"What happened back there in Galicia? Is it true that you killed civilians?"

Oberwieser shoved the beer to the side, stood up, and grabbed a bottle of schnapps from a sideboard.

"And what if?" he spat. "Ever heard of the war code? You must know of it, right?"

Emmerich nodded. The code allowed officers to execute

civilians who collaborated with the enemy without court proceedings. They didn't even need evidence—mere suspicion
was enough.

"Women, children, the elderly, the disabled . . . "
Oberwieser took a sip of liquor and winced. "They could do as
much damage as able-bodied men. They could use weapons
and light explosives. Or worse: they could spy for the enemy.
The adversary you don't recognize as one is the most dangerous of all."

*A group of Royal and Imperial soldiers supposedly massacred
civilians. Women, children, the elderly. Even babies. They were
supposed to have done things so brutal that it would have
shocked Beelzebub,* Emmerich recalled Simon's words. "And
what about babies? They can't talk or pull a trigger."

"Not yet." Oberwieser leaned against the sideboard and
took another sip. "But what do you think will become of them
in a few years? They'll be grown up and out for revenge. You
have to nip the danger in the bud. And besides . . . at the end
of the day we did them all a favor. Better dead than in an
orphanage. You ever seen what those places are like?"

Emmerich's throat swelled with rage. "Nothing, not even
the war code, gives someone the right to kill children. Innocent
creatures who were just born in the wrong place at the wrong
time."

"A lot of people have been in the wrong place at the wrong
time since 1914. The relatives of all the dead will tell you that.
It's just bad luck."

"Bad luck?" Emmerich couldn't believe it. *Things so brutal
it would have shocked Beelzebub,* he heard Simon in his ear
again. "And why the brutality?"

Oberwieser rolled his eyes as if he were dealing with a dull-
witted child. "As a deterrent. After that nobody dared collab-
orate with the Russians. We saved thousands of Imperial and
Royal lives."

"By massacring children? What kind of man are you? Don't you have a conscience?" Emmerich banged on the table so hard that his beer bottle nearly tipped over. "Where's the honor in that? I'd rather drop dead than stoop to that."

"What were we supposed to do?"

"Nothing! You didn't have to do anything!" shouted Emmerich. "Better to die than to bring such shame on yourself and the army."

Emmerich thought of Luise, of Emil, Ida, and little Paul, and looked at the door. He had a burning desire to just get up and leave Oberwieser to his own destiny. Someone who did such things deserved no better.

"It was our duty!" Oberwieser had also gotten loud. He showed no remorse. "We were good soldiers. Obedient and true! We only did what we were told. Whoever killed my comrades had no right to."

"No right to?" Emmerich stood up and looked out the window. A cloud passed in front of the moon. "Because of people like you, ideas like *right* and *just* are meaningless. Nothing more than illusions used to control people so anarchy doesn't break out."

He thought about his job and how hard he had worked to uphold the law. All in vain. For nothing. People weren't worth saving.

He turned back to Oberwieser, looked at his face, which betrayed no sign of understanding or shame, and took his gun from the table. Without another word, he went to the door. Everything he had ever believed seemed lost.

"You can't just leave me behind!" Oberwieser jumped up, ran after him, and grabbed him by the arm. "We just followed orders. The commander was to blame for everything. He ordered it. If someone has to die, then it should be him."

Emmerich ripped himself free of his grip and pushed Oberwieser up against the wall. "Tell me his name."

Oberwieser didn't answer; he stared past Emmerich with his mouth open.

"Tell me his name," he repeated.

The answer was lost in an ear-splitting bang, and Oberwieser jerked.

Emmerich, who still hadn't realized what had happened, put his hands to his ears and stared at Oberweiser's chest, where a dark red stain was spreading.

"Turn around. Keep your hands where I can see them."

The voice sent chills down his spine, and as Oberwieser slowly slid down the wall, Emmerich did as he was told.

"You!" That was all that he could say when he found himself face-to-face with the man with scar on his cheek.

He directed Emmerich over to the table and took his gun. Then he went over to Oberwieser, who was unconscious on the floor. He kicked his body, and when he was sure there was no more life in it, he reached down and pulled the gun out of his waistband.

"Nice of you to make it so easy for me." His German was flawless, with a slight Viennese inflection. He wasn't from Galicia. Or was he?

"I don't understand . . . "

"Scream like there's no tomorrow. I've rarely gotten into an apartment so easily. And the neighbors will all confirm that you were arguing. An easy case for the police." He winked at Emmerich and pointed Oberwieser's weapon at him.

"I wasn't in Lemberg. I didn't do anything to anyone."

"I know."

"Then put down the gun. I understand why you killed these men. Believe me. If my family had been . . . "

The man with the scar began to laugh. "You thought I was one of them? Do I look like a fucking bohunk?"

"No, but . . . " Emmerich was lost. "Are you not a victim of the massacres?"

The laughing got louder. "If there is one thing I am not, it is a victim. Victims are weak. Inferior. Ever heard of Darwin?"

Thoughts were flashing through Emmerich's mind. If this man wasn't a victim of the massacres, what was he? Why had he killed the men of the 13th company? What was his motive? Slowly an even worse thought began to take shape in his mind.

"Oberwieser talked about you. You were the commander and ordered the massacre of civilians. And now that the war crimes commission is starting to ask questions, you're getting rid of all the potential witnesses."

"Shut your mouth!" The stranger's laughter died, and he pulled the trigger.

35

I'm still alive . . . was the first thing that went through Emmerich's head when he opened his eyes again and found himself on the floor of Oberwieser's apartment.

Should he be happy about that? Or disappointed? And how long had he been unconscious? Where was the man with the scar? He sat up with a groan and piercing pain shot through his chest.

He cautiously felt around his ribs and looked at his hands—no blood. He looked down and scanned his shirt. In his chest pocket, directly in front of his heart, was a round hole that was blackened all around. Emmerich ran his fingertips over it and felt something hard. What the hell was that? He frowned, reached into his pocket, and pulled out the amulet—a deformed bullet was stuck in the head of the snake. Emmerich was laughing and crying at the same time.

Lightheaded, he stood up and went over to Oberwieser's lifeless body, which was lying in a pool of blood that was slowly seeping into the wooden floorboards. The man was dead, there was no doubt about it.

He reached for the schnapps, which was still on the sideboard, sat down at the table, and took a gulp. What a day. He'd escaped prison, got involved with a wanted criminal, witnessed a cold-blooded murder, and had come within a hair of being gunned down.

At that moment he heard the sirens.

His first reaction was that of a veteran police detective. He stood up, put the bottle away, and wanted to start to secure the crime scene for his colleagues who would collect evidence. Until he realized that the role of friends and foes had been reversed overnight. He hurried to the door, paused, and looked back. His fingerprints were all over the apartment. He had to get rid of them, but was there enough time?

Doors slamming and the sound of heavy boots on the staircase gave a clear answer.

"Damn it," he cursed, exhaling the breath he had reflexively held. "Have to leave it." He crept out to the hall. Whether they put him away for life for one murder or two didn't matter.

To avoid being seen by the neighbors, all of whose doors were open a crack now, he pressed himself into a window niche and took stock of the situation: he was on the third floor, at the end of a long hallway, a little ways from the only staircase that went up and down. If he went down he would run right into the arms of the police. His disguise was good, but men who had known him for years wouldn't be fooled. And fleeing upstairs wasn't an option. It would only delay his arrest by a few minutes.

The steps were coming nearer. It must be three or more men. In any event, more than he could possibly take on.

"Remain in your apartments!" he heard a voice shout. "There's nothing to see. Stay calm and listen for our instructions."

Murmurs, yells of protest, and slamming doors followed, and Emmerich pressed himself deeper into the window niche. They would soon make it to the third floor and enter his field of vision. He closed his eyes and thought about the interior of the apartment. Was there someplace inside he could hide? No, if the police did a halfway decent job they'd find him regardless of where he hid.

"What did I say? You need to remain in your apartments! Nothing to look at!"

The voices were close now. Even though he was warm with agitation, he could feel the cold air from the window.

The window!

He carefully pushed the latch to the side and opened both sides of the window. "Ach," he whispered as he looked down. It must have been at least twelve meters to the ground, if not more. Undaunted by the thought of death, he climbed out. He had nothing left to lose.

The ornate façade, covered in stucco ornaments, offered enough footholds and places to grab. He could at least consider a dangerous descent.

Thank god Oberwieser didn't live in one of the new-style buildings, he thought, as he placed his left foot cautiously onto the stone shelf that created a visual divider between the second and third floors. The architect Adolf Loos had built a totally unadorned building directly across from the Hofburg a few years before, with a smooth exterior without so much as corbels above the windows, which was why it became known as "the house without eyebrows." Kaiser Franz Josef hated the view of the plain, unornamented building so much that he had the palace windows facing Michaelerplatz nailed shut so he wouldn't have to see the abominable building, as he called it.

"We're going in. You hold the fort out here," he heard a voice say above him, just as he'd found purchase.

He held tight to a stone rosette and was about to jump down the arched top of a jutty when something he overheard caught his attention.

"You hear about Officer Winter?" one of the policemen stationed outside the apartment asked another.

Surely he didn't mean *his* Winter? What had happened to him? Emmerich stayed in place with bated breath, struggling to listen.

"Damn shame," said the second officer. "A real tragedy."

Emmerich had to suppress his desire to ask for details.

What had happened to Winter? His heart beat so loudly that he was afraid it would give him away.

"You think there's anything to the rumors?"

"That it was Inspector Emmerich?"

There was a loud sigh. "I heard he couldn't stand him from day one. He thought he'd be better off without the rookie."

"But that's no reason to run him over."

Emmerich nearly fell from shock. It couldn't be, no, it just couldn't be. He pressed his forehead to the cold plaster and fought off the wave of rage and doubt that threatened to overwhelm him. The man with the scar . . . had killed Winter.

It was all his fault. He should never have dragged the kid into the whole thing. He himself had caused all sorts of problems and his assistant had paid for it. With every instant, a feeling grew stronger and stronger inside him until it had crowded out all other emotions: an uncontrollable thirst for revenge. The man was going to suffer. He was going to hunt him down—if it was the last thing he ever did.

"No idea what's gotten into Inspector Emmerich," he heard one of the two policemen say. They couldn't have suspected the man they were talking about was only a meter or so away. He dug his fingers so hard into the stone that they began to bleed. "Sander said he thought he'd been affected by the war."

"Could be. Hörl said he's been acting strange the past few days. Stranger than usual."

"The war is going to stick with us for a long time."

"Let's wait and see whether Winter wakes up. Maybe there'll be a miracle and he can explain what really happened."

"Let's pray."

Emmerich wanted to cry from relief. Winter was alive. All was not lost. Though this didn't affect his decision to seek retribution. The man with the scar would pay. For the death of the civilians, for trying to kill him, and most of all for trying to kill Winter.

My rage will find you, he mouthed silently as he maneuvered himself into position to make a breakneck leap down to the jutty and then descended the façade with icy resolve.

August Emmerich was on the hunt.

36

Whaat he had in mind was irrational, but he didn't see any alternative.

Before he could devote himself to the hunt for scarface, Emmerich needed to find out what the story was with Winter. He wouldn't be in any condition to think straight and handle things until he knew how his assistant was.

As nonchalantly as possible, he strode into the general hospital, headed straight for the laundry room, and threw on a lab coat. He knew his way around this institution better than he cared to.

"Nurse," he confidently greeted an older woman he encountered in the hall who was dressed all in white.

Only too late did he realize she was the same nurse who had taken care of him after his unfortunate night when he had lost not only his dignity but also all of his belongings, including his service weapon.

She narrowed her eyes and looked him over as he stood there unable to do anything more than simulate a smile. Apparently she didn't recognize him as the man who had fled her custody half-naked a few days before.

"Can I help you, Herr Doctor?"

He was once again surprised how well the simple item of clothing disguised him. "I'm to look at a patient named Ferdinand Winter, a young policeman who was brought in today."

"He's in room three, at the back, behind the curtain. You can't miss him. Some of his colleagues are at his bedside."

Damn it! Police protection. Horvat thought of everything.

"Is he going to make it?" Maybe he could find out what he needed right here, without seeing Winter in person.

The nurse raised an eyebrow. "How should I know . . . It doesn't look good, but . . . you're the doctor."

"Of course. It was possible that one of my colleagues had already made a definitive diagnosis. I didn't mean to offend." He nodded to her and hurried off.

"Room three's upstairs, and the stairs are the other way," she called him back and narrowed her eyes now to slits. Was she suspicious now?

"Of course." Emmerich grabbed his head and then was appalled to see that his hand came away stained. The dye Frau Maria had used was apparently not sweat-resistant. "I'm new here, and it's late," he yammered, trying to paper over the situation.

"I thought you looked unfamiliar, Herr Doctor . . . ?"

"Schwarz." He put his hand in the pocket of his coat. "Dr Schwarz, from orthopedics."

"Got it." She pointed the way and then went on her way. "Vain bunch, doctors," he heard her grumble. "Deal with death every day and still worry about a few gray hairs."

When Emmerich opened the door to room three, he was met by a stale smell. Heat was apparently regarded as more important than fresh air. He walked slowly between the rows of beds lined along opposite walls. He passed heavy breathing, irregular snores, and quiet groans. When he reached a curtain at the end of the room, he held his breath and took a cautious peek through it: in the separated area was an empty chair next to a bed. It appeared he was in luck—there were no police to be seen.

Less pleasant was the sight of Winter, who, just as the nurse had intimated, was covered in plaster from the tips of his toes to his chin. His right leg and both arms were secured with long straps that ran to a sort of pulley that left his limbs hanging grotesquely in the air. There was a thick bandage wrapped around his head and what was visible of his face was swollen and covered with bloody scrapes.

"My God, Ferdinand," whispered Emmerich, sitting down on the chair and looking at his assistant. "Who did this to you?" He leaned forward so his ear was directly in front of Winter's mouth and listened. After a long anxious moment he made out a quiet breath, and the relief nearly caused him to break down laughing and crying at the same time. "I don't know if you can hear me," he whispered, "but you should know how proud I am of you." He would have liked to hold Winter's hand or at least pat his head, but he didn't dare touch him. "You're going to pull through, and when you do I'll tell you everything you need to know to become a great detective. So hang in there . . . And as far as this pig with the scar . . . "

"Be . . . " Winter's eyes opened a tiny crack and he struggled to say something.

"Don't talk."

"Beas . . . " His lips were dry and every syllable an ordeal. "Beas . . . " he pressed.

Emmerich's pulse raced. "Beast?"

"Lem . . . "

"The Beast of Lemberg? Is that what you are trying to say? Is that who did this?"

Since Winter couldn't nod, he winked. "Sca . . . scar."

"The goddamn pig." Emmerich reached into his chest pocket. "He tried to get me, too." He showed Winter the snake amulet with the bullet stuck in it. "But he didn't know who he was dealing with."

Winter pulled his mouth into something like a smile and groaned in pain.

"Don't move." Emmerich stood up. "I'm going to make the bastard pay for his crimes. And you need to get better."

He peeked out of the curtain and since the coast was clear, he said goodbye and crept out between the beds.

The man with the scar was the Beast of Lemberg. It was his face that had been scratched out of the photo. What was it Simon had said? That even his comrades were scared of him.

But Emmerich wasn't afraid. He just needed to find the guy now. But how would he go about that? Without a name, an address, or any other clue? He scratched his head.

The sight of a black-stained finger snapped him out of his reverie. Maria and her miserable dye. What had she smeared in his hair?

He looked around, scanning the labels on the doors. Where were the bathrooms? He needed a mirror.

He found what he was looking for at the end of the hall, and Emmerich saw that the mess wasn't as bad as he had feared. With a bit of balled up newspaper he wiped his hairline and the back of his neck and had another look at himself. He looked good, but strange.

Something else was bothering him. He had no idea what it was, but something was off. Don't get paranoid now, he chided himself. He'd been on the run for only a few hours and he was already imagining things. What was off?

When he heard the sound of a toilet flushing behind him and a stall opening, he dropped his head, turned on the faucet, and acted as though he were washing his hands.

And then he realized what it was: the smell. It was the smell that was bothering him. It didn't stink like a bathroom in here. On the contrary: it smelled like expensive aftershave. An aftershave he'd smelled not so long ago . . .

"Got the night shift, too, eh?" he heard a voice say.

Emmerich's heart skipped a few beats.

He looked up out of the corner of his eye, and the reflection in the mirror confirmed his fears—directly next to him, so close that their shoulders were nearly touching, stood none other than Chief Inspector Carl Horvat.

"Mmm-hmm," said Emmerich, making his voice as deep as possible. With his head down, he tried to maneuver past Horvat, but he took a step back, blocking Emmerich's way.

"Going to be a long night." He leaned over the sink and splashed water on his face.

"Mmm-hmm." Emmerich turned and went as calmly as possible into one of the toilet stalls, closed the door, and locked it.

"*Wiedersehen*," called Horvat, and Emmerich listened, breath held, as Horvat went, step, step, step, door open, door closed. He was gone.

Emmerich slowly exhaled and wiped the cold sweat from his face. That had been a close one. He waited until his heartbeat had more or less normalized, unlocked the door, opened it—and was staring directly into the barrel of a pistol.

"No false moves." Horvat stared directly into his eyes with a penetrating look. "August Emmerich. I knew it." Emmerich, paralyzed with fear, stared back silently. "Hands up!" Horvat directed Emmerich out of the stall. "Bold, just strolling out of the court like that. I have to admit, I was impressed." Emmerich held up his hands and gauged the situation. It looked like his goose was cooked. "Why did you come here? You must have known that Herr Winter would be under surveillance."

"I had to know how he was, otherwise I wouldn't have had a moment's peace," Emmerich heard himself say. "Winter is a good guy, and it's my fault that he's in there. When he was run over, he was looking into something for me." Since Horvat didn't respond, he kept talking. "I heard that his attempted murder will be pinned on me."

"And the murder of Peter Boos."

"And probably the murder of Georg Oberwieser."

"According to witness accounts, Oberweiser had a visitor and there was an argument. Shortly afterwards, shots rang out. The neighbor's descriptions all fit you to a tee. Don't try to tell me that it's just a strange coincidence."

Just as last time, Horvat was the embodiment of calm. Was this guy even human? Or just a well-oiled, perfectly functioning machine?

"I was there, but I didn't kill him. No more than I killed Peter Boos or Josephine Bauer. And I'd never do anything to Winter."

"Ach . . . "

Emmerich would like to have pummeled that dismissive syllable out of his mouth, but he wasn't in a position to just then.

"Who else could it have been?" Horvat looked searchingly at Emmerich.

"In 1915 in Galicia, near Lemberg, there was a gang of men from the 13th Company of the 11th Infantry Division. This unit inflicted unspeakable war crimes on the civilian population. One of the men was so barbarous that they called him the Beast of Lemberg. He did it."

"The Beast of Lemberg," Horvat repeated, wrinkling his nose. "A little theatrical, don't you think?"

"I'm being serious. Horrible things took place. The propaganda machine of the Imperial and Royal monarchy kept it all quiet and swept it under the carpet."

"Ach . . . "

Emmerich wanted to grab Horvat by the throat. "The Beast of Lemberg is a sadist. He cut open innocent women!" he screamed at Horvat.

He was expecting another obligatory "ach," but Horvat didn't say anything. In fact, his facial expression, which had remained the same to this point, suddenly changed. The Chief Inspector was getting pensive. He was about to say something,

282 · ALEX BEER

apparently changed his mind, and then put his poker face back on.

"And what does this have to do with recent events?"

"The war crimes commission has started to ask inconvenient questions, and the Beast of Lemberg is killing off one witness after the next. Dietrich Jost, Harald Zeiner, Anatol Czernin, Peter Boos, and Georg Oberwieser—they were all part of the unit. There's a photo that proves it."

"And Josephine Bauer? She certainly wasn't in Galicia."

"I think she saw something she wasn't supposed to see."

Horvat narrowed his eyes. "This man . . . the Beast of Lemberg . . . what is his name?"

Emmerich shrugged. "I don't know his name. I only know that he's kind of small and unremarkable, and he has a long, narrow scar on his right cheek." He stopped suddenly. Some distant inkling was trying to enter his brain but couldn't quite get through.

At that moment the door was thrown open and a man with a bucket and mop in his hands walked into the bathroom. "I . . . I . . . uh . . . " he stuttered, letting the cleaning tools drop to the floor and cautiously taking two steps backwards with his hands up. The moment he reached the threshold he turned and ran as if the devil himself were on his heels.

"Call the police!" Horvat called after him, reaching with his free hand for a set of handcuffs tucked in his waistband and tossing them to Emmerich. "You can go ahead and put those on. Backup will be here in a moment."

Emmerich held the cool metal in his hand.

"What is it? What are you waiting for? Put them on! You know how this works."

Emmerich closed his eyes for a moment and took a deep breath. "No," he said, looking at Horvat without blinking. He had decided to go all in, praying that he wasn't making a fatal error.

"No?" Horvat seemed truly surprised. "I'm not sure if you've noticed, but I have a gun. And you don't."

"They say you have a brilliant knowledge of human nature. So you must sense that it wasn't me. Look at me. Look me in the eyes. I've done a lot things in my life that I'm not proud of. I've broken the law and brought shame upon myself. I'm a lot of things, but I'm not a murderer." He slowly lifted his left foot and moved it backward.

"What are you doing?" Horvat flipped the safety off his pistol.

"I trust my judgment of human nature." He moved his right foot. "You're no more of a murderer than I am. You're not going to shoot an innocent man." He leaned down and picked up the mop the other man had dropped.

"But . . . " Emmerich had succeeded in convincing Horvat. "You can't just . . . "

Emmerich jumped out of the bathroom, closed the door, and blocked the handle with the broomstick. As he went to test the strength of his blockade, a shot rang out. A few centimeters above his head the wooden door splintered. A bullet had flown past him.

"Next time I won't hesitate!" called Horvat, rattling the door.

"Ach . . . " said Emmerich. Then he ran off.

37

E mmerich hastily removed the doctor's coat, threw it away, and turned with quick steps into the next street. He had to get out of here quick, the cops could show up at any moment. In a dark corner he carefully snorted another pinch of heroin.

"He can't have gotten far," he heard the familiar voice behind him. Horvat. "He has a war wound and can't run fast. Bring him to me." He sounded angry.

Emmerich hurried on. The street smelled of sewage and rotten potatoes.

"You heard what he said. Spread out!" came another voice through the night, and soon he could hear the sound of heavy boots. Lots of boots, all going the same direction.

Emmerich was startled when, running in the dark, he knocked into a garbage can, which fell over with a loud clang.

"Did you hear that?" he heard a man's voice say. From nearby. Too nearby.

"Let's have a look. That way."

Emmerich ran and ran until he found himself in a street that dead-ended in a high wall.

He felt his way along the brick wall. But it was too smooth. No footholds. No holes. No way to get over.

"Goddamn vermin," cursed one of the policemen from what sounded like just a few meters behind him. He heard squeaks. Rats.

Emmerich looked down and saw one of the rodents go into

a sewer grate almost directly next to him. Quickly he lifted the grate and lowered himself into the sewer, replacing the grate above the culvert, which went to the right beneath the street.

"You see anything?" A beam from a flashlight crossed above him.

"He's not here." They were right above him.

"Okay, let's backtrack. Horvat wants his head."

Even though it was claustrophobic and stank to high hell, Emmerich decided not to go back out. His chances were better underground. The Fortress represented the perfect hideout to plan his next move. He just had to find it.

He crawled beneath the streets of Vienna while Horvat's men searched for him above, through the sewers until he ended up in a chamber. There, using rusty metal rungs, he climbed down another level and scuttled in absolute darkness through the underworld until he had lost all sense of time and orientation.

And then he heard it. A dull bubbling. A subterranean river he would have to cross. Emmerich felt his way ever closer to the rushing, until it was directly in front of him.

"Hey!" he yelled into the noise. "Can somebody get me across?"

A few meters in front of him a gas lantern went on, and a heavily-built man with a brush cut and big ears held it up toward him. "Shit!" he cursed. "The cops!" The lamp went out and the man disappeared into the dark.

"Tell Kolja that it's me. August Emmerich."

The lantern was soon lit again, only this time it was Simon who was holding it. "It's alright," he yelled behind him. "He's okay. He's one of us."

The plank was shoved across the chasm and Emmerich cautiously balanced his way across the decaying wood. When he reached the far side he looked around. Once again there was much activity. He felt as if he'd landed in the middle of an ant colony.

"What the . . . ?" He rubbed his eyes when he saw a man who looked exactly like Xaver Koch. Was it really him? Had the bastard managed to get in with Kolja's people? "You there, stop!"

He didn't have a chance to try to talk to Koch because Kolja came toward him. "Are you crazy? What are you doing here? You were supposed to stay in the apartment!"

"I can't wait any longer," said Emmerich. "I have to catch the Beast of Lemberg." He sat down on a wooden crate and borrowed a cigarette from a man rolling a barrel past.

"And just how do you expect to do that? Even I wasn't able to figure out the man's identity." Emmerich took a drag and thought for a moment. "You never recognized your limitations," Kolja lamented. "And patience is something you could afford to finally learn. Sometimes I really wonder . . . "

Emmerich stopped listening to him. He thought about the encounter with Horvat and his reaction to the gruesome acts that the Beast had committed. Death and brutality were part of Horvat's daily life, but for an instant he had displayed an emotional reaction. It hadn't really been revulsion or shock exactly, it had been something else. But what was it?

"Recognition," he blurted as it hit him. "It's not the first time he's seen such things."

"Who? What?" Kolja frowned. "I think maybe you shouldn't drink so much."

"Carl Horvat . . . When I mentioned the gutted women, he looked as if he knew what I was talking about. You understand?"

"When the hell did you run into Horvat? Jesus, Emmerich, I leave you alone for a second and you just get deeper and deeper into the shit. Just like the old days."

"He must have dealt with such crimes before," Emmerich continued. "And that makes sense. Perversions like that don't just pop up from one day to the next." He looked Kolja in the eyes. "The Beast of Lemberg must have been active here in the city. Before the war."

Kolja slowly realized what Emmerich was saying. "Or he got a taste for it during the war and couldn't stop."

"Before or afterwards. Doesn't matter. But he's definitely committed murders. In Vienna. In Horvat's jurisdiction."

Kolja sat down on the crate next to Emmerich. "Horvat's reaction is all well and good. But it doesn't help you. He isn't going to be too keen on discussing his cases with you, of all people."

"I know. That's why I have to get hold of the files somehow, so I can at least get a peek."

"And how do you propose to do that? You plan to break into the offices of the *Leib und Leben* division?" Kolja started to laugh.

"Exactly." Kolja's laughter reverberated so loudly through the Fortress that some of the men stopped working and looked over at him. But Emmerich was so deep in thought that he didn't notice. "I need a skeleton key from you, and . . . " he began.

The laughter died like a flooded engine. "You lunatic, you're serious?"

"It's my best chance. I've got to take it. And besides . . . If there's anyplace they won't be looking for me, it's there."

"I don't know if you're a genius or if the heroin has eaten into your brain." Kolja looked at Emmerich and frowned. "If, for the sake of argument, I were to help you . . . how would you go about it?"

"If I learned anything during the war, it was camouflaging, deception, and tactical maneuvering."

Kolja rubbed his chin. "I'm afraid it's too dangerous for me. I can't afford to blow my cover. Half the city depends on me and my deliveries."

"Not to worry. I can manage the break-in alone. Or, as good as alone. All I need is a skeleton key, one of your men, and this." He pointed to a barrel. "Oh, and do you know where the nearest telephone is?"

38

L *eib und Leben* division," said Emil Mandl, a young policeman who had been working for Horvat for barely a month, with a yawn. "Uh-huh . . . *ja* . . . really? Can you describe him?" He stretched his back and rubbed his eyes. "Uh-huh . . . *ja* . . . and where exactly, did you say?" Suddenly wide awake, he took notes, hung up the phone, and waved over two colleagues. "He's been spotted. August Emmerich. At the Prater."

"Prater? You sure?"

"You better get going right away."

"Someone else just called and said he was at the central cemetery. That's the opposite direction. You sure they're not just idiots trying to feel important?"

"The guy described the elegant clothes and the dyed hair. And none of the wanted posters say anything about that. Get going." Mandl clapped his hands excitedly.

The two men pulled on their jackets. "Will you be alright by yourself?"

"Of course."

A few minutes after the two police had left the division offices, the entrance door swung open again and a delivery-man entered pushing a meter-high barrel on a hand truck. "*Leib und Leben?*" he asked, slapping a clipboard down on the desk in front of the surprised Mandl.

"Yes, but . . . " He tried to decipher the writing on the barrel. "Rum?" he asked in wonder. "What? Who?"

"Not rum. A body. For the evidence vault." The delivery-man pulled his cap down over his face and pointed with a dirty finger at the form on the clipboard. "Sign here."

"Halt, halt, halt." Mandl stood up, leaned over the desk and stared at the barrel. "You're not really delivering a body, are you?"

"Come on." The courier rolled his eyes. "The barrel's empty. But there was a body in there, and I'm bringing it for the evidence vault, get it?"

"Understood. Who sent you? And which case is it related to? And does Herr Horvat know about it?"

"The medical examiner sent me, and the rest . . . no idea. Please sign this and point me in the direction of the vault. I'm tired and want to get home to bed."

"The evidence vault is at the end of the hall. Just around the corner. Last door on the left," Mandl explained, and the deliveryman started to take his load there.

"Wait a second." Mandl came out from behind the desk and pointed to the barrel. "Open it!"

The courier made a face filled with disgust. "Get out of here. The barrel and the body were stored in a warm ware-house for a long time. And my stomach is not so strong. Understand? If you don't want me to throw up all over your place here, then let's just leave the top on." Mandl thought for a moment. "Have you ever smelled a rotten corpse? I have. Summer of 1916, Brussilow Offensive. I can tell you. The smell really gets to you. You never get it out of your system. But if that's what you want, go right ahead." He took a few steps back and held a filthy handkerchief in front of his nose and mouth. "Go ahead."

"That's okay."

Mandl went back behind the reception desk again, signed the form, and handed it to the deliveryman.

The man stuck the clipboard under his arm. Before he

disappeared in the direction of the evidence vault, he knocked his knuckles on the top of the barrel.

"Be back in a minute."

Emmerich waited a moment and then slipped out of the barrel. "Phew." He gasped for air and stretched.

Light-headed from the rum fumes, he took a peek out into the hallway. Kolja's call had indeed had the desired effect. The offices of *Leib und Leben* were empty.

He crept out, smiling. He liked the idea that the entire elite division of the Vienna police department was out looking for him tonight while he was strolling around their offices. On tiptoes he snuck to the next door, and his grin broadened. CHIEF INSPECTOR C. HORVAT was written in chunky letters on the door. Exactly what he had been looking for.

With Kolja's skeleton key it was a piece of cake to get into Horvat's innermost sanctum, and Emmerich whistled quietly through his teeth when he turned on the lights. It made the station house where he and his lower-ranking colleagues worked look like a run-down broom closet. He locked the door and looked around: the floor of the spacious room was covered with carpeting, on the huge desk was a personal telephone, and the walls were lined with file cabinets and shelves.

Emmerich sat down on an upholstered chair, opened the desk drawers, and inspected the contents. A pistol, a leg holster, a silver picture frame with a photo of a woman in it . . . Who was she?

Doesn't matter. He didn't come here to investigate Horvat's private life. He had to find out whether there really were cases in which women had been gutted. On a whim, he grabbed the pistol and tucked it into his waistband, then he stood up and turned his attention to the file cabinets.

Horvat had organized his files by district, and Emmerich

mulled things over. Where should he begin? Not in the neighborhoods where the elite and well-to-do lived—that was clear. A murder in those circles would have caused such an uproar that he would surely have remembered it. If there were cases, the victims would have to have been women from working-class areas. Favoriten, Simmering, Ottakring . . .

Following a hunch he grabbed for files for Ottakring. He just had a vague feeling. Some fragmented thoughts from the not-so-distant past. He put the surprisingly extensive stack of folders down on the desk, sat down, and started to leaf through the papers. *Strangled, shot, poisoned, crime of passion, suicide, infanticide* . . . , he read. A chronicle of horror, clinically sorted, labeled and noted.

He leafed on—and there it was. Exactly what he was looking for: *The Vienna Slasher.* A newspaper clipping stared up at him.

"Of course," he mumbled. He could vaguely remember. Back in 1898—he was just fifteen when forty-one-year-old Francisca Hofer was discovered murdered in Haymerlegasse. Because of the brutality of the crime, everyone had talked about it.

She was completely unclothed, her feet dangling down from the divan. The entire body, up to the chest, was cut open. The innards spilled out of the abdominal cavity, Emmerich read, looking at the attached sketch with disgust.

Professor Alwin Hirschkron had undertaken the autopsy and noted in the forensic report: The murderer went out of his way to mutilate the body in an extraordinarily ghastly and unusual way. The cause of death was loss of blood, which occurred as a result of the hideous wounds to the abdominal wall and entrails.

In addition, the file contained various witness statements, which offered no usable evidence, as well as sketches of the crime scene and the report of a psychiatrist who spoke of an extraordinary case of sadism. A handwritten note referred to similar crimes which had taken place in 1902, 1905, and 1907. As a result of the panic that broke out among the citizenry after the Francisca Hofer case, the public was left in the dark. When no further murders occurred after 1907, it was assumed that the perpetrator had either died or been conscripted, until . . .

One other note, very recent, concerned body parts that had been found by coincidence in the Danube floodplains just a few days ago. The identity of the woman had yet to be established, but the modus operandi was clearly the same as the other murders.

Wiesegger's assessment: probably a cigarette roller, Emmerich read, shaking his head. How small the world was.

A clock striking the hour startled him. He didn't have a lot of time, and he still had no concrete information.

I am operating under the assumption that all the murders were committed by one and the same perpetrator, Horvat had written. The long gap between murder number four (1907) and murder number five (1919) can in my judgment be explained only by a prison stay and/or military service during the war. Given the sparse evidence, potential perpetrators include L. Elsner, A. Stephan, H. Damian, C. Liebert, C. Hendrich, and J. Rau.

Emmerich thanked his stars for Horvat's meticulousness. The guy was incredibly well organized. He had attached the criminal files of all the potential suspects, with personal descriptions and photos.

Ludwig Elsner was out of the question because at nearly two meters in height he was a head too tall. Andreas Stephan's chin was too prominent. Emmerich flipped the pages and then froze. There he was. He looked younger than now and didn't yet have a scar, but it was him. Definitely. The Beast of Lemberg, also known as the Vienna Slasher, finally had a name: Heinrich Damian.

A noise outside reminded Emmerich of the time. Time he didn't have left. He stuck Damian's file into his shirt, hurried to the door, and peered out.

"What is that supposed to mean . . . prematurely approved?" he heard the voice of the young policeman echoing down the hall.

"Sorry. But it's not my fault. I just do what I'm told."

"So what does it mean exactly?"

"That I have to take it back. Apparently the assistants didn't clean out the barrel properly and they're missing a few pieces of the body. Whatever. All I know is that I have to take it back. It's better for you and your colleagues, believe me."

Emmerich smirked as he crept back into the evidence storeroom.

"A wise decision," was the last thing he heard before he curled back into the barrel.

39

S o? Success?" asked Simon.

The "deliveryman" had loaded the barrel back onto the horse-drawn carriage in which they'd arrived. Now he lifted up the top and looked inside, where Emmerich was hiding—bent like a pickle.

"I think I found what I was looking for."

"Wow . . . broke out of the Landl and into the coppers' offices. The world is going to hell in a handbasket."

Emmerich waited until Simon had swung himself up onto the coach box and then wriggled out of the tight container and stretched. He had really pulled it off.

"Where to?"

"Wait a second." Emmerich pulled the stolen file out of his shirt and scanned it in the dim light of a match. *Heinrich Damian . . . born Dec 23, 1870, in Vienna . . . widowed . . . carpenter by profession . . . remanded to the Landl from 1908 to 1913 for grievous bodily harm as a result of a bar fight . . . during the war stationed in Galicia and Poland . . . residence . . .* "Richard-Wagner-Platz!" he said to Simon as he continued to read.

Damian apparently lived in 16th district and owned a successful carpentry shop and an apartment above it, where he lived.

Simon flicked the reins and the carriage started off bumpily. About a quarter of an hour later he whispered, "We're here," and stopped the carriage. "No police in sight. Coast is clear."

"Thanks." Emmerich climbed to the front and shook Simon's hand. "You're a hell of a lot better at acting than you are at tailing someone. You should think about a career in the theater. It's also more legal than working for Kolja."

"But less well paid." Simon yanked off the fake mustache he'd been wearing and pointed to the building in front of which they had stopped. "Does he live in there?"

"I think so."

The young man looked at the façade. "You sure you want to go in there alone? The guy's a dangerous nut. He wouldn't think twice about doing the same things to you he did to people in Galicia."

"Let him try." Emmerich patted the gun in his chest pocket. "I have surprise on my side."

"I'm happy to come along. Between the two of us we'd take him easily."

"Thanks, but I promised Kolja not to put you or the organization in danger, and not to take advantage of your help for any longer than I absolutely needed. Besides, this guy belongs to me and only me."

"Whatever you want." Simon gave a sign to the skinny nag in front of the carriage. "Good luck."

He sang a song from Nestroy's *Der böse Geist Lumpazivaganbundus* as he slowly drove toward the Gürtel and disappeared into the night.

Emmerich put up his collar and looked to the east, where dawn was already breaking. What would the new day bring? There was a lot at stake. Everything, really. He gathered himself and headed to the doorway.

HEINRICH DAMIAN, MASTER CARPENTER. TOYS AND FURNITURE. EVERYTHING YOUR HEART DESIRES, it said in large letters on the door, and Emmerich spat on the ground. He knew what Damian's heart desired.

When he was sure that nobody was watching, he picked the

lock and opened the door. A cheerful jingle rang out. Emmerich flinched. If Damian was home, he now knew he had a visitor. He held his breath and listened for a while as he took stock of the situation, then, when he was satisfied that he was alone, he looked around, happy that the moon was with him. On one side of the room were hobbyhorses, dollhouses, and wooden cars lined up neatly on shelves. On the other side were stools, tables, and chairs stacked on each other. The place smelled of resin and turpentine. Behind a sales counter that was decorated with ornate carvings hung a child's drawing.

Emmerich rubbed his eyes tiredly and let his gaze wander. What had he expected? A torture chamber and the stench of decomposition? *The adversary you don't recognize as one is the most dangerous of all*, he heard Oberwieser's words ring in his ears. And Damian was dangerous. There was no doubt about that.

He pulled out Horvat's pistol and once again looked around. With his free hand he picked up a piece of wood from a shelf. He pressed his back to the wall next to the door and waited.

From his apartment upstairs, Damian must have heard the jingle in his workshop. A man like him was observant and always on the lookout. Just like Emmerich now.

Time went by. Emmerich heard a dog bark, he heard the scurry of mice and . . . the creak of wood.

Come on, he mouthed. Where are you?

In the next instant the door opened and a hand reached for the light switch. Emmerich didn't wait any longer. He swung the piece of wood.

"You goddamn . . . who the hell . . . ?"

"We meet again," snarled Emmerich aiming the pistol at Damian's heart. "Give me your weapon." Damian pressed his lips together and his nostrils flared. "Don't even think about it." Emmerich cocked the hammer of Horvat's pistol.

With a look of pure hatred on his face, Damian handed over his revolver and, with a groan, grabbed his arm where Emmerich had whacked him with the wood. "You're supposed to be dead, you bastard."

"But I'm not."

"What do you want? Why aren't you underground? Half the city is looking for you?"

"And for you, Vienna Slasher. Or shall I call you the Beast of Lemberg?"

Emmerich motioned to a chair. That Damian actually sat down surprised him. "So the day has finally arrived," he said, grinning.

Emmerich sat down opposite Damian. Cautiously. He had to take care. Someone like Damian could pull a trick out of his hat at any moment. And then the tables would be turned.

"Exactly. You're finally going to pay for your crimes," said Emmerich, aiming the pistol directly between Damian's eyes.

"You're not going to kill me. Not with your own hand."

"True. I have something better in mind. You're going to spend the rest of your life in jail and slowly rot. Death would be a merciful fate compared to that."

Damian smiled wider. Aside from the scar he really was a small, unremarkable man. Someone who could melt into the masses without inspiring any negative suspicions. He didn't look like a sadistic killer, more like a friendly uncle.

And then the thought that had been trying to work its way back into Emmerich's consciousness for a long time finally succeeded: *Big and broad-shouldered, he was. An attractive man. He looked a little like Emil Jannings . . . only he was older.* That's how Josephine Bauer had described the third man, but that didn't fit Damian. So why did she have to die?

"And now? What are you going to do now, August Emmerich?"

"Talk," he said, leaning back without lowering the gun.

Damian crossed his legs. "I'm not sure where I should begin. So much has happened."

"Don't flatter yourself." Emmerich's tone made clear how serious he was.

"Then we'll begin with Francisca Hofer. She was my first. I was still a little awkward back then, which is why it got so much attention."

"Forget the slasher murders. You can chat with Horvat about those. I'm not interested in Lemberg, either. I want to know what happened with your comrades. Why did you kill them?"

"Wouldn't you like to know?" He smiled broadly again.

"It was about the war crimes commission, right? If everything had come out, Horvat would have put two and two together and you'd have been caught. So you had to get rid of the witnesses."

"Why do you ask if you already know the answers?" snapped Damian.

"I'm asking the questions here," barked Emmerich. "And I want to know why Josephine Bauer had to die, and why you dragged me into the whole thing. That was no coincidence."

Damian laughed. "True. I don't believe in coincidences. Do you?"

"If you answer one more of my questions with a question of your own . . . " Emmerich gestured to the piece of wood and Damian's arm. "Now talk."

"Do you really think your life will ever be the way it was before? Are you really so naïve? Do you have no idea what is really behind the whole thing?" When he saw Emmerich's agitated look, he broke out laughing. "Poor August Emmerich. You're going to spend your whole life on the run or in prison. Or what's even more likely: you won't live past Christmas."

Emmerich's rage gave way to uncertainty. "What the hell are you talking about?"

Damian didn't answer. Quick as lightning he pulled a long knife from his sleeve.

Emmerich shot to his feet. "Put it on the ground! Now!"

Damian leaned back, grinning, and breathed calmly in and out as if he hadn't a care in the world.

"Get rid of the knife!" shouted Emmerich. "Do you think you've got a chance against this?" He motioned with his head to the pistol. "Believe me, I know how to use it. You're definitely not fast enough."

"But smarter . . . and more determined."

"Enough with the cryptic blabbering. Got it? What do Josephine and I have to do with it?"

"So many questions . . . " Damian laughed loudly.

"That's enough. Do I have to shoot you in the leg? Either you talk voluntarily or I'll make you talk. I've got no scruples when it comes to you."

Damian nodded approvingly. "You really mean it. I'm impressed."

"What is it now?" He released the safety on the gun.

"No need for that." Damian put the knife to his throat. "I'm not going back to the Landl. You said it yourself a minute ago: death is a merciful fate compared to that."

"Stop, don't do it!"

"I've prepared for this day for years. Since Francisca Hofer. I never thought it would take so long for someone to find me out. Be well, August Emmerich. See you in hell."

Damian winked, and before Emmerich could do anything he slit his own throat.

40

L ost in thought, almost as if he were in a coma, Emmerich walked aimlessly through the streets in the soft light of the new day.

There was nothing more he could have done to keep Damian alive, and so he died without giving Emmerich the answer he needed so desperately.

He could still hear the gurgling sound Damian had made as the life seeped out of him. Emmerich stared at his hands, which were soaked with blood. Evil. Inhuman. The Beast. In the end he was just a man. It was this thought that troubled him most.

He knelt down next to a puddle. He scrubbed off the blood, splashed dirty water on his face, rubbed his chin, nose, forehead, and cheeks in the hope that he could wash away the horror, the fear, and the grief that had settled on him like a deadly disease.

When his hands and face were numb from the cold, he let himself fall to the ground, leaned against the wall of a building that reeked of dog piss, and began to sob. He had lost. He was damned and would remain so forever. In his final act, Damian had taken his only chance for redemption with him to the grave.

The sound of approaching footsteps snapped Emmerich out of his despair. Was he prepared to go back to the Landl? Or maybe . . . to take the same measure Damian had?

No. He wasn't going to give up. Not yet. At least not

voluntarily. He reached beneath his cape, put his hand around Horvat's pistol, and looked up.

"Here." Before him stood a broad-shouldered man, who, to judge by his calloused hands, was a worker on his way to an early shift. His simple clothes were patched but clean. He handed Emmerich a piece of bread and nodded encouragingly. "Here. Take it."

Emmerich wiped away the snot and tears from his face with his sleeve and took the kind offering, since he wasn't sure what else he could do. "Thanks," he said, forcing a smile.

"It'll be okay. Just don't give up." The worker turned away and headed off.

Think. He had to think. What had Damian said? *Do you have no idea what is really behind the whole thing?* Had he been serious, or was he just trying to unnerve him? And if it was true, what had he meant? Or more to the point, who?

Emmerich closed his eyes and went through every sentence he had exchanged with Damian. With Damian and with Oberwieser. What had he said?

He snorted a pinch of heroin and waited until he was clear-headed again. Exactly, that's what it was: *The commander was to blame for everything. He ordered it. If someone has to die, then it should be him.*

Emmerich smacked himself on the forehead. Of course. He had made a mistake in his reasoning. How could he have been so stupid?

The commander and the Beast of Lemberg . . . they weren't one and the same person. The commander had ordered and the Beast had followed orders. Both during the war and afterwards. Now Josephine's statement made sense. *Big and broad-shouldered, he was . . .*

Emmerich ate the rest of the bread, put his head down, and walked in the dawn light. There was one last chance.

"August, it's really you. What are you doing here? What happened?" Minna, standing in her usual spot waiting for a client, put her hand in front of her mouth in shock. "I saw your photo in the paper and couldn't believe it. Do you need a hide-out?"

"Don't you even want to know whether I did it?"

"Even if you did. I'm sure you had your reasons. So tell me: do you need a hideout?"

"No, it's okay." He pulled her deeper into a recessed entry-way. "I need to speak with Maximilian Neubert. You know, the former judge you were with in Chatham Bar. It's important. Do you know where he lives?"

"No, but I know where he is. At the Winter Ball at Palais Coburg. I was actually supposed to go with him, but I guess he thinks I'm too . . . "

Emmerich looked at her face and understood. Minna looked bad. Her cheeks were sunken, her lips pale, her glassy eyes set deep in their sockets. Not even the makeup she had on could hide the fact that she was a deathly ill woman.

"Here." He gave her a couple of heroin tablets. She needed them badly.

Minna took one and nodded. "Let's go there."

"Now? It's already too late. Or more accurately: too early."

Minna smiled sadly. "You've never seen the wealthy people party, have you? Max took me a few times. The moneybags live it up into the early morning or even longer. It's not like they have to get up the next day to go to work."

"At Coburg Palace, you said . . . " Emmerich thought about how he might best try to sneak into the party unnoticed.

"There's a dress code. You can't go there dressed like that," said Minna, reading his thoughts. "But I can."

"No way. You belong in bed."

Her smile grew sadder still. "It doesn't matter anyway," she said, buckling over from a frightful coughing fit. Emmerich could see that the handkerchief she'd held in front of her mouth was full of blood. Minna needed a minute to collect herself. "I'll go home quickly and change," she said. "Wait for me behind the palace. In a quarter of an hour." She turned to leave, but Emmerich stopped her.

"You don't have to do this."

"I know. But it's better than standing around here for no reason. At least we can save your life . . . "

"I don't think you understand what you're getting yourself into. I'm being sought for murder. Think about your moral compass."

"Screw my moral compass," she answered. Before she left, she turned to him one more time. "Coburg. In fifteen minutes. Don't get caught."

Emmerich stood behind a coach, trying to look as normal and calm as possible. He'd made it unchallenged to the Asparagus Palace, as city residents called the place because of the slim free-standing columns in the middle section of the façade.

"Psst. August. Here."

He turned around. "Minna! You look . . . "

She had on a floor-length white gown with snowflakes embroidered on it, the collar lined with silver fox fur. She had put her hair up with a feather-covered brooch. Minna looked enchanting and tragic at the same time, like a bride who was about to stand at the altar with Death.

"Max gave it to me. It was supposed to be for tonight . . . " She squinted. "If he's inside, I'll find him and bring him to you."

Before he could do anything to stop her, she hurried off. Emmerich watched her with a wistful look. She seemed so frail, so eternally lost. Almost translucent. He could tell how much she struggled to climb the few steps that led to the entrance. She had to pause and catch her breath several times.

304 - ALEX BEER

She wasn't going to live to see Paraguay. She'd need a lot of luck to see Christmas. As a group of drunken ball guests stumbled out of the palace and nearly ran over Minna, Emmerich balled his hands into fists.

"Watch where you're going!" A woman in an opulent gown cast a disdainful look at Minna. Then she whispered to her companion, who handed her a bottle of champagne. The woman took a swig and laughed shrilly. Better sorts were what these high society types called themselves. But these sorts weren't better.

Emmerich watched the people leaving the palace. He saw clothes and jewelry that could have been sold for enough money to get hundreds of children through the winter, and he noticed how poorly they treated the footmen.

"Miserable vermin," he mumbled and spat on the ground before warning himself to be inconspicuous.

Soon Minna came through the portal, and she had actually managed it—her companion was none other than Maximilian Neubert. He was all in white and looked exasperated. He didn't like the fact that she had dragged him into harsh reality from the warm, colorful world of people who reveled in luxury and excess.

"Will you tell me now what is so important? Or did you make all that drama just to punish me for coming here with someone else? Minna, what we had wasn't a relationship. It was strictly business. I can do what I want, with whoever I want. Do you understand?"

"Of course. It's just that . . . " The rest of the sentence was lost to a fit of coughs, and Neubert jumped to the side.

"I'm going back in. If I wanted to have problems with girls I would have gotten married."

"*Halt!* Wait. It's all my fault. I sent her." Emmerich walked up to the two of them, put his cape around Minna's shoulders, and glared at Neubert angrily.

Neubert looked intimidated at first, then looked Emmerich up and down. "Do we know each other?"

"You are head of the war crimes commission, right?"

"It's called the Commission for the Inquiry into Military Breach of Duty. But yes, I am." Neubert narrowed his eyes and looked Emmerich over again. "You look familiar. What was your name again?"

"Do you know what happened in the vicinity of Lemberg in 1915?" Emmerich said, ignoring his question.

Neubert frowned with surprise. "Yes, I know the rumors . . . but . . . what have you . . . " He shook his head and looked toward the palace, where loud music was now playing. "This is not a suitable time for such things. If you want something from me, come to see me tomorrow afternoon in my office. Riemergasse 7, on the fourth floor."

"I can't wait that long. I need the information now."

"What information? Who the hell are you, and what do you want from me at . . . " he paused to look at his watch, " . . . seven in the morning?" Neubert ran his hand over his face. "You know what? I have no appetite for this drama. I'm going home. If you need something from me, come to the office."

Neubert wanted to turn and go, but Emmerich grabbed his arm. "I'm a police inspector. That's all you need to know for now. People have been murdered, and more may still die if you don't answer my question. Who was the commander?"

Neubert pulled himself free of Emmerich's grasp. "The unit was under the command of Georg Oberwieser."

"He was the noncommissioned officer. Who was his superior?" Emmerich's tone was so urgent that Neubert no longer put up any resistance.

"Lieutenant Wilhelm Engelhard. He was the platoon commander."

Emmerich, who was now sweating despite the cold, wiped

his brow. Engelhard . . . Wilhelm Engelhard . . . He had never heard the name in his life.

"What did this Engelhard look like, and what does he do now?"

"No idea what he looked like. But it doesn't matter. He's dead. Killed in 1918."

Emmerich looked at him in disbelief. "That's not possible," he mumbled, massaging the tip of his nose. "I don't understand."

"It's all I know. And that's the way it's going to stay. The case was shelved. Like most of them," added Neubert quietly. "Nothing but rumors . . . nothing confirmable. What am I supposed to do?"

"But you can't just let these people off the hook!"

"First you harass me, and then you lecture me." Neubert's tone was harder now. "I won't put up with this!" Once again he prepared to leave.

"Please. We're on the same side. We both want justice."

Neubert sighed and pushed a strand of hair out of his face. "Do you have any idea how difficult my task is? You can't imagine how many barriers are put up by all sides. Nobody in this city wants to shed light on war crimes," he said, enraged. "The conservatives don't want to sully the memory of the imperial army, and the social democrats don't want anything to do with the history of the monarchy. They want to draw a line and start over. It's a daily tilt against windmills. Files disappear or can't be located, witnesses don't want to admit to knowing anything . . . "

Emmerich wasn't listening. Had he misinterpreted everything? Falsely construed the evidence? Had Damian, as a final act of malice, caused him to lose his mind? Was there no sinister power behind it all?

The commander was to blame for everything. He ordered it. If someone has to die, then it should be him.

"Who was above him?" he asked in the middle of Neubert's stream of words.

" . . . and the judges are all still from the era of the monarchy and are biased . . . " Neubert paused. "What?"

"Who was above Engelhard? Who was the commander of the company?"

Neubert thought for a moment and then said a name.

"What's wrong?" Minna asked when she saw the stunned look on Emmerich's face.

He didn't answer her question. "You have to do me a favor," he said instead.

"Of course, whatever you need."

Emmerich thought for a moment, grabbed her by the shoulder, and looked directly into her eyes. "It's important that you listen carefully to me now . . . "

41

As he looked out the window, he gritted his teeth so hard that his jaw hurt. August Emmerich tried to get his rage under control.

From the next room came soft snoring, but he couldn't, no, he mustn't wake the man now. He was too enraged still. One false word, one false look would be enough, and he couldn't guarantee anything. He was clutching Horvat's pistol with such anger that his knuckles were bulging out white. Never in his life had he felt such an urge to kill someone as he felt now—not in the orphanage or the war, not even in Damian's workshop.

With a bright red face he looked out at the city as it woke up, bathed in the cool silver light of the winter sun. Its architecture was so imposing and the imperial luster so bright that nobody who didn't live here could possibly fathom the melodrama that took place behind the curtains. What seemed and what was diverged so violently—like this miserable piece of work a few meters away from him.

The man in the next room rolled over in his soft, warm feather bed and smacked his lips comfortably. Apparently the sleep of the unrighteous was just as deep and peaceful as the sleep of those with a clear conscience.

Emmerich stepped away from the window. He couldn't put off the confrontation any longer. Waiting was only making it worse. Instead of settling down he was getting more upset with every passing second. He quietly closed the curtains, switched the safety off his pistol, and went into the bedroom.

"Wake up!" Inhale. Exhale. The man murmured something incomprehensible, then started to snore again. "Get up!" Same order, louder and sharper, accompanied by a kick in the ribs.

Stay calm. Don't pull the trigger. Don't beat him to death.

The man opened his eyes and groaned. "What in god's name . . . " The rest of the sentence got stuck in his throat when he saw who had so rudely awakened him. "Emmerich," he mumbled, staring at the barrel of the gun aimed directly at him.

Emmerich snorted. "You . . . " He searched for the right words, but what he was feeling just then couldn't be put into words. "I know everything," he said, looking at his boss with a level of disgust he had never felt for any other human being.

Leopold Sander. When Neubert had said this name, the world had stood still for Emmerich. He had come within a hair of choking on the flood of realization and emotion.

"How did you get in here?" Sander, who was wearing a silk nightshirt, sat up and wanted to swing his legs out of the bed. Emmerich stopped him.

"Just lie there." He felt under the pillow and then threw off the covers to make sure Sander didn't have a weapon within reach.

"What do you want? Do you want to kill me now on top of all the others?"

"Don't play dumb. You know it wasn't me. You know it was Damian—because he was acting on your orders." He was in such a rage that the veins in his neck were popping out.

"You're worked up, I get it, but we're not going to get anywhere like this." Sander's tone was gentle and sonorous. "Put down the gun, and then we can talk in peace."

Emmerich cast him a scathing glance.

"I have money and connections," Sander changed his tune. He seemed to sense that his previous strategy wasn't working. "You can start fresh. As a rich man in a new land. How would you like that?"

Emmerich snorted again. "Never."

"Then what do you want?"

"I want to know why. Why did all those people have to die?"

"Isn't it obvious? Through the death of a few I prevented a partisan war, and thus the destruction of many. My orders saved thousands of lives. The lives of honest, upstanding soldiers. It's unfathomable insolence to try to make me out as a war criminal. I should be given a medal."

"A medal for the slaughter of innocent women and children? You're crazy."

Sander knitted his brow and dug his fingers into the bedcover. "What do you want?" he asked again.

"I want to know why Jost and the others had to die. If they said anything to the war crimes commission they would only be incriminating themselves." Sander mumbled something into his mustache. "Speak up!" Emmerich smacked him with the butt of the pistol.

"Jost blackmailed me. He had nothing left to lose and wanted money to emigrate. A lot of money."

"And Zeiner?"

"He had figured out that I had something to do with Jost's death, and had dragged Czernin into it."

The meeting at the Poldi Tant . . . the man Josephine Bauer had seen . . . Sander . . . All the puzzle pieces were slowly forming a complete picture.

"How convenient that Jost, Zeiner, and Czernin belonged to the lower rungs of our society. Nobody cared about them in the slightest."

"Except you."

"Except me. Which is why you set Damian on me. Let me guess . . . You had noticed in Galicia how much pleasure he took in cutting open women and had put two and two together. You realized he had to be the Vienna Slasher, and you had him at your mercy as a result." Sander's expression told Emmerich that he'd hit the target. "Damian was supposed to find out how much I knew," he continued. "And while keeping an eye on me he saw me get robbed. Savvy as he was, he had my service weapon . . . "

"If you had just let it drop," interrupted Sander. "If you had just stopped investigating, as I ordered you . . . " His words began to tumble over each other. "It's you who put the others in danger. Your stubbornness killed them all and made Winter a cripple."

"Leave Winter out of it!" Emmerich punched Sander.

"Are you happy now?" Sander asked as blood ran from his nose, over his lips, and down his chin, dripping onto his pretty silk nightshirt. "Can we talk to each other like two grown men now?"

"You're not a man. You're a monster, a beast. No better than Damian, if not worse."

"I can't undo the past, but I can shape the future. Your future. Just imagine what kind of life you could have abroad . . . "

"I'd rather sell my soul to the dev . . . "

All of a sudden Sander threw up his arms. "Help!" he cried. "This nut wants to kill me."

Emmerich glanced to the side and then opened his eyes wide. In the open door stood two uniformed patrolmen.

"This is August Emmerich," said Sander. "The escaped murderer."

Emmerich stared into space and lowered his weapon. It was over.

"Arrest him!" It was none other than Horvat himself who

came into the adjoining living room and gave the patrolmen the order.

They hurried over to Emmerich as Sander exhaled, got out of bed, and, with his arms spread wide, went toward Horvat. "Carl, am I glad to see you."

"Not him!" shouted Horvat at the patrolmen. "Sander!"

The two looked surprised for a moment, but then did as they were ordered. They cuffed the stunned district inspector and led him to the door.

Horvat nodded to Emmerich. "I've heard enough. You can put the pistol away. He's not worth it. Give me your weapon. I'll make sure justice is served. You have my word."

"Let him go!" yelled Sander, widening his eyes. "Shoot, Emmerich. Shoot! End this, you son of a whore." He looked almost grotesque standing there in his blood-spattered nightshirt, his eyes wide open. "These miserable creatures, these subhumans . . . they deserved to die!"

Emmerich looked back and forth between Horvat and Sander. "No mercy . . . " he mumbled. "No mercy . . . " Then he lowered his gun.

Emmerich watched as Sander was taken away, protesting loudly. A leaden fatigue had suddenly overtaken him. He slowly realized that he'd made it through everything, and yet he felt no satisfaction.

"Clever move," said Horvat. "And bold. It could have gone wrong. How did you know I would come?"

"I was certain that Minna would be able to convince you, and I just had to take the risk." He sighed. "And now? Transition to the order of the day?"

"Good that you mentioned that." Horvat scratched his neck. "As I'm sure you are aware, since the war the mood of the people hasn't been exactly friendly towards uniforms and authority. As a result, the police cannot afford a scandal."

Emmerich breathed heavily. "What is that supposed to mean?"

"That means we'll hold the proceedings against Leopold Sander behind closed doors, and it would please both myself and the police superintendent if you would refrain from talking about these events. It won't work against you."

"What are you trying to say?"

"I'm saying that I could use somebody as good as you. What would you think about a transfer to *Leib und Leben*?"

Emmerich rubbed his eyes. "To be honest, I don't know. My belief in the rule of law is not exactly the strongest at the moment."

"Think it over."

"I will."

"Oh yeah, I believe that's mine." Horvat took the pistol from Emmerich and snorted. "Concerning the circumstances under which you came into possession of it, we should also maintain silence. Sound alright to you?"

Emmerich nodded, closed his eyes, and nearly fell asleep in another strange place.

With his hands buried deep in his pockets, Emmerich watched the door on the opposite side of the street while fat snowflakes swirled around him as they fell to the ground. Winter had definitively arrived and covered the roofs and streets with a layer of snow and ice that veiled over the many blemishes and left Vienna looking tranquil and clean.

But appearances were deceptive. Emmerich knew this. He knew all too well the depths and shallows—of the city and its residents. The Second Rider had left a trail of destruction behind and created more societal flashpoints than ever before. The war may have been over, but the ravages had just begun. There were many demons to battle. Too many wounds that needed healing, too many loose ends that needed tying up.

Tying up a couple of loose ends was the reason he'd come here today. To a place that had once been his home. He touched the amulet hanging from his neck, and gulped. Let go. As easy as it sometimes was, it could be just as difficult at other times.

There were too many losses. Still.

When he went to Minna's to thank her for everything, he'd found her dead. She was lying in bed in her white ball gown, infinitely fragile and pale. The dress had become her funeral garb. "*Auf Wiedersehen*, my plucky princess. May the place where you are now offer you all that you dreamed of," he whispered.

Emmerich wrapped his arms around his body. The cold had

crept into his bones and he could barely feel his feet anymore. At that moment, he saw Luise at the end of the street. She broke his sad reverie and made his heart jump. Though she had her head down, he recognized her instantly. She had a bucket full of coal briquettes in one hand and was holding little Paul's hand with the other.

He took a step toward them. "Lu . . . " he called. He swallowed the rest of her name. Xaver Koch had appeared behind her—a cigarette in the corner of his mouth, his hands buried deep in the pockets of a warm jacket. "What the hell . . . "

Emmerich hid behind a horse cart parked on the side of the road, and stuck his hands in his pants pockets. He felt for his new badge and clenched it. August Emmerich, detective in the *Leib und Leben* division. He had accepted Horvat's offer with the condition that Winter—whether he was disabled or not—would remain his assistant. Horvat had agreed with gritted teeth. Now the little guy just needed to recover.

Just before they entered their building, Luise paused. As if she had sensed his longing gaze, she turned and scanned the street.

And that's when he saw it: not just that she had been crying, no, but that her right eye was swollen and her upper lip split.

Emmerich balled his hands into fists and admonished himself to stay under control. Paul was with Luise. He couldn't settle the score with the father in the presence of the child. He would have to wait. But one thing was clear: he was going to do something about it.

This story was not over.

AFTERWORD

Many of the locations and individuals in this novel are based on reality—Poldi Tant, for instance, on Nußdorfer Platz, was for a long time known as the most seedy bar in 19th district, until the Renner family took it over in 1970 and made it into a wonderful pub (Gasthof Zum Renner, Nußdorfer Platz 4, 1190 Wien).

The Chatham Bar also existed. The renowned Café Hawelka has occupied the space since 1939 (Dorotheergasse 6, 1010 Wien). The adjoining room that once held booths is today a storeroom.

The traditional Café Central has stood the test of time and still shines with imperial luster (Herrengasse 14, 1010 Wien). Also still around are the Hofburg (Michaelerkuppel, 1010 Wien), the Schönbrunn Palace (Schönbrunner Schloßstraße 47, 1130 Wien), the Vienna Skating Club (Lothringerstraße 22, 1130 Wien), and the Palais Coburg (Coburgbastei 4, 1030 Wien). As is the building so hated by Kaiser Franz Josef, "the house without eyebrows," designed by Adolf Loos (Michaelerplatz 3, 1010 Wien).

The medical examiner's office was indeed led by a Professor Albin Haberda in 1919, and his assistant was an Anton Werkgartner. Haberda was the medical examiner in charge of the case of Francisca Hofer in 1898. The murder was never solved. My characters Alwin Hirschkron and Aberlin Wiesegger are based on Haberda and Werkgartner.

The apartment building called the Beehive was torn

down in the 1930s. The building on Blattgasse where once a homeless shelter had been housed is still there. It is now apartments.

Fortunately, these days nobody needs to live beneath the city anymore, the Fortress has been abandoned, and the entrances to the sewers are properly secured. Anyone who wishes to have a look at the city beneath the city can do so as part of the Third Man Tour (www.drittemanntour.at or +43 1 4000 3033).

Many of the events and circumstances are also rooted in facts. Everyday life after the war was plagued by hunger and hardship. The economy was destroyed, there were housing shortages, and unemployment was higher than ever before. Sicknesses, epidemics, and suicide were common.

Since fuel was scarce, thousands of Viennese went out into the nearby forests and cleared entire sections. Fuel for heat wasn't the only thing in short supply; food, clothing, shoes, and medicine were as well, which led to a booming black market.

Many people tried to mitigate their plight by planting garden plots, upstanding women turned tricks to supplement income, and at some stage the shortages were indeed so extreme that even zoo animals from Schönbrunner Zoo were eaten.

The activities of the American Relief Administration were unable to help much. A multitude of citizens saw no future in Austria and opted to try their luck abroad, aided in many cases by emigration agencies, as described in the book.

Another way to make it through the hard times was with alcohol (there are many mentions of a liquor epidemic) and drugs. Diacetylmorphin was brought to market in 1898 by Bayer under the name Heroin. It was initially considered a cough medicine, but it soon came to be seen as effective against pain, depression, high blood pressure, and many other ailments. A true wonder drug. Because of low dosages and the slow rate of ingestion through oral usage, there was little addiction. Only when people realized its effects were enhanced through intravenous use or snorting did the number of addicts explode.

Another core theme of the book is the atrocities of the First World War. The victors insisted on investigating them, leading in 1919 to the foundation of the Commission for the Inquiry into Military Breach of Duty. The commission's work was cursed from the beginning because nobody had an interest in bringing the atrocities to light. The conservative powers of the new republic did not wish to besmirch the reputation of the imperial army, while the social democrats made every effort to leave the Habsburg past behind and look forward instead. Files disappeared, witnesses failed to come forward, and information remained hidden. The commission was also poorly funded. Four hundred and eighty-four complaints were brought, but only eight cases were ever taken to court. These led to just two convictions. The commission shut down in 1923.

I could not have written this book without reports and descriptions from eyewitnesses. I must mentioned first and foremost the two pioneers of social reportage, Max Winter and Emil Kläger, but other writers and historians also contributed important information about the times through their works.

Another great help was ANNO (AustriaN Newspapers Online), the virtual reading room of the Austrian National Library. Available there, for free, are more than 15 million pages of historical newspapers and magazines (Anno.onb.ac.at).

ACKNOWLEDGMENTS

There are people without whom this book would not be what it is. First and foremost my agent Kai Gathemann, the man who makes it all possible, who can motivate like no other, and who always finds the right word at the right moment. I would like to thank Kathrin Wolf for the warm welcome in the Limes publishing family and her engagement with Emmerich and company. Margit von Cossart made very valuable contributions in the form of excellent tips along the way; with her patience, accuracy, and understanding of the historical context, she greatly helped polish the manuscript. Last but not least, a huge thank you to the people without whom nothing would be possible—my readers. You're the best!

Alex Beer

ABOUT THE AUTHOR

Alex Beer was born in Bregenz, Austria, and now lives in Vienna. *The Second Rider* is her English-language debut.